Not Even If You Begged

Also by Francis Ray

In Another Man's Bed
Trouble Don't Last Always
I Know Who Holds Tomorrow
Somebody's Knocking at My Door
Someone to Love Me
Rockin' Around That Christmas Tree
Like the First Time
Only You
Irresistible You
You and No Other
Any Rich Man Will Do
Dreaming of You

ANTHOLOGIES

Rosie's Curl and Weave
Della's House of Style
Welcome to Leo's
Going to the Chapel
Gettin' Merry
Let's Get It On

Francis Ray

Not Even If You Begged

 St. Martin's Griffin ♏ New York

NOT EVEN IF YOU BEGGED. Copyright © 2008 by Francis Ray. All rights reserved. Printed in the United States of America. No part of this book may be used or reproduced in any manner whatsoever without written permission except in the case of brief quotations embodied in critical articles or reviews. For information, address St. Martin's Press, 175 Fifth Avenue, New York, N.Y. 10010.

www.stmartins.com

Library of Congress Cataloging-in-Publication Data

Ray, Francis.
    Not even if you begged / Francis Ray.—1st ed.
        p. cm.
    ISBN-13: 978-0-312-94817-7
    ISBN-10: 0-312-94817-4
    1. Women lawyers—Fiction.   2. African Americans—Fiction.   I. Title.

PS3568.A9214N68   2008
813'.54—dc22

                                                              2007039760

First Edition: February 2008

10 9 8 7 6 5 4 3 2 1

To Elaine Koster, my fabulous agent, for your guidance and wisdom. This one is for you.

Acknowledgments

I would like to thank my agent, Elaine Koster, for her continued support and guidance. I am forever indebted to you.

I would also like to thank, as always, my daughter and friend, Michelle Ray, who reminds me of why I write.

Prologue

Man had fallen from grace again . . . just as Traci Evans knew he always would.

Standing amid the hushed and tensed selective few in the wings of the auditorium at one of the largest churches in Charleston, South Carolina, Traci watched her client, Andrew Crandall, struggle to maneuver his wheelchair to the lone microphone positioned at the center of the stage. The moment he'd appeared, the standing-room-only audience had surged to its feet, applauding loudly. The ovation was deafening.

Waiting with Traci, Brianna Ireland muttered a curse. "He can walk!" she hissed. Since she was the lawyer for Justine Crandall, Andrew's soon-to-be ex-wife, Traci thought the other woman was entitled to be angry.

"But not for long distances," Traci said, which was the truth, but both women knew the wheelchair would elicit more sympathy. Andrew was going to need every bit he could get. It was time for him to pay the piper, to a degree, of course. That was where Traci came in.

Once in front of the microphone, Andrew glanced at Traci. She tipped her head slightly, their signal for him to begin. Instead he bit his lip. Perspiration dotted his forehead. His manicured hands clenched. He didn't want to do this. Tough. She stared straight back. People needed to know the high price he had paid, was still paying, for his adultery.

On the other side of the stage, the side Andrew had wheeled himself from, stood his number one fan and staunchest supporter, his mother, Beverly Crandall. Traci and the overprotective woman had clashed at the first meeting. But Traci had to give it to his mother; she'd backed off and kept out of the way once she saw that Traci was running the show and wouldn't stand for any interference. Beverly wanted Andrew out of the mess he had gotten into, and their best bet was Traci.

Finally understanding that Traci was not going to come out and rescue him, Andrew reluctantly reached for the microphone, then momentarily bowed his dark head just as he and Traci had rehearsed. When he spoke his voice trembled, stumbled. "G-good ev-evening."

A hush fell over the crowd. Gone was the smooth baritone voice that had persuaded thousands to shell out their hard-earned money to hear him speak about relationships. Personally, Traci thought it a fitting punishment. Each word was now an effort. The grimace in his handsome face showed his embarrassment. She hoped the audience would see it as remorse.

People began to slowly sink to their seats, their eyes glued on Andrew. "I-I com-mitt-ed t-the un-for-gi-givable sin." He visibly swallowed, bowed his head once more. When he lifted it, tears glistened in his brown eyes. "It-it c-cost m-me m-my m-most cher-ished po-possession, my-my wife."

Tears pooled on his lids, rolled down his cheeks. Traci thought that a nice touch and totally false. Andrew loved himself most of all, first and foremost.

"M-my wife, Justine, ha-has asked for a d-divorce and I have to gi-give it to her." There was a collective gasp. Andrew had made his considerable fortune, his sterling reputation on reconciling couples, yet he was unable to help his own marriage.

He swallowed, his grip on the microphone tightening. "Sin co-cost me ev-everything, p-put m-me in this chair, almost killed m-me. I'm ma-making this pu-public con-confes-sion so you won't blame Justine."

"And because you don't want the whole truth coming out," Brianna muttered.

Out of the corner of her eye, Traci saw Brianna's fiancé, Patrick Dunlap, run his large hand up and down her arm in a loving, soothing gesture. The pending marriage was three weeks away. Traci suspected there was a reason for the short six-week engagement. Her gaze drifted to Brianna's stomach, concealed by a long black tailored jacket. With another lawyer Traci might have tried to use her intuition to press for more leverage for her client, but Brianna was known as a badass.

And Andrew deserved a bit of payback. Just like most men, he couldn't keep his zipper zipped.

"S-she'll forever be the light of m-my life. S-she stuck by m-me, pulled m-me back from m-my coma knowing I had betrayed her trust, her love." Tears rolled faster down his cheek. "I-I ask for her forgiveness and yours."

Silence was his answer. Another idol had fallen. Such was life, Traci thought with a bit of sarcasm. You play, you pay. To her and the party you wronged. Andrew's divorce settlement could have made his ex, Justine, a very rich woman. Instead she had donated it to the senior center Andrew's foundation was building.

Andrew saw the move as wasteful, even spiteful, instead of what it really was. His wife simply wanted no reminder of him.

Two of the most influential ministers in the country stepped around Andrew's mother and continued until they flanked Traci's shaky client. He had a right to be. If things went badly tonight, his once bright future was in the garbage. What happened in the next few minutes was crucial.

Each minister placed a comforting hand on Andrew's slumped shoulder. Traci had personally picked them: one young, charismatic, handsome, and the other older with a balding head, a kind face, and no-nonsense manner. Both had balked until Traci had reminded them that her client wasn't the only one who had sinned. She hadn't meant metaphorically either. A nice personal check had further convinced them.

"Who among us has not sinned or committed a fault?" asked Reverend King, his eyes sweeping the audience as he had done for thirty years in the pulpit. "Which of us would not want forgiveness?"

Reverend Coggins took up the plea. "Jesus was the only perfect man. Man is sinful by nature."

Which has made me a very rich woman, Traci thought.

"How many in this audience are happier today because of this man?" Reverend King asked softly, his husky voice carrying his conviction. Andrew's mouth tightened and Traci knew it was with envy.

Good. Payback is a bitch in high heels and she's doing a tap dance on Andrew's once proud neck.

"Judgment is not ours, but a higher power's," Reverend Coggins said. "We have counseled with our brother and find him truly remorseful and have forgiven him."

Andrew lifted his face, tears still sliding down his cheeks. He was probably thinking of all the money he'd lose. He certainly wouldn't be able to afford the custom suits, expensive sports cars, and life in the lap of luxury he had become accustomed to if things went badly.

"I-I am going to Los Angeles to work with Reverend Coggins's foundation. I pray that I can take your forgiveness with me," Andrew told the audience.

Several seconds passed before one person in the middle section stood to applaud, followed by another in the balcony, and another, until almost the entire audience was on their feet.

"How can they forgive that creep?" Brianna asked, her voice sharp with anger.

Because I made sure of it. Traci had discreetly hired twenty actors from Atlanta, then sprinkled them among the audience. The two renowned ministers were further insurance. She didn't believe in taking chances.

Once was enough. Her eyes momentarily chilled as an old memory surfaced. Thrusting the image away, she faced Brianna. "Justine's good name is clear. You have what you wanted."

Brianna shot her a look that would make most people cower. Traci wasn't the cowering type. "If I had my way he'd be hung up by that part of his anatomy that thinks for him."

Traci shrugged. She'd heard and thought worse. "He's a man."

"Not even close," Brianna said. "If he was, he wouldn't have strayed."

Traci's gaze again flickered to the man standing so protectively by Brianna's side. Broad-shouldered, strikingly handsome, and dressed casually in a sports coat and slacks, he hadn't said a word after he'd greeted Traci. Yet his silent presence showed he trusted Brianna to handle the situation. He supported her. He'd fight the world for her. But what about six months, six years from now? She hoped Brianna might be one of the lucky ones. Her best friend, Andrew's soon-to-be ex-wife, certainly hadn't been.

"Perhaps. If you'll excuse me, I have another engagement. Good night." Traci turned and saw people coming on the stage from the audience. Many of them were women. No one had to tell her that the majority of them were wondering if they could be the next one Andrew did a little sinning with. The tears were gone but, in keeping with their plan, his face remained remorseful, his shoulders slumped.

A young, slender woman in a stylish suit and killer heels bent to kiss Andrew on the cheek, pat his chest. If Traci was a betting woman, she'd wager the woman had also slipped her phone number into his jacket pocket.

Shaking her head in disgust, Traci left the stage using the back stairs. Some women didn't mind taking leftovers or stepping over another woman to get a man. She should know.

Shoving open the back door with more force than necessary, she spied her car waiting for her. The driver snapped to attention and rushed to open the back door of the black Lincoln. Nodding her thanks, she slipped inside the plush luxury of the automobile.

Love made fools of people, shattered lives. And she collected big bucks helping the guilty party skate the blame.

She reached for the crystal whiskey decanter and poured a shot just as the car pulled away from the curb. She was looking forward to the weekend with her best friend, Maureen

Gilmore, and the rest of the lovable ladies of the Invincible Sisterhood where she could forget sin . . . including her own.

With a flick of her wrist she tossed back the amber-colored drink in one quick motion. The liquid burned a trail down her throat to her stomach. Her hand clenched on the glass.

Helping the guilty was what she did best. People said she was a natural. They didn't know how right they were.

1

"What do you miss most about your husband?"

Nettie Hopkins asked the question of the four women sitting around the spacious great room in Maureen Gilmore's lavish beach house on the Isle of Palms. The ocean was less than two hundred feet away. As usual, when Nettie was in charge of leading the book club discussion, no matter what the plot, somehow she always managed to turn the conversation to her deceased husband.

Since Nettie had been married to Samuel Hopkins for forty-one years, neither Traci nor any of the other women minded. Samuel had passed away of natural causes quietly in his sleep eight years , leaving the woman who loved him with millions. Mo important, he had left the good-hearted woman with wonderful memories and children and grandchildren who adored her. Priceless.

There was a discernible yearning in Nettie's soft eyes, a wistful look, then she quietly said, "I'll start. The tender way he always held my hand when we went out or strolled in the park or in our garden."

"The smell of his cigar," Betsy Young said just as quietly, her hands for once still instead of knitting. At sixty-five she had been a widow for seven years. Her husband, Rudolph, a successful trial lawyer, had been a womanizer, but she had loved him despite his unfaithfulness. Never once had she said a word against him or her twin adult sons, who were unfortunately following in their father's faithless footsteps. "I've kept his humidor all these years."

"The way he used to tease me out of my anger." Sixty-five-year-old Donna Crowley sighed. She was a robust, large-boned woman with a boisterous laugh. She was also the best cook in the county, and had a hair-trigger temper but a heart of gold. Gary, a financier, hadn't made it off the operating table for his quadruple bypass five years ago. "And you all know that's not an easy thing to do."

"My Raymond always made me feel safe." Ophelia Simmons, sixty-four years old, told them quietly, her apple martini, her favorite drink, forgotten. She'd married her high school sweetheart a week after graduation. They had been inseparable. She'd held him as he took his last breath due to lung cancer six years ago. "I still remember him walking me home after band practice the times my mother was late picking me up. I lived two miles from the school and enjoyed every step."

Quietness and good memories settled over the room. The only way to be considered for membership in the Invincible Sisterhood was to be a widow who overcame, a woman who had lost a great love, but who refused to let that loss dominate her life. Maureen had started the group six months after she had lost her husband, James, four years ago.

Traci was a guest of the Sisterhood and considered it an honor. In an overstuffed wing chair near the massive stone fireplace, her bare feet tucked under her hips, she took another sip of the scotch she had switched to when she arrived an hour ago.

It was her second for the night and she was on her way to a comfortable buzz. Usually she didn't drink more than a glass of wine during social engagements, and she never drank alone at home. She'd seen the disastrous consequences in her clients too many times. Then too, the stronger stuff often made her morose and talkative. Although tonight she didn't have to worry. The Sisterhood was sworn to secrecy. What happened in these meetings was sacred.

Traci took another sip and let the aged liquid fuzz her brain so she wouldn't have to think about the cheating bastard she had just helped or the one she had married. She refused to miss anything about Dante Babers. Although a recent graduate of SMU Law School in Dallas, she'd remained naïve and insecure, and was still trying to prove something to a mother who would never love her.

Dante had given Traci the love and acceptance she had longed for all of her life . . . or so she thought. She often wondered afterward if she would have known about his infidelity were it not for the accident.

"Thinking of Dante?" Betsy asked, her hand paused over one of Donna's high-calorie chocolate brownies crammed with pecans. "I miss my Rudolph the same way. I keep his smoking jacket in a plastic clothes keeper so I can still smell the aroma and remember him."

Traci had donated every stitch of Dante's designer clothes to Goodwill. She had wanted nothing to remind her of her stupidity.

"He didn't suffer. You have to remember that," Maureen said.

Traci almost choked on her drink. The policeman and the mortician had mouthed the same thing. He'd been dead from the massive heart attack when his twin-engine plane crashed. They'd said it with a straight face, although she'd learned from a not-so-discreet attendant at the funeral home that her husband's pants were undone and that there were teeth marks on a part of his anatomy that shouldn't have been exposed.

Dante's companion had been ejected from the aircraft. They had found her by accident when they were searching the area for her husband's downed aircraft. Dante hadn't listed her as a passenger when he'd filed his flight plan. Traci didn't want to think of the two-timer. She wasn't as forgiving as Betsy.

"Maureen, you're next," Traci told her.

Maureen looked around the room, a light dancing in her laughing almond-colored eyes. Traci took another sip, for the first time glad she wasn't an official member of the Sisterhood. Even she didn't think she could lie that good.

"Well, let's see," Maureen said. Next to Traci, Maureen was the youngest of the widows. At fifty-nine she had a size-six body she ruthlessly kept trim. She also had a wicked sense of humor. "You all might tap-dance around it, but I miss the sex."

Amid the girlish giggles and laughter, Traci scrunched further down in her chair. *That* was the last thing she missed about Dante.

Never at a loss for words and with a knack for living life to the fullest, Maureen continued, "While I was leaving the Crescent Hotel this afternoon this gorgeous man tried to pick me up."

All the women scooted forward in their seats, their eyes

wide, their collective breaths held. Traci took another sip of scotch.

"Well, don't leave us hanging," outspoken Ophelia said. "Details, and don't leave anything out."

Maureen smiled. "You mean details like six feet plus of conditioned muscles stretched over a chocolate frame, sexy dimples, and a heart-pounding smile?"

Traci barely listened. A man was the last thing she wanted to hear about. *Fool me once, shame on you. Fool me twice, shame on me.*

"He was so charming and sweet." Maureen wrinkled her nose. "He almost made me forget I have my sixtieth birthday in two months."

"He was younger?" Nettie asked, her brown eyes twinkling.

"Why else do you think I didn't say yes and cancel tonight," Maureen said with real regret, all teasing gone from her voice.

Traci lowered her glass. Nothing and no one interfered with the Invincible Sisterhood meetings every two months. Their calendar was scheduled eighteen months out for that very reason. If an unavoidable engagement came up, you were still expected to get to the meeting as soon as possible. Their family and friends knew this.

"You look great," Traci said, meaning it. Maureen had the kind of trim figure Traci had once longed for, until she'd finally accepted that her C-cup-size breasts and child-bearing wide hips weren't going to go away. "Obviously the man thought so."

"Thank you, but so do you." Maureen, in peach-colored slacks and knit top, gracefully sank down on the arm of Traci's chair and stared down at her. "You're always so giving. That's one of the reasons we want you to join us."

A furrow marched across Traci's brow. Perhaps she hadn't heard right. She gave to Maureen and the Sisterhood because they had reached out to her first. Traci thought herself the least giving or friendly person she knew. "I beg your pardon."

Donna, who had retired from teaching high school English after her husband died, leaned forward in the silk sofa in a fragrant cloud of X, one of the most expensive perfumes in the world. "We want you to be a part of us."

Traci glanced around at the other women. She was being given an honor, but, damn it, she was only . . . her mind did a quick calculation and she was stunned with the number she came up with. She couldn't be. She took another swig. *Thirty-seven.*

"You'd be the youngest member, but you're so sensible and settled. You'd fit in perfectly," Maureen continued.

Traci looked at the group of gracious, well-meaning, perfectly dressed women—another thing the Sisterhood had in common was a love of shopping—and wanted to run from the room. Their life was settled. They'd had their great love and life. But she hadn't lived, had tried and fallen flat on her face. Now there might not be another chance; she didn't even really know if she wanted one.

She was a coward. Worse, she didn't live up to the Sisterhood creed. She hadn't gone on to live life to the fullest. Dante's betrayal had knocked her down hard and she still struggled with her anger.

"I-I don't know what to say," Traci finally mumbled, which was the truth. She admired all of them, especially Maureen, she just wasn't like them.

The women traded worried glances. "We thought you'd be honored," Nettie finally said.

"I am. I just . . ."

"Not ready to be over the hill yet," Maureen said with a teasing smile.

She wasn't. She appreciated that they had welcomed her into their circle for the past four months. She wouldn't have missed a meeting for anything. She had a lot of associates, but not friends outside of the Sisterhood. "I admire you so much."

Maureen patted Traci's knee. "We were married for years before we lost our husbands. You had less than a year."

Nine months and eighteen days too long. Traci had known from the honeymoon that it wasn't going to work. She'd been analytical instead of emotional in choosing a husband and still ended up making the wrong choice. She raised the glass to her lips and found it empty.

"Regrets?" Maureen asked.

Traci had to bite her tongue to keep from blurting "More than you know." She averted her gaze. Maureen was too intuitive. "A few."

"Do you want to talk about it?" Donna asked gently. The mother of five had had a lot of practice listening to problems.

I'd rather roast on a spit. "I just don't know what all the fuss *is* about sex," Traci blurted, then went still. Not even with Maureen had she discussed *that* side of her marriage. She placed the empty glass on the side table. That was her last drink for the weekend.

"Blame it on the man," Maureen said with that straightforward attitude of hers that Traci admired and, at times, envied. Maureen wouldn't take crap from anyone. If they tried, she'd tell them off so fast their heads would swim.

She would have set Dante straight from day one. Or would have been smart enough to see through that handsome face and polished charm. With her knack for reading people she probably surmised that Traci had blamed herself for her failed marriage. Frigid was one of the nicer names that Dante had called Traci. She shrugged as if throwing off the old hurt. "It was a long time ago."

Maureen sighed dramatically. "Don't remind me."

Traci blinked and laughed with the other women. "You're incorrigible."

"If I were, I would have let Simon pick me up at the hotel."

"Simon's a good, strong name," Betsy said, knitting another pair of booties for the premie nursery where she volunteered once a week.

Maureen sighed again. "I bet the name fit." She stared down at Traci. "He might be too young for me, but he's just right for you."

Shock raced across Traci's face. Her nice buzz evaporated. In the six months since Traci had moved next door to Maureen in Charleston, the other woman had tried to fix her up a couple of times, but had quickly gotten the message that Traci didn't want to date.

"She's too young to be by herself," Nettie commented.

"I agree," Ophelia said.

"So do I." Maureen gently grasped Traci's arm and brought them both to their feet. "Perhaps he's still there."

"Maureen, we had this conversation before," Traci said, realizing she had to talk fast. Maureen would steamroll over your objections if she thought it was for your own good.

"That was before I saw the gorgeous hunk at the hotel," Maureen said.

"I could care less," Traci said, trying to free her arm. Maureen's hand tightened. She might be forty-five pounds slimmer and twenty-two years older, but she was strong.

"You'll change your mind once you've seen him." Maureen turned to the other women. "My car is out front. Let's go find out if he's still there."

Drinks, knitting, and chocolate were hastily cast aside. In less than a minute the women were assembled with their handbags, ready to leave. They'd done some crazy things in the past and usually Traci was as game as the next person, but not this time. "Maureen, I'm tired. I've had a hard week at work."

"You're also stalling." Maureen handed Traci to Nettie and Ophelia. "Hold her until I get my keys. We're going man hunting."

This is for Traci. No regrets.

Maureen repeated the words over and over as they piled out of her BMW 750 in front of the hotel. The soft evening breeze from the nearby sea teased her nostrils. Couples, hand in hand, strolled by. A soft yearning stole through Maureen.

A smiling young valet rushed past his counterpart to reach her first and take her keys. She usually smiled at their playful antics, but somehow couldn't tonight. She glanced around as Ophelia and Donna practically dragged Traci out of the backseat.

Maureen tried not to sigh. *No* regrets. Traci needed this. Since she had moved into the Georgian mansion next door, she hadn't been out on one date. Maureen wasn't a nosy neighbor. Traci had told her as much.

Traci was too serious and settled for someone so young. Maureen's son, Ryan, a noted OB-GYN, might have a serious and grueling profession that he loved, but he also enjoyed having a good time. Too much at times, Maureen thought with a shake of her head. She'd be eighty before he made her a grandmother.

Giving the keys to the valet, Maureen grasped Traci's arm, personally taking charge of her. "Smile." A creed of the Sisterhood was to help the other members even if they didn't want it. Traci might not be a member yet, but they all loved her. "You'll thank me if he's still here."

Traci grunted.

"Wait a minute, Maureen." Nettie opened the purse dangling from her arm and took out a comb and a tube of lipstick. "We need to make a few adjustments."

Traci's unpainted lips curled, but Nettie just stood there. Traci blew out a breath, uncurling her lips. Nettie rewarded her with a smile.

Traci might act tough around others, but she was really a softie, Maureen thought. Traci respected and loved the older members too much to appear ungrateful. Maureen suspected that a man had hurt her. One bad apple doesn't mean the entire bushel has worms, Maureen's mother had always said.

A picture of a tall, chocolate-skinned man with teasing midnight-black eyes flashed into her mind. Maureen's teeth gritted. *No, you're for Traci.*

Nettie put away the lipstick and comb. "Now, you look pretty."

"Thank you," Traci mumbled dutifully, not sounding at all pleased.

"Let's go." Entering the hotel, Maureen went straight to the bar on the far side of the lobby, which was filled with palm trees and milling people, some with conference badges.

They were barely inside the crowded, laughter-filled bar

before Maureen saw him. Her heart thudded. *What a man, what a man.* Her fingers tightened on Traci's arm. She swallowed before she could speak. "That's him."

Maureen hardly recognized the husky whispered words as being hers. Despite her best intentions she couldn't help but wish that the man looking directly at her with such interest could be for her.

Slowly he came to his feet. He wore a wheat-colored sports coat, white shirt, and chocolate-colored slacks. He was tall, athletically built with broad shoulders and a wide chest. His muscular body would make most women's heads turn, their bodies hum. Maureen's body certainly was.

"Come on." Before she weakened, Maureen skirted the tables and people, heading for Simon.

"I—" Traci began.

"This is for you," Maureen said, cutting her off. She didn't know if she said the words to bolster Traci or to chide herself. She didn't stop until she stood in front of Simon's gorgeous body. She barely registered the three other men at the table.

Damn it, he still made her heart beat like a drum. But he was too young. People often said she looked fifty. Simon looked to be in his late thirties or early forties. If she added ten or even fifteen years to what she thought his age was he'd still be too young.

"I'm glad you came back," he said softly. "You ready for our dance?"

Shocked pleasure raced through Maureen before she could suppress the emotion. He hadn't forgotten her or even glanced at Traci. Her silly heart skipped in joy. "I—"

"Please," he said, his voice a deep baritone that made her nerve endings stand at attention.

Maureen's grip on Traci's arm loosened. Yearning curled through her. What would it feel like to be held against that broad chest, held securely within his muscular arms?

"Enjoy the dance."

Caught off guard, Maureen watched as Traci took the opportunity to escape before Maureen could stop her. Traci quickly went to the table in the round booth just inside the door, from where the Sisterhood was watching them. Helplessly, Maureen turned back to Simon, a man who made her remember too much about being a woman.

Simon smiled, showing perfect white teeth and the most gorgeous dimples. "My name is Simon. Simon Dunlap, in case you've forgotten."

She hadn't forgotten one thing about the incredible man standing in front of her. In fact, she had thought too much about him. She liked tall men and he was at least six inches taller than she was even in her three-inch heels. Maureen's heart beat so fiercely she felt light-headed. Since Ryan had insisted she have a thorough checkup, including a complete cardiac workup, a month ago, she knew Simon caused the anomaly.

But that wasn't the only thing he was causing. The sexual thoughts that had been plaguing her lately returned with a vengeance. Her clinging to a man while he loved her until she was weak with pleasure, their bodies locked in passion. She had a healthy sex drive that was apparently tired of being repressed for four years.

Simon looked as if he were just the man to fulfill her fantasies and create a few more to heat up the night. She felt her face flush with embarrassment and something else—hot desire. "Excuse me."

"Please don't go." The light touch of his calloused hand on her bare arm sent a jolt of excitement to her nervous system. What would happen if he touched her in more intimate, softer places?

She licked her lips, watching his smoky black eyes narrow on her mouth, and wanted to taste him, savor him. Her hand tunneled through her short hair in desperation. Something must be wrong with her.

"How about I buy you a drink and we can just talk?"

Talk? She wouldn't be able to get out a complete sentence for thinking of him naked in her bed to do to him as she pleased. Her face and body heated even more. Hurriedly she glanced away. "I can't. I'm sorry."

"So am I," he said, unmistakable regret in each word. "At least tell me your name."

"Ashley," she mumbled, then hurriedly walked away. She might change her mind if she lingered. She'd given him her middle name, in a way wanting to give him something of her, hoping he might think of her beyond tonight, as she knew she would think of him.

"We can leave now," Maureen said, stopping at the table. None of the women moved.

"Traci said he asked you to dance," Nettie said.

"He was just being nice," Maureen said, in spite of herself wishing it had been more than that.

"From the hot way he's looking at you he was being a lot more than nice," Traci said, nodding toward Simon.

Maureen ordered herself not to look, but she lost the battle in less than a second and got that light-headed feeling all over again when her gaze met Simon's. Her eyes drifted to his well-shaped mouth. Her stomach quivered.

"The naughty boy," Ophelia said.

"Go slap his face," Donna told her. "A man would never be that bold in my day."

"Teach him a lesson he won't forget," Betsy urged.

"My Samuel would have never acted that way," Nettie said with a shake of her gray head.

"Go give it to him, Maureen," Traci urged. "We'll wait here until you get back. Sock it to him."

Maureen saw through their outrage and loved them more for it. They were goading her to forget her age and just have fun. She wished that she could. From the smoldering look Simon had given her, he wished the same.

"He's still too young," she said firmly. "The car is leaving as soon as the valet can bring it around."

"I'm comfortable here," Traci said, leaning back in the booth. "We all are."

Maureen frowned at them. They were using the Sisterhood creed on her—the promise to help the other out even if they didn't want it. She'd have to fight dirty. "How about Godiva chocolate martinis for nightcaps?" That got them moving. One of the pleasures of the Sisterhood meetings was answering to no one and indulging themselves when the mood struck.

Another thing the Invincibles did was know how to have fun. Maureen tried not to sigh as they piled back into her car. They just couldn't have hot, glorious sex.

2

Late Sunday night Maureen dropped Traci off in front of her two-story Georgian house in Charleston. Traci's overnight case sat at her feet; her garment bag was draped over her arm. The Sisterhood had ended the weekend early due to the weather forecast of a thunderstorm for the Isle on Monday.

With the exception of Traci and Nettie, who didn't drive and had come with Donna, all of the ladies had driven themselves and none liked driving in the rain. Since Traci had dismissed the driver after she'd arrived at Maureen's Friday night, she'd grabbed a ride back with Maureen.

"Thanks for the lift," Traci said through the open passenger door window.

"Yeah, it was a big hardship since you live next door," Maureen teased.

"Smarty." Traci picked up her overnight case. "Good night."

"Good night."

Maureen waited until Traci entered her house and the lights came on in the entryway and the door closed before pulling away from the curve. Feeling tired and a bit off, she parked in the circular driveway of her two-story French-style house instead of going to the four-car garage in back as usual.

Maureen got out of the car and removed her overnight case from the trunk, then went up the curved brick steps. Opening the double door, she stood in the sixteen-foot vaulted entryway and stared at the lyrical sweep of the Carrara marble staircase that curved to the master suite. The sense of home, of happiness that she usually felt, was missing. Loneliness hit her.

Before she could stop herself she thought of Simon, his smile, the regret in his beautiful smoky black eyes.

She wasn't the type of woman to deal with regrets or indecisiveness. With Simon she was dealing with both.

Sighing, she continued to the stairs. At least she didn't have to drag in any clothes, since the family always kept a rather extensive wardrobe at the beach cottage in case they decided to visit on the spur of the moment. But only she used it now. James was gone, and Ryan seldom had time away from his busy practice, the clinic where he volunteered, and his social life to visit her, let alone go to the beach.

"Stop feeling sorry for yourself. You have friends, a wonderful successful son, and more than the basic necessities of life."

Before she could stop herself, she wondered if a man could be considered a basic necessity. Probably not in today's culture where women were independent and cracking the glass ceiling, running Fortune 500 companies and countries.

She might not *need* a man, but a man did have his uses.

Lost in her musing, Maureen was almost to her bedroom before she saw the light coming from the open door. She frowned, and her steps slowed. She'd left midafternoon Friday.

The maid who came daily had left at the same time to visit friends in Memphis. She wasn't due back until Monday around noon.

Still puzzled, Maureen opened the door wider to her bedroom. And gasped.

A naked man lay sprawled facedown in her bed.

The overnight case dropped from her hand to land with a soft thud on the Oriental rug. The snoring man on top of her custom-made silk duvet didn't budge. Several empty wine bottles scattered around the room were probably the reason why. She fought down a mixture of rage and fear.

Not only had he broken into her house, he'd made himself at home in her bed and in her private wine cellar. Her first thought was to grab him by his long, unkept dark hair and pull the thief out of her bed.

Sanity prevailed.

He might be drunk, but that didn't mean he was incapacitated. Then she noticed something else, the outline of a smaller figure beneath the covers. Woman or man, she couldn't tell.

Maureen took one step backward, then another until she was in the hallway. She stopped at the landing by the house phone. Easing up the receiver, she dialed 911. She'd considered hitting the police button on the alarm pad in the bedroom next to hers, but she didn't want to risk waking the thieves when the alarm went off.

"911 operator," answered a female voice.

"Two people broke into my home and they're asleep in my bed," she whispered, her voice unsteady. "I just got home."

"We have your address. A patrol car is on the way. Are you alone?"

Her hand clenched the phone. "Yes."

"Go outside immediately. Do you have a cell phone?"

"No." She'd lost hers last week and hadn't had a chance to get another.

"Please go outside and wait."

"Thank you," Maureen whispered, her gaze on the door to her bedroom. Hanging up, she immediately hit the speed dial button for Ryan.

The phone answered on the second ring. "How's the love of my life?"

"Ryan." Just hearing his strong, steady voice made her knees shake.

"Mother, what's the matter?" All playfulness left his voice.

"Two people broke into the house." She swallowed before she could go on. "They're asleep in my bed."

"Where are you?" he asked sharply, then said something she couldn't understand.

"Down the hall on the phone," she whispered.

He muttered an expletive. "Get out of there! Now! We're on our way."

"Please hurry." She hung up the phone, turned to go, then swung back. The last mementos of her husband were in her bedroom. They were valuable, but worth much more to her, to Ryan, and to the grandchildren she hoped to have one day. They might take her precious mementos.

While she was cowering outside, the thieves could wake up and go out the bedroom window . . . if they knew she was there.

But they didn't. So they'd come out the bedroom door. Taking a deep breath, she picked up the heavy brass candlestick as long as her arm by the side chair at the top of the landing and went midway to her bedroom door. She'd be ready.

It seemed like an eternity before Maureen heard the front door open.

Her breath caught. Was it Ryan or was it an accomplice of the thieves? Ryan still had a key. Would the police come in unannounced? Have a master key?

She swallowed and started down the hall to the bedroom next door to hide. Then she heard Ryan's familiar footfalls on the stairs. They'd moved into the house when he was nine months old. There were so many wonderful memories here that she hadn't wanted to move after his father died.

Ryan, his face lined with fear and annoyance, came around the sharp turn of the stairs. Reaching the landing, he sprinted toward her. Her fingers loosened, letting the candlestick fall to the silk Oriental runner. She met him halfway.

In the security of his arms, she closed her eyes and allowed the fear and tension to ease out of her. His arms tightened around her as if reassuring himself that she was all right. She marveled again that this strong, handsome man was her son.

"In there."

Hearing Ryan's voice giving directions, she opened her eyes and caught a glimpse of a wide-shouldered man wearing a black sports coat before he disappeared into her bedroom. Moments later she heard a yelp, then a curse. She tensed.

"Don't worry. He has it covered," Ryan told her.

"There are two of them," Maureen said, tucking her lower lip between her teeth.

"It would take more than that to throw him, from what I've heard." Ryan pulled his mother closer as two uniformed officers appeared. "Second door to the left."

"You're sure he's all right?" she asked as the patrolmen rushed past them. There were no more sounds coming from her bedroom.

"Yes." Taking her arms, he stared down into her face. "Why didn't you do as I asked you?"

"I didn't want them to get away with your father's things," she answered.

Ryan shook his head, then gently shook her. "You were the most precious thing to him, to both of us. Dad would have understood."

"Or fussed a blue streak if he were here," she said, fondly recalling the occasions when she had done something her husband thought might have placed her in harm's way.

"I still recall the time you picked up a hitchhiker on your drive to Greenville." Ryan shook his head again.

Since that *had* been foolish, she said nothing. But in her defense she had felt sorry for the young black man, and so thankful her son was in college and safe, not standing in the drizzling rain trying to get to the next city to find work to support his family. People had to consider the risk, but also the reward if they reached out to help each other.

A commotion at her door caught her attention. Instinctively she stepped closer to Ryan. The scruffy man, now in jeans and a T-shirt, and a young woman dressed similarly were escorted past them by the two policemen. Both thieves were in handcuffs.

"Be sure to repeat the Miranda to them before you put

them in the squad car and once you arrive at the station. They're both pretty plastered," ordered the man who had arrived shortly after Ryan.

Maureen went still as she stared straight into the smoky black gaze of Simon Dunlap. She saw the recognition, the appreciation in his gaze, felt her heart race. Then she glanced at her son, and felt a different sort of fear.

Simon Dunlap always believed himself lucky.

His luck was holding, he mused, as he stared at the beautiful woman from the bar in the hotel on the Isle of Palm. She'd turned him down. Twice. A first since he never asked again once a woman said no. For her, he'd ask as many times as it took for her to say yes. Now she looked nervous, refusing to meet his gaze. He had a pretty good idea why.

"Mother, I'd like you to meet Simon Dunlap, a second lieutenant with the Myrtle Beach Police Department Burglary Division. Simon is on loan to the Charleston Police Department to help curb burglaries. My mother, Maureen Gilmore," Ryan introduced, his arm still around Maureen a.k.a. Ashley's shoulders.

"Mrs. Gilmore. I wish we could have met under different circumstances," Simon said, sensing that she didn't want her son to know they had met earlier. Her son. She looked too young to have an adult son in his late thirties. Simon had thought she was in her late forties, the same as he.

Finally, her head lifted, her dark amber eyes met his. "Lieutenant Dunlap. It was fortunate that you were in the city. Thank you."

"Simon and I were having drinks when I got the call," Ryan explained.

"He went through a caution light or we would have arrived together," Simon told her, trying to put her at ease and let her know her secret was safe. "If I had been in a police car I might have followed. I'm sorry you had to be alone one moment longer than necessary."

A pleased expression flickered across her beautiful face, then it quickly disappeared. "It couldn't have been helped."

"Ryan said you had planned to be away until Monday. I don't think they expected you back so early," Simon told her. "Looks like they were more interested in drinking and partying. The other patrolman reported a car in the back. A wrecker will tow it within the next couple of hours."

Maureen moistened her lips, lips that he had spent a lot of time thinking about in the past two days. "Can I go into my room?"

"Yes. I'll need you to make a complete list of missing items, but as I said I don't think they had taken anything yet." Simon followed her into the bedroom. "Another patrolman will wait with the car until it can be towed."

Maureen didn't answer, just glanced around. Except for the bed and the empty bottles, the elegant blue-and-white room was picture perfect as far as Simon could determine. She slowly crossed the room and opened one of the top drawers in a triple dresser and removed a small jewelry box and opened it.

She turned to them, an unsteady smile on her face. "I was almost afraid to look, but your father's watch and other things are still here."

Simon had known Maureen was a woman of worth. If he needed any proof, she had just given it to him. The first things she checked were the possessions of her deceased husband. If the sparkling diamond ear studs in her ear, her watch, and ring were any indication, she probably owned other expensive jewelry pieces, yet she hadn't bothered to check them.

Ryan's arm tightened around her. "Your safety is the important thing. They couldn't take what's in our hearts."

"I know, but I want your children to have these one day." She bit her lip, looked around the room, and shivered.

Ryan gently turned her stricken face to his. "We'll take everything off the bed and call Willie in the morning to replace the bedding."

"Willie?" Simon asked, hoping to get Maureen's mind on something beside the invasion of her room.

"The decorator," she answered, staring at her tumbled bed.

Having dealt with people in the past and their feeling of violation, Simon didn't expect to feel the anger or strong regret. He wished he had yanked harder when he'd pulled the man out of the bed by his hair. "Why don't we go downstairs? You and Ryan can go over your room later."

She turned firmly toward him. This time her gaze met his. "Would you like a cup of coffee?"

She was as gracious as she was lovely. And for a while it might help her forget. "That sounds good. Thank you."

"Please follow me."

Simon did as requested, wishing they could have met again under different circumstances. For a moment upstairs she'd looked shattered. Not for anything would he have wanted this to happen to her.

Downstairs in the spacious and ultramodern stainless steel kitchen with its hand-painted vaulted ceiling and large island, Maureen went to the automatic coffeemaker on the immaculate granite counter to put on the coffee. "Please have a seat," she said.

Ryan waved Simon to a padded chair at the antique rectangular oak table that would easily seat eight. "This is nice. My oldest brother and his wife just remodeled their kitchen."

"Thank you," Maureen said over her shoulder as she set the carafe under the spout. "They just finished last Thursday."

He stood and pulled out a chair for her as soon as she finished. "Please take a seat. Ryan and I can take it from here when the coffee is ready."

Maureen sent him the briefest hint of a grateful smile, then sat, placing her trembling hands in her lap. "Thank you."

Simon took a seat across from her and tried to keep his mind on procedure rather than the way Maureen kept licking her lips. He shifted in his seat. "I suppose the remodeling crew were in and out a lot."

"Yes," she answered, her gaze sliding to his, then away.

"Is your alarm a fixture or do you use it?" Simon asked— time to get back to business.

Her head lifted. A chagrined expression crossed her beautiful face before she glanced at Ryan. "I use it."

"Now. I nagged her until she did." Ryan got up to grab three cups. "This is a pretty crime-free neighborhood, but it pays to be safe. Or at least it was," he said with a grimace.

"Did you turn on your alarm before you left?" Simon continued.

"Thank you." Maureen accepted the cup of coffee from her son before answering. "I thought I did, but I must have forgotten. It wasn't on when I returned." She glanced guiltily at her son. "I guess I was in a hurry to leave."

"I wouldn't be so sure about that," Simon told her, then went on while she looked puzzled. "There was a pay stub from a kitchen remodeling company in the pocket of the man's jeans. A Fine Touch Remodeling. Sound familiar?"

Maureen's eyes widened. "They did the kitchen."

"And you gave them your code since they were in and out so much. Once they finished, you never changed it," Simon guessed.

Briefly her eyes closed. "I was at the store and the maid was on vacation when they began the project." Her shoulders straightened. "I'll call the alarm company tonight after we finish and change the code."

Simon almost reached across the table to take her agitated hands. "It could have happened to anyone. Apparently you trust people."

"The wrong people," Ryan said.

Maureen tucked her head. Simon didn't want to see the worry on her face. He made a quick decision. He didn't care for the idea of her being vulnerable or feeling incompetent. "If you'd like, I could come back and check the place over to see if there is anything that we can do to make the house safer."

Maureen felt gullible, a bit naïve, and embarrassed that a man she'd lusted after was a friend of her son, but the hard fact was she wanted to feel as safe as possible. At the moment she didn't. "I'd like that. Thank you."

"Is Tuesday around three all right?" Simon asked. "I check in at the station at eight in the morning and will probably be there all day. I coach a boys' basketball team on Tuesday nights."

Had she imagined the pleased look in his eyes when she'd agreed? Did he see the same undeniable look in hers? "Three would be fine. Do you mind if I invite a few friends?"

"No. The more knowledgeable people are about protecting themselves, the better for all concerned. I'll see you then." Flashing her a smile that made her heart sigh, he stood. "I'd better go and file that report."

Maureen slowly came to her feet, her hand pressed on the tabletop for support. If his smile made her weak what could his hands, that wicked mouth of his do? "I'll see you out."

"That isn't necessary," Simon told her as he moved toward the door.

"To Mother it is." Ryan slung his arm around his mother's shoulders. "She is a true Southern lady."

Maureen had always been proud to be Ryan's mother, but at that moment she wished he hadn't reminded Simon she had a grown son. Perhaps it was for the best. No matter how she might wish or fantasize, Simon wasn't for her. She hadn't thought of what Simon did for a living. He seemed much too easygoing for that profession, but perhaps not. His understanding and caring had certainly been what she needed in order to cope.

Simon smiled again. "She's also a very brave lady. I hope this doesn't happen again, but if it does, please wait outside."

"She will," Ryan said with finality.

The best way to win an argument with a man was to not start one, just do as you pleased . . . another lesson her mother had taught her. "This way." Maureen left the kitchen and started for the front door, the two men following close behind.

At the front door, Simon stepped in front of her to open the door, accidentally brushing lightly against her arm. She started. Her wide-eyed gaze jerked up to meet his; her breathing accelerated.

"I'm sorry. I didn't mean to startle you," he said, a frown marring his handsome face.

"You didn't." Which was the truth. He excited her. She swallowed and wrapped her arms around herself, felt the tingling of her bare arm where he had brushed against hers.

Again she wondered what it would feel like if he had the freedom to touch her as he pleased.

He stared at her a long moment as if he might be wondering the same thing, then mercifully he gave his attention to Ryan and extended his hand. "Thanks for the drink and the warm welcome to Charleston."

"I'm the one who should be thanking you." Shaking Simon's hand, Ryan glanced at his mother. "We owe you."

"Just doing my job. Good—"

"Maureen!"

Maureen jerked around at the sound of Traci's worried voice and saw her running across the adjoining yard. Maureen stepped off the porch and went to meet her.

3

Are you all right? Why were the police here?" Traci asked, her voice frantic as she clutched Maureen's arms.

"I'm fine, Traci," Maureen quickly reassured her. "Thieves broke into the house, then made themselves at home in my bed."

"Your bed!" Traci shrieked her outrage.

Maureen's eyes narrowed, her teeth clenched. Her own simmering anger resurfaced with a vengeance. "I wanted to drag the man out by his hair."

"Mother, please tell me you wouldn't be so foolish," Ryan said. He and Simon had stepped off the porch, but remained on the sidewalk.

"Your mother has more sense," Simon told him.

Maureen felt a small spurt of pleasure that Simon thought her sensible. "Luckily, Ryan was with a policeman. They rushed over," she explained. Looping her arm through Traci's, Maureen started toward the men on the walkway.

Maureen had taken only a few steps before realizing things could become awkward if Traci revealed that they knew Simon. Hoping Traci would understand the unspoken need for discretion, they joined the men on the walk.

"Traci Evans, Lieutenant Dunlap from Myrtle Beach. Traci lives next door."

"Pleased to meet you, Ms. Evans, but I wish it could have been under different circumstances," Simon said, extending his hand.

Traci was slow in lifting hers. "Hello, Lieutenant Dunlap." Almost immediately she released his hand and faced Maureen, "Would you like me to go in and help you straighten things up and spend the night or do you want to stay at my place?"

"Thank you, Traci, but I plan to help her and spend the night," Ryan said with just the tiniest bit of displeasure in his deep voice, which always made her think of moonlight and magnolia.

Traci finally looked at Ryan, all six feet two of conditioned muscles. He looked as delicious as usual. He wore one of his Italian suits that fit his glorious body perfectly, this one charcoal pinstripe. He was drop-dead gorgeous with a killer smile that made her stomach muscles dance a jig. "Of course."

His smile was slow and easy as his assessing gaze ran the length of her. "Simon is going to give Mother a home evaluation Tuesday afternoon. Perhaps he should do your house as well."

"I'm fine," she said, trying not to grit her teeth. Ryan irritated the hell out of her and he knew it.

"I wouldn't mind checking," Simon said. "The reason I'm here is to help decrease the number of home robberies."

"Come on, Traci. I'd feel better if you did," Maureen coaxed, her voice a bit unsteady. "Believe me, you don't want this to happen to you."

Simon lifted his hand toward Maureen, only to let it fall.

"Strip the bed, get rid of the mattress if you have to. Do whatever it takes to reclaim your room. Create a memory that will take away seeing them there."

Maureen's eyes widened as if she was surprised he understood. She nodded. "I will."

Traci felt Ryan looking at her again, and she ignored him. From their first meeting shortly after she'd moved here, there had been this "thing," this "awareness" between them. She planned to ignore whatever it was and thought he was doing the same. But the last two times they had been together, she'd felt his hot gaze on her, weighing, examining as if he were trying to figure out if she was worth the effort.

And she wanted to sock him. He was just playing with her. Maureen had dragged Traci to an award banquet where Ryan was honored, and she'd seen the sleek, model-thin woman he'd been with. Where it counted to most men— hips and breasts—Traci would make two of the woman.

"Is there someone else in your household who could come if you're busy?" Simon asked.

"I live alone," Traci said. *Just the way she liked it.*

"Traci and Mother are both widows," Ryan explained. "Which means they both need your services."

Traci's eyes narrowed. "I don't need anything from a man."

Ryan's eyebrow cocked in disbelief. Was that a challenge? "That remains to be seen."

"I—"

"Traci, I plan to invite the others," Maureen interrupted. "You know we'll all nag you until you come. Besides, if one of us forgets something, you'll remember."

"That's blackmail," Traci said.

Maureen smiled into her angry face. "Yes, it is, isn't it?"

"I promise it will be painless and not bore you." Simon, a smile on his face, glanced at Maureen. "I get the impression that you're very close. She'll worry if you don't come, and I don't think you'd want that."

Traci and Maureen both stared at Simon. An intuitive man could cause a woman a lot of trouble. Traci's gaze traveled to Maureen. She had that wistful look on her face again. Or a lot of pleasure.

"You're right. She'll be there."

Traci's attention snapped back to Ryan. He was too self-assured and too used to having his own way. She'd like to— her thoughts abruptly halted. Heat flushed her cheeks. The image that had popped into her mind hadn't been that of slapping that know-it-all look off his too-handsome face, but had involved two naked bodies locked in an erotic embrace.

Thoughts like that could get a woman into a lot of trouble, but Traci was too smart to fall for that trap again. A man could make a woman's life hell. Dante had taught Traci that, and she had learned her lesson well.

"Please," Maureen said, as if knowing Traci was considering not showing up just to show her son he couldn't speak for her.

"I'll come only because I have a lot of work this week and I don't want the Sisterhood nagging me." Traci firmly turned to Simon. "If it's boring I'm going to tell you."

He chuckled. "I wouldn't have it any other way."

His easy response pleased her. From the way he kept sneaking glances at Maureen, he had more on his mind than burglar-proofing her home. Maureen might have hit pay dirt the second time as well. Traci remembered another man with the same name. "Are you any relation to Patrick Dunlap?"

Surprise briefly flitted in Simon's eyes. "My younger brother. Do you know Patrick?"

"We met briefly the other night," Traci told him, hoping Maureen had gotten as lucky as Brianna seemed to be. But Traci of all people knew how looks could be deceiving.

"I'm staying with him." Simon shook his head and smiled. "He's getting married in three weeks and counting the days."

"With Brianna as the bride, I can see why," Ryan said. "She's something. We went to school together."

Traci's mouth firmed. She might have known Ryan would know the stunning woman. "And why aren't you the one marrying her?"

Ryan's gaze centered on her. "Contrary to some people's belief, I don't date all the beautiful women I know."

Traci didn't know why, but his words made her think he was taking a swipe at her. "Yeah. Some of them have more sense."

Maureen cleared her throat. "I'll see you Tuesday at three, Lieutenant Dunlap."

"Three it is," Simon said.

Ryan finally pulled his hard gaze from Traci. "I'd also like you to go over the security system at her store if you don't mind and have the time."

"I don't mind and I have the time," Simon spoke to Maureen. "I could stop by Friday afternoon if that would be convenient?"

"I don't want to take up too much of your time," Maureen protested.

Simon shook his dark head, a smile on his lips. "Your safety and peace of mind are what counts. I don't want you feeling vulnerable," he said with feeling. "I promise not to interfere with your business."

"All right," Maureen said. "Thank you."

Traci watched as Simon's and Maureen's gaze clung together, and she decided to help before Ryan caught on. There was one sure way to grab his attention. "Maureen, I don't mind helping you. Then Ryan can go home." Traci kept her gaze on Maureen and off her son.

"I'm staying and taking Simon's advice," Ryan said firmly. "We're going to make another memory."

"That we will," Maureen said.

Ryan curved his arm around his mother's shoulders. "You and Dad spent many happy hours in that room."

"I'd better be going," Simon said. "The tow truck should be here shortly. Good night."

"Good night," Maureen, Ryan, and Traci chorused.

Traci watched him walk away and wondered if he would have left if Ryan hadn't mentioned his deceased father. In any case, it was time to leave as well. "Good night."

"Maybe I should walk you to your door," Ryan suggested.

Traci gritted a smile. "Just take care of Maureen. I'm fine." Giving her best friend a quick hug, making sure she didn't accidentally touch Ryan, she hurried back to her house, feeling Ryan's gaze every running step.

Let him look all he wanted, but it wouldn't do him any good. No man would ever take advantage of her again. She'd made that promise when she stared down into Dante's still face at the funeral, and she'd kept it.

Opening the front door, she went inside her house. She hadn't gone three steps before a little voice inside her head whispered, *"But no man had ever tempted you the way Ryan has. No one. He makes you wonder how making love with him would be."*

"Shut up," Traci muttered, then cursed. If it wasn't bad

enough that Ryan had her hearing voices, now she was answering them. "Damn."

In her lifetime she'd only met one man she'd cared about, who loved her unconditionally. She mustn't forget. She was too smart to be tripped up by hormones.

In control once again, she raced up the winding staircase.

Ryan woke up the next morning with a plan.

Once he saw that his mother was back to her calm, caring self, he saw no reason not to put it into action. He wasn't a player. In this day, it was not only stupid but dangerous. He wasn't conceited, but there had never been a woman he had wanted that he hadn't gotten. And one had never given him the cold shoulder the way Traci seemed to enjoy doing.

He didn't mind, because he knew eventually she'd be in his arms and in his bed. Patience was required. He was willing to stay the course. According to his mother, Traci wasn't dating anyone. Unless she was working, she was at home. His mother thought Traci should get out more. Ryan planned to take care of that. Starting today.

He was sticking around until Traci showed. This time she wouldn't be able to ignore him. She might be the last to show up, but she wouldn't leave for work until she'd checked on Maureen. She cared for his mother. She just didn't care for the son.

Or so it seemed at times. Then there were those other fleeting moments when he'd catch her looking at him with pure female speculation in her beautiful eyes. In the next instant, she'd go cold and haughty on him. But those brief glimpses gave him hope.

He wasn't sure why he just didn't move on. Perhaps

because she tried so hard to irritate him. More than likely it was because the first time he'd seen her she'd been in shorts and a halter top. Her lush body had filled out both nicely and made his body harden. She'd quickly made an excuse to leave his mother's house, but the view of her rounded backside kept him awake half the night and made him itch to get his hands on her.

Five months and he wasn't even close, but he wasn't giving up. She'd be here just as the Invincibles were.

Nettie and Betsy arrived first with indignant anger and a pan of fresh-baked cinnamon rolls and quiche. They were quickly joined by an outraged Ophelia with a platter of thick slices of honey-cured ham, smoked links, maple bacon, and pan sausages. Donna, minutes behind Ophelia, had a basket of fluffy brown biscuits, and her own harsh words for the burglars.

All brought sympathy and encouragement. Ryan watched the Invincibles flutter around the large kitchen, consoling his mother and ordering her to eat. In the Southern tradition, food was a panacea for everything.

Not for what he wanted, which was Traci Evans naked in bed.

He was as surprised by the attraction as she seemed to be. The women he dated were slim, beautiful, and agreeable. Traci had lush breasts, a rounded bottom, and was pretty and mouthy. His lips curved. He'd like to teach her something else to do with those lips.

"Ryan, you're not eating." Nettie, the eldest and self-appointed mother figure, frowned at his plate piled high with a bit of everything. "Don't tell me you don't eat quiche."

He forked in a bite of the ham and cheese quiche. If he had to put in extra time at the gym, it was worth it not to hurt any of their feelings. For the rest of the week he'd stick to a sensible low-fat, low-calorie breakfast. "This man does. This is delicious. Thanks for coming over this morning."

"Where else would we be?" Donna served everyone biscuits. "Maureen needed us."

Standing by the large slate island, Maureen set down her coffee cup. "I'm having the bedding cleaned, then donating everything to the Salvation Army. The cleaning company is coming by after nine."

"Have you called Willie yet?" Ophelia asked.

Maureen nodded. "Shortly after eight this morning. She's going to check and see if she can find the fabric to redo all the bedding and swags."

"She will." Betsy nodded emphatically. "Willie is a gem when it comes to decorating. She certainly did wonders with Traci's house."

"By the way, where is she?" Nettie asked, her brow furrowed. "She called us last night. I would have thought she would be the first one here this morning."

Maureen's gaze flickered to her son. "She said she had a lot of work to do today."

Starting with evading me. Score another point for Traci. "Well, I'd better get to the office." He came to his feet, then kissed each of the women's offered cheeks. "Stay out of trouble, ladies."

"What would be the fun in that?" Ophelia asked, laughing boisterously.

Ryan smiled and kissed his mother. "I'll come by tonight."

"Maureen will be fine. We have the day all planned." Nettie escorted him to the kitchen door. "We probably won't be back until late afternoon, so don't be alarmed if you can't reach her. You have our cell numbers."

"One of those stops should be to replace Mother's cell," Ryan suggested.

"It's on the list. That was the second thing Traci said," Donna told him.

The first was probably to be there this morning to support his mother. Even if she did avoid him, she made sure Maureen was cared for. Waving good-bye to the women, Ryan closed the door, then followed the bricked path to the front of the house where his car was parked.

Opening the door to the sports car, Ryan stared at Traci's house. She was probably peeping through a window, waiting for him to leave. She definitely didn't like the sensual awareness between them.

Too bad. He wasn't giving up. She was a challenge he couldn't resist. Opening the door, he slid inside and started the motor. The car had barely straightened out on the palmetto-lined street when he looked into his rearview mirror and saw Traci, holding a covered dish, cutting across the adjoining yards. He slowed, then stopped.

She stopped as well. He wondered what she'd do if he backed up. He glanced at the clock on the dash. Eight thirty-seven. His first patient was at nine and he was twenty minutes away from his office. He shifted the car into drive and pulled off.

Someday, somehow he'd see that she didn't get a chance to run from him or avoid him.

Traci's hands began to tremble when Ryan's car stopped. She didn't like it. She liked it even less that she wasn't sure if the reason was because Ryan irritated her or excited her.

She wasn't sure she wanted to find out. That cowardice

notion did irritate her. After Dante she'd promised herself that no man would ever make her feel helpless, insecure, or a coward again.

Ryan, during the months that she had known him, had made her feel all three. But she had to admit not in the same way that Dante had done. She couldn't tell how she recognized the difference. She just did.

Even now, after he'd pulled off, her hands continued to tremble just the tiniest bit. She let out a pent-up breath. After a sleepless night, she was in no mood for a verbal battle with Ryan.

Maureen's front door opened and all of the Sisterhood came out. "We were wondering where you were," Nettie said.

"There was no answer when we called, and we got worried," Donna continued.

"I'm fine. Sorry I'm late." Traci lifted the dish in her hands. "Cheese grits."

"We have enough food for a dozen people." Maureen studied her closely, no doubt not missing the dark circles beneath her eyes. "Did you sleep all right?"

Traci shrugged. "Thinking about the new client. How is everyone this morning?"

"Better than you and Maureen," Betsy said. "Come on in here and get yourself a plate."

Traci was more than happy to obey. Not because she was hungry, but because the topic would shift from her to Maureen, the reason they were all there. In the kitchen, she placed the Crock-Pot on the granite counter and plugged it in. She turned and Nettie handed her a cup of coffee that she knew would have two teaspoons of sugar and a generous dollop of cream. Just the way she liked it.

"Thanks." She sipped. "Perfect."

Nettie smiled. She was happiest when she was mothering others. Her two daughters lived in Seattle with five children among them. Both were wives of busy executives. Nettie usually flew out to visit them every couple of months. They managed to talk almost daily. They had the strong bond that Traci would never have with her mother. Traci told herself she no longer cared. And on good days she actually believed the lie.

"Here you are." Maureen sat a plate of food by Traci's elbow. "Anything we can help you with?"

Traci's hand, reaching for the quiche, stilled. Her head lifted. Despite all Maureen was going through, she wanted to help Traci. She was still getting used to that kind of selfless caring. "That's what we should be asking you."

Maureen waved Traci's words aside with her hand. Folding her arms, she leaned back against the island. Ophelia and Betsy, drinking their coffee, flanked her. "I'm over being mad and just thankful we cut the trip short. I'm very lucky."

"Have you told them how else you're lucky?" Traci smiled at the sudden flush in Maureen's checks.

Ophelia whirled on Maureen. "What?"

"You're blushing," Betsy said.

"A man," Donna guessed. "You met a man."

Nettie frowned. "You went out after your house was burglarized?"

"She didn't have to." Traci picked up the cinnamon roll oozing with cream cheese icing and took an unladylike bite. Delicious. Now this was something she could indulge in without consequences . . . well, almost. "Maureen had another surprise last night."

Maureen held up her hand as all the women except Traci

surged toward her, demanding answers. "The police lieutenant with Ryan last night was Simon."

"Your Simon from the bar?" Nettie asked, her eyes wide.

Maureen blushed again. "He's not my Simon."

"Yet," Traci put in. "Just like at the bar, he couldn't keep his eyes off Maureen. Personally, I think he has another reason for wanting to talk about burglar-proofing our homes."

"He's too young," Maureen cried out, but the words lacked conviction.

"Are you trying to convince us or yourself?" Ophelia asked quietly.

"Myself, and I'm having a hard time," Maureen admitted. "He . . . he—"

"Excites you," Donna whispered.

Maureen nodded, then made a face. "I have a birthday coming in less than two months."

"I read an article that said older women and younger men were becoming more commonplace," Ophelia offered. Ophelia was a former librarian and usually was never without a book. "You're following the trend."

Maureen wrinkled her nose. "Somehow that makes me feel worse."

"That's because you're thinking too much." Traci went to her. "Just see what happens. Have a drink, go out to dinner. You'll always wonder if you don't."

"He might not ask me again," Maureen said, misery creeping into her voice.

"My money says he will. You just be ready with your answer," Traci said. "Now, I have to get to the office."

"You're sure you can't get away to go with us?" Donna asked. "We're going to the spa and have the exfoliating body polish and the moisturizing massage."

"These eyes of mine could use the eye massage and moisturizing mask," Betsy said. "I could carry luggage in these bags."

Maureen touched her arm. "What can we do?" Before she finished speaking, the other women were standing around Betsy offering their support as well.

Betsy patted Maureen's hand and produced a shaky smile. "I'm fine." She looked around at the women. "We're here for Maureen, not for me."

"We're here for each other," Nettie said. "That's what friends, good friends, are for. They don't judge because they know we're all different with different needs and lives. But most of all, we realize that it's His blessings that have gotten us this far, and none of us can brag that we did it on our own."

Traci thought of her grandfather, the man who had raised her, loved her when no one else had. He'd prayed for her when she was too stubborn and too stupid to do it for herself.

"Nettie is right, Betsy," Maureen said. "When you're ready, we're here. Now, let's get this show on the road." She hooked her arm through Betsy's. "Do you think a massage will take a couple of years off so I won't feel quite so guilty for thinking about accepting a date with Simon . . . if he asks?"

"There's one way to find out," Betsy said, her expression grateful. "Let's get moving."

"I wonder if I can get a male masseuse," Ophelia said as the women began putting away the food.

"Ophelia, what a thing to say!" Nettie admonished, but she was smiling as she pressed the plastic top on the quiche.

"If you get one, I want one, too." Donna covered the plate

of ham. "I want to see if I can remember what a man's hand felt like."

"I'll never forget," Traci said tightly. The absolute quietness in the room told her she hadn't hidden her anger or disgust. Unable to meet any of their gazes, she turned to the back door of the kitchen. "Have fun, and don't get into too much trouble."

"As I told Ryan, what would be the fun of that," Ophelia said with a laugh. The other women joined in. "We'll be at Bliss, trying out the day spa if you change your mind. You know how much fun we had the last time we were there."

At the door, Traci looked over her shoulder. They all watched her. Not with censure, but with affection. Good. She didn't want their pity. She'd had enough of that to last a lifetime.

Forever Yours was the culmination of a twenty-year dream for Maureen.

Her husband had traveled extensively with his import-export business; she had traveled with him once Ryan was in college. She'd fallen in love with the beauty and craftsmanship of the fine furnishings abroad and at home. She'd wanted to preserve the history and the craft. She'd opened the shop two years before James's death. He'd been so proud of her.

Tuesday morning, Maureen unlocked the half-leaded glass door that dated back to the eighteenth century and smiled. The area looked elegant with groupings of furniture. She'd wanted the customer to get a sense of how the pieces would look in their home, so she had rooms without walls, leaving plenty of aisle space for people to wander, touch, and imagine.

The door opened behind her. Henrietta Rudley, her full-time assistant, entered. Henrietta was on the far side of sixty. She knew and loved antiques as much as Maureen. Forever Yours was in good hands when Maureen was away.

"Good morning, Henrietta."

"Good morning." Henrietta studied Maureen's face closely,

then nodded. "You look well. You didn't let the break-in get you down."

"I realized I was lucky. Plus too many people wouldn't let me," Maureen said, thinking of one in particular. "I see the eighteenth-century English desk is gone. Did Mrs. Miller finally decide to take it?"

Henrietta shook her head. "Nope. A young woman came in late yesterday morning and purchased it. She came back with two strapping men to pick it up."

"Mrs. Miller will be disappointed."

"She should have bought it instead of coming in here every week to look at it," Henrietta said without sympathy. "It isn't as if she didn't have the money. Sometimes when you see something you want, you have to grab it."

Maureen frowned. Henrietta had buried one husband, and had been married to a retired postal worker for the past twelve years. "Have you been talking to the Sisterhood?"

"Should I have been?"

Maureen laughed at herself for jumping to conclusions. "No. Any other sales?"

"Four. Business was good as usual." Henrietta started to the back and Maureen fell into step with her. "Your other browser was here looking at the paintings again."

Maureen opened the door to her office. "Did you get any more out of him?"

Henrietta harrumphed and put her large bag in the bottom of a cherry filing cabinet and her lunch in the refrigerator in the corner. "Not a peep."

"Maybe one day he'll let down his guard and talk." Maureen placed her purse in the bottom drawer of her desk. "Everything go all right with Avery?"

"It would go better if she didn't talk so much." Henrietta

opened the closet and took out a dustcloth and a can of beeswax. "I'm sure glad you and the Sisterhood don't meet every month. I'm not sure I could stand it."

"She's young." Avery, nineteen and perky, was a sophomore college student majoring in interior design. She worked part-time in the store on weekends and when Maureen was away. "She's a good salesclerk."

"Why do you think I put up with her?"

Maureen eyed the clean white cloth and the wax. "I thought Avery was supposed to do that."

"We were busy," Henrietta said by way of explanation and went out the door.

Maureen grabbed another cloth and followed. Avery had broken a vase her second day working there. It had been an expensive and irreplaceable piece. Avery had cried, afraid of being fired. She needed the job to help her pay for college.

Maureen had understood that it had been an accident, but since then Henrietta had assigned the young woman to duties that didn't demand anything be moved.

People made mistakes. Her thoughts unerringly went to Simon. Was she making one in thinking of going out with him? She visualized the warmth, the sheer male appreciation in his eyes, and knew, if given the opportunity, she was going to take the chance.

"He's early today," Henrietta said, then shook her head and went back to dusting.

The front door opened and a teenager entered. He was tall and lanky, his feet long. Maureen wasn't sure if she should try to approach him again. He'd been coming since the beginning of summer.

He moved easily around the store, his backpack securely fitting his lean frame, presenting no danger of breaking anything. A couple of times before he came in, she'd seen him drag it off one shoulder and put it on properly. Obviously he was cautious and valued the antiques.

She thought he must be in summer school since most teenagers, if they didn't have a job, weren't out of the house and prowling stores, at least not an antique store. It was unusual to see a teenager return again and again to an antique shop.

As usual he didn't make eye contact with her, just moved aimlessly around the shop before ending up, as always, in front of one of the oil paintings. She'd caught him a few times with his hand following the sketch or peering closely as if trying to figure out what kind of brush had made the stroke.

Maureen waited until he stood in front of an oil painting by Henry O. Tanner before joining him. "It's beautiful, isn't it?"

He tensed.

"The painting is one of his earlier works. Do you want to be a painter?"

His gazed snapped to her as if he couldn't make up his mind whether she was making fun of him or being serious. But he didn't answer.

"Well, I'd better get back to dusting. Feel free to stay as long as you like." She turned away, wondering if she would ever reach him. She knew he could talk because she had gotten a one-word answer from him before.

She had barely made it back to the chest of drawers she was dusting before the door closed behind him. She sighed.

"I don't think he knows what to think of you," Henrietta said as she came to stand by Maureen.

"That makes us even." Maureen went to the plateglass window and watched him, as he, head down, continued along the street. "I don't know what to think of him either."

"But you want to," Henrietta said.

Maureen nodded. "I look at Ryan and know how blessed James and I were. I also know we couldn't have been with him every moment. He learned from other people as well. I don't want to miss an opportunity to help someone else's child."

"You won't. Now, let's get this dusting done before the real customers start coming."

Maureen wasn't fooled by Henrietta's gruff words. Underneath she cared. She just didn't like people to know. Her first husband had abused her and it had taken a long time for her to trust people, to stop being angry at God and everything that breathed. "Have I told you lately how much I value your friendship?"

Henrietta's arthritic hand paused. Her face lifted. "If you try to kiss me, I'm going to sue for sexual harassment."

Maureen grinned and began polishing the chest. "I'm on to you, Henrietta Rudley. I happen to know you've been taking Avery to her classes and picking her up on the days she works here since her car is in the shop."

"Self-preservation." Henrietta moved to a commode table. "If she has a job and pays taxes, my Social Security just might last."

The smile Maureen had been wearing slid from her face. A woman a few years away from Social Security certainly shouldn't be having the thoughts she had, but she didn't seem to be able to help herself.

No matter how Maureen wanted to convince herself that the meeting she had called was just to help her neighborhood and the Sisterhood better protect themselves against burglaries, as she watched Simon stride up the sidewalk, her racing heart told her she'd lied to herself.

Her breath fluttered over her slightly parted lips. *My, my. What a man.*

Today he was dressed casually in a lightweight tan-colored sports jacket, white shirt with an open collar, and creased jeans that caressed his muscular thighs. His jet-black hair gleamed in the afternoon sun. His skin was the color of rich chocolate. She couldn't see a spare ounce of fat on his muscular frame, and she was looking hard.

Her hand fluttered to her stomach. She was in good shape herself. For a woman her age. Reality hit her just as the doorbell rang. She jumped away from the curtained window. Yesterday the spa had been invigorating, but she remained fifty-nine.

The chime came again. Stop being silly, she admonished herself, and started for the door. He's just a man. No big deal. She opened the door.

Simon, who had been looking around, turned and smiled at her, causing her body to throb, her throat to dry. He might be just a man, but what a man.

"Good afternoon, Mrs. Gilmore."

She felt old. "Lieutenant Dunlap, please come in and please call me Maureen."

He entered and waited until she closed the door. "I guess Ashley is out."

She flushed, then smiled because he was. "Thank you for not mentioning we'd met before Sunday night."

His smile faded. "How have you been? Did you sleep all right?"

"I did. Ryan and I took your suggestion," she told him.

"I'm glad."

She caught herself smiling and gazing at him, the same way he was smiling and gazing at her. Perhaps Traci was right. Perhaps he would ask her out again. "This way to the terrace." She started through the foyer and great room.

"You have a beautiful home," he said.

"Thank you. My late husband and I moved in when Ryan was nine months old," she told him, a subtle reminder to both of them.

"Then this house must hold a lot of fond memories for you," he said, stepping ahead of her to open the French doors leading to the terrace.

Pleased that he understood and hadn't choked at the mention of her late husband, she stopped. "It does. Ryan and I made more after we changed the bedding. We looked at family films and pictures. Played cards. He let me win."

"Your smile is as beautiful as you are," Simon said, still holding the latch. "To have stolen that would have been a travesty."

Pleasure went through her before she could stop the reaction. She simply stared at him.

"Simon, right on time." Ryan strode toward his frat brother, extending his hand.

Simon turned to shake hands with Ryan when what he really wished was that he could send everyone away and be alone with Maureen. Soon, he promised himself. "I didn't expect you here."

"Mother might not want to follow through on your suggestions." Ryan looked at his mother. "I plan to make sure she does."

"I'm quite capable of taking care of myself and following through with Lieutenant Dunlap's recommendations, Ryan."

Her son kissed her on the cheek. "Never said you weren't."

"Would you like something to drink or do you want me to introduce you to everyone and get started?" she asked Simon.

"Why don't you introduce me?" Simon suggested, wondering if Ryan had caught his mother's brief annoyance. Women hated being made to feel as if they were incompetent or stupid, and he couldn't blame them. They were as smart as men. Sometimes smarter. "I can talk to them and see how I need to gear the discussion. The needs of a woman living alone will be different than a couple's."

"That sounds good. This way," Maureen said.

He was watching her. Again.

Every time Traci looked at Ryan, he was looking at her . . . which meant she was watching him as much as he was watching her. Annoyed with herself and him, she went to the kitchen for another tray of food. With the attentive way Maureen was listening to Simon it wasn't likely she was going to get it. Traci supposed she couldn't blame her. If she hadn't known of their history she might not have paid any attention to all the times Simon looked at Maureen. Since she was sitting with the Sisterhood, he could have been looking at any of them.

Tracy knew better.

Simon hadn't been boring. In fact, he was a hit. The Sisterhood liked him even before he volunteered to inspect each of their homes to improve safety. Simon was proving to be a nice guy.

In the kitchen, Traci opened the side-by-side refrigerator and bent to take out the covered meat-and-cheese tray. Picking up the tray, she bumped the door closed with her hip and turned. She almost dropped the tray on seeing Ryan.

It ran through her mind that he had seen her use her wide hips, bringing more attention to them. Her temper spiked.

"Why are you sneaking up on me?"

"Sorry." Ryan glanced over his shoulder. "I wanted to get you alone."

Her pulse sped up. Her hands clenched on the tray.

"I need your help to plan Mother's birthday party," he whispered, coming closer.

Traci blinked. "What?"

"Let me have that." Ryan took the tray out of her hands and set it on the island. "I'm not sure if she wants a large to-do at the country club or a girl's night out with you and the Sisterhood. Maybe a private pampering spa thing."

Traci was having trouble taking it in. "You want help planning her party?"

"It's more involved than that." Ryan folded his arms and leaned back against the island. "I could hire a party planner, but I want it to be special. After the break-in Sunday night, a special night is even more important."

Surprised and oddly annoyed, Traci didn't know what to say. How could she have been so wrong?

"I hate to throw this on you, but I've been trying to catch your attention for weeks. The Sisterhood is a great group and, no offense, but I thought since Mother is younger and you two are such great friends, you might have a better idea of what she wants."

He didn't want her body: He wanted her mind. She could really hate Ryan Gilmore.

"I'll take this. It will throw Mother off if she saw me follow you." He picked up the tray. "We'd better get back before she misses us. Do you think you might be able to get away one night this week to have dinner and discuss things?"

She had let a man fool her again and, although it wasn't in a sexual way, she wanted to disappear. How could she have read him so wrong? She had almost made a complete fool of herself. How could she have been so blind, so stupid? She knew the type of women he dated and they certainly didn't resemble her.

His smile faded. "You aren't going to refuse, are you?"

Not if she ever hoped to be able to look him in the face again and, since he was Maureen's son, there was no way she could ever get around that. "No, I was just thinking of where we could meet," she lied, and suggested the first place that entered her mind. "Circa 1897."

"Great. It's quiet enough so we can plan and talk," he said. "Is eight tomorrow night all right? There shouldn't be any danger in Mother seeing me. I'll make reservations."

The restaurant was quiet all right, and very intimate, but it was done. "Why don't I meet you there?"

He shook his head. "If I pick you up we'll have more time to talk." He turned away, then turned back. "Thanks. See you tomorrow night at eight sharp. This is going to be great."

Traci watched him leave, her pride in tatters, but she had done it to herself. She should have known Ryan wasn't interested in her. It took all of her courage to go back to the patio where all the guests were converged.

She was in time to see Celeste, the single daughter of the couple at the end of the block, slide up to Ryan. Celeste was in her late twenties, a college dropout, and still trying to figure out what she wanted to do with her life while living at home. From the way she was curled against Ryan, she had found one thing she was interested in. Ryan, just like a man, was grinning from ear to ear at the attractive brunette.

Traci took a seat and gave her attention to Simon, who

was discussing how outdoor lighting served the dual purpose of beautifying your home and keeping burglars away. Too bad there wasn't something that kept men faithful. Their conscience and morality certainly never got in the way.

Celeste could have Ryan. Traci wasn't interested in being cheated on again.

W ould you have dinner with me tomorrow night?"

Simon had kept it professional until all the people Maureen had invited had gone home and he'd finished his inspection of her home and given her a written list of his recommendations. They'd just finished and were in the great room.

"Lieutenant Dun—"

"Simon, please," he coaxed. "I'm off duty as of an hour ago."

"Yet you stayed?"

"I'd stay longer if necessary," he said. "I want you to feel safe. To feel as if you have control over your life again."

"I do, thanks to you, Ryan, and the others," she told him.

"Good. The woman's parents bailed her out, but the man is still in jail," Simon told her. "From what I heard, they've been trying to get her to stay away from him."

"I guess it would be too much to hope that this will show her that her parents are right," Maureen said.

"Probably. I've seen it played over and over too many times." He shook his dark head. "We're losing too many of our young people to crime."

"I know. That's a big part of the reason the Sisterhood has a mentoring program with Kirk High School."

"You're a good woman, Maureen."

She blushed. "I'm not doing this alone."

He smiled. "You're all good women. It should be interesting inspecting their homes."

Maureen laughed. "Glad you already know that. They like you."

"I like one member in particular." He stepped closer. "A late dinner Thursday night? Wherever you choose."

She glanced away, then stared straight at him. "Why?"

He frowned. "Why let you choose the restaurant?"

"Why me?" she asked, her shoulders straightening.

"When I first saw you I thought you were beautiful and I liked that you were smiling. Some people walk around frowning at nothing."

Her shoulders relaxed. "I had just sold a dining set, and was looking forward to the weekend with the Sisterhood."

"Then I witnessed your courage, your resiliency, your graciousness and caring for your friends. You're a woman I'd like to get to know better," he told her. "Please."

"All right."

A wide grin split his face. "Great. Where would you like to go and what time should I pick you up?"

She smiled back. "Why don't you pick someplace casual? I'll be ready at nine."

"Patrick said Sticky Fingers is good."

So she'd have barbecue sauce on her fingers and mouth. Perhaps he could suck it off. "Yes."

"Good." He picked up his briefcase and went to the door. "I'll see you Thursday night at nine."

"Good evening. And thanks again."

He looked at the dark exterior of the house and frowned. "How soon do you plan to get the spotlights on the house?"

Her lips twitched. "Is that a nice way of telling me it should be done sooner rather than later?"

"Yes."

"I plan to call the first thing in the morning and ask if it can be done immediately."

"Good. One more thing? Is Ryan coming back tonight?"

"Yes. Later. He's at the hospital," she told him.

"Do you want me to stay until he returns? We could play cards and I'd let you win."

For just a moment she looked tempted. "No. That won't be necessary."

"Good night," he said, then just stood there until she smiled and closed the door and locked it. Simon went to his car, parked at the curb. He was due at the YMCA in an hour to coach the basketball team. The chances of another burglary happening were slight, but it wouldn't hurt to keep watch until Ryan returned.

Simon pulled out his cell. As soon as he saw Ryan's headlights he was leaving, but until then he had no intention of going anyplace.

5

Wednesday morning Traci pulled into her assigned parking space and got out of her Benz convertible.

She would have preferred a truck, had loved driving them ever since she'd learned how to drive in one, but the luxury sports car was part of the image she and Dante had created. Traci delicately snorted. They were as phony as their clients. They'd just hid it better. Dante was gone and she was sole owner of Images, and becoming increasingly tired of the charade, and many of the clients she had to work with.

"Traci, wait up."

Traci recognized the voice immediately and muttered under her breath. Briefcase in her hand, she turned to see Craig Walker, a three-time all-pro athlete, come down the sidewalk toward her. His movements were stiff, sluggish. Either he was coming off a night's drunk or had gotten an early start on drinking. He had everything going for him and was tossing it all away with both hands.

Winded, he stopped in front of her. His eyes were red, his expensive sports coat and tailored shirt rumpled. He smelled of cigarette smoke and expensive whiskey. "Walker."

His unsteady hand raked across his unshaven face. "I got problems."

As long as he let his fondness for booze and drugs rule him he always would. It was useless to remind him of that simple fact. His agent, his coach, and his pastor had all tried. "I told you after the last time that I could no longer represent you."

"You didn't mean it," he said, smiling. "Not at the price I pay you."

Since money had once been her primary reason for taking a client, she didn't take offense. "If you'll check with your accountant and lawyer, I returned your last check and sent you and your lawyer a certified letter severing our relationship."

His expression hardened. "I'm Craig Walker. People all over the world look up to me."

The ego of some athletes was unbelievable. "That was before you broke a very popular newsman's nose, before you were busted twice on possession, before your last incident with a fellow football player."

Fury leaped into his eyes. "That fag. He's lucky I didn't beat him to death."

There was no sense pointing out the "situation" had been consensual until they'd been discovered by the man's agent. Then all hell had broken loose. Accusation and fists started flying.

The only reason the police hadn't become involved was that the other athlete's agent had put a lid on things. Unfortunately, the doctor the agent had called hadn't been discreet and news of him treating the beaten player had leaked. With bruises on Craig, it wasn't difficult to tell with whom he had been fighting. She'd been called in to help the team and the players handle the explosive situation.

"If you'll excuse me, I have clients waiting."

His hard hand on her arm stopped her. His foul breath beat against her face. "Don't you walk away from me. Sunny is threatening to tell my wife about us if I don't tell her first."

Traci's first instinct was to knee Craig so hard his balls would pop out of his mouth. As satisfying as that thought was, it would only lead to more problems. He wasn't the type to back off if she hurt him, hurt his pride. Craig also had a zipper problem. She didn't know or care about Sunny's gender. "I'm not going to represent you, Craig, and if you put one bruise on me, I can guarantee I'll file charges. Your tenuous place with your team will be shot to hell."

His mouth tightened, his fingers uncurled. He wasn't that stupid. "You've got to help me. Dee Dee will take the kids."

"And what's left of your money," she said. If he spent half as much time with his children as he did out partying he wouldn't be in the mess he was in.

His gaze narrowed, he stepped closer, his foul breath washing over her face. "You think you're so smart."

Perhaps he was that stupid. "Walk—"

"Is there a problem here?"

Ryan. Relief swept through Traci.

Craig spun around to glare at Ryan. "Move on! This is none of your business."

"That's where you're wrong, Walker." Ryan stepped in front of Traci. "Traci is a friend of mine and my mother's."

"You know who I am?"

"Who doesn't know the great Craig Walker," Ryan said to him. "If you'll excuse us." Nodding, Ryan took Traci's arm and started toward the office building, leaving Craig on the sidewalk.

Inside the building, they saw him walking away. Traci

couldn't help the slight shiver caused by Ryan's touch until she recalled he just wanted friendship. She stepped away. "Thanks."

Ryan's face was harsh. "Why don't you have security?"

She was surprised at the venom in his voice, then guessed it had something to do with his mother's recent break-in. Craig represented another man wanting to take advantage of a woman. "Because that's the first time an incident like that has happened."

"Who's to say it won't happen again?" Ryan pressed.

"Point taken under advisement." She was grateful for his intervention, but she ran her own life.

"Meaning you'll do as you please," he said.

"I'm not careless or foolish, Ryan," Traci said.

He studied her for a moment. "Perhaps you should think about severing your relationship with him."

Ryan was a smart man. Suggestion was always better than telling a woman what to do. "Already done."

His beautiful eyes narrowed. "And he was trying to get you to change your mind."

"Yes. He's in a sticky situation," she told him.

"That's no excuse."

Traci looked at Ryan's clenched fist. Her gaze jerked back up to his. "You wanted to hit him."

"If I didn't have surgery in an hour I would have. I was on my way to the hospital when I saw the two of you and stopped," he told her. "Walker's reputation isn't the best with men or women, and I wanted to make sure you were all right."

Despite telling herself it shouldn't matter, she was pleased that he had wanted to protect her. Perhaps she could relent a little bit. After all, he was Maureen's son. "Is the surgery a difficult one?"

"Yes," he said, the one word speaking volumes.

She briefly touched his arm. "If anyone can do it, you can," she said, surprising herself by the words and the contact.

He seemed just as surprised. "Thank you. I'd better get going. See you tonight."

" 'Bye." Sighing, she turned toward the elevator. Watch it, Traci. Ryan is a risk you can't afford to take. Stepping on the elevator, she hoped her silly heart was listening.

That night Traci dressed with care for her dinner engagement with Ryan.

She'd selected a blue midcalf lightweight dress that complemented her dark brown skin tone, lush curves, and generous breasts and hips. Ryan might not want her, but that didn't mean she wasn't desirable . . . if she was foolish enough to want a man in her life. At least that's what she told herself until she opened the door that night and greeted Ryan. She looked hard for a hint of appreciation, if not desire, in his eyes.

"Hello, Traci," Ryan greeted. "You're ready. Great."

Traci swallowed her disappointment when she didn't see even the briefest gleam of lust. "Hello, Ryan. I didn't want to take a chance on Maureen seeing your car."

"Good thinking." He stepped back as she came out the door and waited until she used her key to lock the second lock. "Have you always taken that precaution?"

Straightening, she slipped the keys into her small handbag. "Simon's doing," she confessed.

"Same here." His warm hand closed around her bare upper arm, sending a tingling sensation up it. She fought to ignore the feeling as they continued to his car, which was parked in the driveway by the side of the house leading around back to the garage. "He made me more safety conscious. I'm glad he's taking a closer look at Mother's house and business."

That's not all he's looking at, Tracy thought. She slipped inside the car, thought of all the skinny, beautiful women who had sat in the seat before her, all those who would come after her.

Getting in and fastening his seat belt, Ryan started the motor. "Any more problems with Walker?"

"No." She'd put in a call to his agent and his attorney to ensure that there wouldn't be. "How did the operation go?"

"Good, thanks. She's in ICCU, but I expect her to move to the regular floor in the morning if she continues to do well." He slowed and looked at his mother's house as he passed. "The accent lights look good." He shifted the car into third. "Perhaps you should think about speeding up your timetable as well."

"Perhaps." Why she didn't just tell him they were installing the lights Friday she wasn't sure. "About Maureen's birthday celebration, I think she would like to have something casual with all her friends."

He nodded. "I kind of thought of it being a surprise, but I'm not sure how we could pull it off." Flicking his signal, he pulled up into the restaurant's parking lot. The parking gods smiled and he found a spot near the entrance. "It's hard to believe she'll be sixty."

"She doesn't look it or feel like it."

"Yeah." He cut the motor and unfastened his seat belt. "One of the new doctors in our building saw her with me and wanted to know who she was. He couldn't believe she was my mother."

"Did you give him your mother's number?"

Shock raced across Ryan's face. "No."

"Why not?" Traci asked, but she had a pretty good idea.

"She's almost sixty." Getting out of the car, he came around to her side and opened her door.

"Women much older date," she said and came to her feet. "Your mother is a beautiful, desirable woman."

At the word "desirable" his mouth flattened into a hard line. "Mother is happy the way she is, just like the other women in the Sisterhood. She loved my father. She's not thinking about a man." He started for the restaurant, then abruptly stopped. "She's not, is she?"

"No." Traci lied with a straight face. Whatever was said in the Sisterhood stayed with the Sisterhood.

The grip on her bare arm loosened. "I thought not. At her age, Mother has better sense."

Traci remained quiet. Ryan might be a top-notch doctor, but he knew squat about women.

Their table was in a quiet area of the restaurant as he'd requested, the service was impeccable, the food delicious. Or was everything right because Traci was sitting across the table from him? She looked beautiful. He wished he could tell her that, but he didn't want her to become suspicious. She was too smart and too independent.

He got angry each time he thought of Walker towering over her. She'd just stood there. She hadn't even looked around or yelled for help. He'd considered calling a frat brother who was a close friend of the team's owner, but he hadn't. He knew instinctively she wouldn't want him interfering.

"I'm thinking a garden party. Perhaps casual elegance with draped tables, sterling flatware, and centerpieces of her favorite flowers." Traci leaned across the table, excitement gleaming in her pretty brown eyes. "She's commented a couple of times how inviting my backyard is with the pool and waterfall and the flower gardens. The woman I purchased the house from used to belong to the garden society. I understand she gave some wonderful parties there."

Ryan was delighted—if the party was at Traci's house, they'd have to be in contact even more to coordinate things. This was working out better than he had expected. "Thanks. I'll take you up on the offer. Since her birthday is on a Saturday I can take her to brunch and have her back around two."

"I think we can do a surprise party. We'll have all the guests meet at Nettie's house since she lives the closest, and have a van to shuttle them over so the cars won't give the party away," she suggested. "So she won't become suspicious, the Sisterhood will tell her we're going antiquing after she returns from brunch with you."

He smiled at her. "You seem to have thought of everything. I guess you have to in your profession."

The smile slid from her face. "I guess."

"I meant that as a compliment, Traci," he said, wanting to bring the laughter back in her face and eyes.

"Don't mind me." She leaned back in her chair.

"Long day?" he asked.

"Try a long month." She blew out a breath and reached for her glass of wine.

"Owning your own business has its disadvantages," he said. "Everything stops at your door. The good and the bad."

"Lately it's been bad," she said, and then was startled that she had admitted that to him. "But that's to be expected in my profession."

He heard the tenseness underneath the blithe words. "Ever thought of changing professions?"

"Nope. That would be committing financial suicide," she told him, then put her glass down. She never talked about her business to anyone. It had to be the wine. "Could we leave? I have an early appointment."

He didn't believe her. "Certainly." He signaled to the waiter for the bill. "Will you be able to meet tomorrow night to go over the details of the party? The best caterers might already be taken for that date."

"I guess so," she said slowly.

"Great." He paid the bill, then stood to hold her chair. "Will seven be all right? We can go to North on Broad."

"All right."

Ryan placed his hand on the small of her back, felt the slight tremble of her body. Oh, yes. She wasn't immune to him, just fighting him. He felt there was more to it than just being cautious.

Outside, they walked silently to his car. Opening the door, he helped her in, hating that he couldn't keep on touching her. For some odd reason, he thought she needed touching. Not just sexual, but shared caring.

In the car he started the motor, then backed out of the parking space and pulled onto the busy street, still thinking about the silent woman beside him. Traci was attractive, successful. She moved in the circles of some of the most successful people in the community. Yet, she was home most nights.

Not once did he recall her mentioning her deceased husband. The Sisterhood often spoke fondly of their spouses. Perhaps he was off base, but he was beginning to think her marriage hadn't been a happy one.

He sped through a green light and glanced over at her. She

was looking out the window so he couldn't see her face. He wondered what she was thinking. He didn't like to think of her being unhappy, but clearly something else was going on.

If he thought she'd confide in him, he'd gently push. Her backpedaling at the table earlier told him that wouldn't work. He'd just have to show her that she could come to him with any problem, any time.

"You're very quiet." He glanced over at her as he turned onto her street.

"Just thinking about my schedule tomorrow," she told him.

"I—" he broke off abruptly, slowing the car.

"What is it?"

"That's Simon's car." He stopped behind a late-model Ford and cut his lights. By the time he was out of the car, Simon was, too. "Is Mother all right?" Ryan demanded.

"She's fine." Simon's gaze flickered behind Ryan. "I was in the area working a case and thought I'd drive by to see if your car was here. When I didn't see it in the driveway I thought you might be at the hospital and decided to stay for a bit."

"Thanks."

"Hello, Simon," Traci greeted.

"Hi," he said, his quizzical gaze going from Ryan to Traci.

Ryan saw the exchange. "Traci and I were out planning Mother's surprise birthday party. I'd appreciate it if you didn't say anything."

"She won't hear it from me."

"In that case, you're invited," Traci said. "If you're in the neighborhood you can drop your address in my mailbox."

"I will and thanks. Good night." Returning to his car, he got in and pulled off.

"He's a nice guy. He takes his job seriously," Ryan commented. "I'm glad he's here."

"You're not the only one."

"What?" Ryan stared down at Traci.

She stared up at him with a hint of puzzlement. "The class he taught. He helped a lot of us."

"Oh, right." For a moment, he'd been afraid Traci was attracted to Simon. He supposed some women might be swayed by his good looks. Thank goodness Traci wasn't one of them. He took her arm, enjoyed the zing. He was going to take every opportunity to touch her. "Let's get you home."

She balked when he started to his car. "I can walk from here. You go on in and check on Maureen."

"Traci, if you want to walk, we'll walk, but I'm seeing you to your door." Still holding her arm, he guided her to the sidewalk, then continued down the quiet street.

"I'm only agreeing because it would take more time to tell you off and, being a man, you'd have to think of a comeback . . . eventually," she said, with just enough pique for him to believe. "I want you to check on Maureen."

They started down her walk. "I appreciate you being considerate of my manhood and thinking of Mother. She likes you, too."

She unlocked her door. "She's great. I sometimes wonder . . ."

"Wonder what?"

"How did she end up with a son like you?" Stepping inside, she closed the door.

He laughed, then headed for his car. Seems she was right. He hadn't been able to offer a quick comeback, but perhaps that was because she had been smiling.

6

A blast of furnace-hot air enveloped her.

Maureen came awake in an instant, kicking the covers off. She sat up in bed. Her hand swept across her forehead, which was beaded with perspiration. Her silk nightgown stuck to her body, her scalp was damp. Her first thought was that the central air had gone out.

Flicking on the lamp on the night chest, she went to the thermostat on the other side of the room. The gauge read 74 degrees. She frowned, then pushed the control button, checked the setting, and found everything in order. Even as she tried to figure out the problem, the unit came on and she felt the brush of cool air against her skin.

It must have been a dream, she mused. She changed into another nightgown and went back to bed, snuggling under the down covers, intent on going back to sleep. Ryan had early surgery and she planned on getting up with him and cooking him breakfast. It felt good, safe having him under the same roof, if only for a few nights.

Her eyes closed as sleep claimed her. It seemed like only seconds before she was jerked awake again by the hot breath of the furnace. She scrambled from under the covers, clicking on the light and sitting on the side of the bed.

Her chin dropped to her chest as she tried to deny the truth. "No. This can't be happening."

Slipping out of bed, she went to the small built-in refrigerator in the sitting area of the bedroom and grabbed a bottle of water. Twisting off the cap, she drained the bottle. This time the heat subsided more slowly.

Leaving, she caught her reflection in the long swatch of mirrored glass over the triple dresser. Her cheeks were flushed, her short hair spiked and damp, her gown clinging to her moist body. She couldn't deny it any longer.

She was having hot flashes.

Cautious was not being afraid.

Just because Traci had waited to see Ryan's car leave the next morning before she went over to Maureen's house didn't mean anything. Just as teasing him before she said good night hadn't. The only reason she was seeing him was for Maureen's sake.

Traci blew out a disgusted breath as she went around the side of the house to the kitchen entrance. She detested liars. So where did that leave her? She wished she knew.

She passed the bay window and saw Maureen with her elbows propped on the table, her head resting in the open palms of her hands. Traci sprinted to the door, thankfully found it open, and rushed inside. "Maureen, what's the matter?"

Maureen lifted her head, her face miserable. "I've started having hot flashes."

Traci plopped down in a chair. "You scared me half to death over a hot flash?"

Maureen was incredulous. "Don't you understand what this means?" At Traci's stare, she continued. "I'm old. I'm going through the change. I thought I was going to be spared them because my mother was." Sadly, Maureen shook her head. "The hot flashes show me how foolish it is to think of dating a younger man."

"Maybe you're mistaken," Traci suggested.

"No. I thought the same thing at first. After the second one I stayed awake and waited for the next one. The insidious flash of heat swept over me in one instant; the next time it crept from my face to my feet." Her hands clenched. "I'm not mistaken."

"What did Ryan say?"

Maureen jerked upright. "I'm not discussing these with my son."

Traci, used to handling volatile situations, was failing badly. Ryan might be a doctor, but he was also Maureen's son. "What about the Sisterhood? Or your gynecologist? An herbalist?"

"They all had them to varying degrees. Nettie suffered through hers. Donna and Betsy took prescribed medication. Ophelia took herbs." Maureen put her head in her hands again. "None of them could remember how long they had them. Like childbirth, they said, they'd blocked it out of their minds."

"Since they're older, the medical profession must have advanced," Traci encouraged. She'd never seen Maureen this down.

"After I couldn't sleep I went to my home office and looked on the Internet. There's risk with prescribed medicine as well as over-the-counter medicine." Maureen's hands lifted to curve around her coffee mug. "I haven't decided which course to take."

"Then you're being premature in giving up on you and Simon." Traci brightened. "Medicine could take care of them."

Maureen got up from the table with her cup and poured the coffee down the drain. "It's not that simple. Whether they're controlled or not, I have them. They prove I'm too old for Simon."

"Bull crap." Traci went to her. "They don't prove anything of the sort. You're vibrant and fabulous. Until last night you would have pitted yourself against any woman, no matter her age."

"Maybe you're just too young to understand."

Nothing sent Traci over the edge faster than telling her she didn't understand. It was too close to Dante always calling her stupid. "I understand you're miserable. Don't let something you can't control ruin your life."

"You mean like you've done," Maureen tossed back. "You couldn't control the way your mother pushed you aside or that Dante cheated on you. Yet, because of them you don't trust love and won't let another man in, and only a few people get close to you."

Traci jerked as if she'd been sucker-punched. She had. She never thought Maureen, her closest friend, would use a confidence against her.

"At least I'm not panting after a man."

Maureen gasped. "At least I have desires. You're cold."

You're cold. The words slapped Traci down hard and left her reeling. How many times had Dante called her a cold, heartless bitch? Making love to her was like lying on top of an ice cube.

Hurt, angry, oddly embarrassed, Traci swung around for the door. She had to get out of there.

"Traci, please don't go," Maureen called. She grabbed

Traci's arm when she didn't stop. "Please. I'm so sorry. You're kind and loving."

"Just let me go." Her voice was hoarse, thick with tears she refused to shed.

Maureen hugged Traci's stiff body. "Please forgive me. I don't know what I would do if I lost your friendship."

Traci heard the hitch in Maureen's voice, felt the tears seeping through her blouse. Only her grandfather had cried for her. She'd told Maureen things she'd never confided to another human. "Let go of me."

"No. If I do, this will be the end of our friendship and I don't want that," Maureen cried.

True. Traci didn't give second chances. But hadn't she been just as harsh? Traci tried to hold on to her anger. Couldn't. "You're right."

"No," Maureen protested.

"I don't trust love. I never want to be vulnerable again. Not even if a man begged," she said. "James showed you how love, how marriage is supposed to be."

"I loved James with all my heart, but I want that again." Maureen lifted her head, tears shimmered in her eyes. "Will you forgive me?"

"If you'll forgive me. I wanted to hurt you."

"Because I hurt you first." Maureen sniffed and rubbed the heels of her hands across both eyes. "Men. They can complicate a woman's life."

"If you let them," Traci said. "I have no intention of letting that happen."

"I want to love and be loved again by a man," Maureen said quietly. "Perhaps there is a man out there closer to my own age."

"At the risk of going at each other again, are you sure?"

"I've had all night to think about it." She wiped her eyes one last time. "I might as well call Simon now and cancel tonight."

"I have an engagement, but I can cancel and we can have a girl's night," Traci offered.

"No. I have paperwork to do. I'll be fine." Maureen's smile wobbled. "Who knows? I might meet a man today at work."

"He'll be distinguished and completely taken by you," Traci said, trying to help. "I'll check with you later today. Take care." Letting herself out, she followed the curved walk to the front of the house. There was no way she was putting herself in a position to feel all the pain and heartache Maureen was feeling.

No man was worth that risk.

Maureen picked up the kitchen phone and dialed Simon's cell number before she lost her nerve. She'd never acted as bitchy as she had today with Traci. She honestly didn't know if it was her hormonal imbalance, anger at her body, her lust for Simon, or a little bit of all three.

"Hello. Simon Dunlap."

Just hearing his voice increased her heart rate, her yearning for something that would never be. Perhaps it was better that the hot flashes started before they went out.

"Hello?" he repeated.

"Simon, it's Maureen."

"Are you all right?" he asked.

"Yes." Her grip on the receiver tightened. "Something has come up and I need to cancel tonight."

There was a slight pause. "Are you sure you're all right? Your voice sounds strange."

Trying to break a date with a policeman, at least a

discerning and caring one like Simon, wasn't easy. "I'm fine. Well, I'd better get going. Good-bye."

"Wait," he said. "Are you free tomorrow night?"

Briefly she closed her eyes and leaned back against the counter. If she just told him she didn't want to see him again, he'd ask why. She'd never tell him the true reason so she just had to keep saying no until he got the message. "I'm afraid not."

There was another pause. "Then when?"

"I'm not sure. I'll call. Good-bye, Simon." She disconnected the cordless phone before he had a chance to ask her any more questions. Almost immediately the phone rang again.

She knew who it was before she glanced at the caller ID. Simon. She was sure he wouldn't call Ryan, but she didn't put it past him not to come by. And, if she saw him, she wasn't sure she was strong enough to keep saying no. The phone stopped after the eighth ring.

Pushing away from the counter, she grabbed her keys and purse. She was on the steps before she remembered she hadn't set the alarm. Quickly retracing her steps, she pushed the "on" button and hoped that, unlike now, she wouldn't think of Simon each time she activated the alarm.

Maureen's bad day continued once she arrived at the shop.

She put the blame squarely where it belonged: her hot flashes. They kept her from thinking and appeared at the most inopportune time. A browsing male customer thought she was coming on to him when she removed her jacket and unbuttoned the top two buttons of her blouse.

A shipment from Florence for a customer was being held

up in customs and nothing she could say or do would get the officials to move faster. Mrs. Miller had come in to look at "her secretary" only to learn that it had been sold, and she created such a scene that a customer about to purchase a bedroom set left. Henrietta had become so annoyed with Mrs. Miller for acting irrationally and with Maureen for not calling the police, she'd left for the day.

Alone in the shop, an eighteenth-century fan dangling from her wrist, she felt miserable and alone. All the members of the Sisterhood had dropped by with sympathy and encouragement. Traci's doing. She'd forgiven her and was trying to help. There wasn't any.

Trying not to mope, tired of trying to anticipate the next hot flash, she moved around the shop touching, straightening, rearranging. The door opened and a distinguished gray-haired gentleman came in. She smiled despite the inward sigh. The man appeared to be in his late sixties. He was well dressed with a straight back and a warm smile. He was just what Traci had ordered, but Maureen didn't even feel a flutter.

"Hello." She moved to greet him just as the door opened again and the taciturn teenager came in. She greeted the silent young man, who ducked his head and moved toward the painting he favored. She gave her attention to the older gentleman, then inwardly winced at her description. He might not be that much older than she was. "Was there anything in particular that you were interested in?"

"I understand that you have an eighteenth-century Louis XV double pedestal dining table with the original chairs," he said. "My wife was in here last week. She wanted me to have a look."

"Certainly. This way." Maureen led the man to the table and chairs, planning on telling Traci she'd met a distinguished man, but he was already taken. "By the way, I'm Maureen Gilmore. I own the store."

"Edward Johnson," he said.

"Here it is. The rectangular dining table is the most traditional shape and well suited for formal dining."

"It's beautiful," he said, running his hand over the back of a chair. "We've been looking for some time. We're renovating a farmhouse in Georgia for our retirement home, but we still plan to entertain a lot."

"This is a beautiful set. You'll note the chairs have the original seat coverings." She moved to pull out the chair and saw the teenager in the Sheraton mirror over the sideboard just as he picked up a cut-crystal inkwell from a nineteenth-century Italian inkstand. He slipped it into his backpack, and headed for the front door.

Her first reaction was shock, quickly followed by anger. Despite her anger, she kept her voice pleasant when she spoke to Mr. Johnson. "Please excuse me. I want to check on the other customer."

"Go ahead," he said, pulling out the dining room chair and examining the covering and carving.

Maureen reached the door seconds before the teenager. "I saw what you did."

Fear flickered in his eyes. His shoulders slumped. "I didn't ta—"

"Shut up and keep your voice down," she hissed. "Give me the backpack and sit down until I deal with this customer."

"I don't have—"

She pulled her cell out of her jacket pocket and held it up. "Yes, you do."

"Mrs. Gilmore, when you're finished, I'd like to ask you a question," Mr. Johnson said.

"Certainly." Maureen held out her other hand for the backpack. The teenager eyed her, then the door. "Thinking of trying to get by me is a bad idea. I can promise you I won't let you go without a struggle, and I'm tired of waiting." She reached for the backpack herself. He stepped back.

"Is everything all right?" Mr. Johnson called.

"Have it your way." She pressed 9, letting him see her do it. He quickly shrugged off the backpack and handed it to her. "Sit down until I finish." Holding his backpack, she went to Mr. Johnson, casually putting the bag on a nearby loveseat. "How can I be of assistance?"

"Are you able to ship merchandise?"

"Yes. I deal with a very reputable firm. Of course, if there's any damage during shipment your money is refunded," she told him. "But in the six years I've been in business, that's never happened."

"Thank you. We're definitely interested." He glanced at his watch. "I'd better run. I teach at the Citadel and I came on my lunch break."

She handed him her business card. "Please feel free to come back as many times as you'd like. Good afternoon."

He nodded and was gone. Maureen turned to see that the young man had grabbed his backpack and was hurrying to the back. He wouldn't get far. The rear door had a coded combination lock.

Maureen picked up an iron poker as she passed the fire tool set. She had no intention of using it but, after the break-in, she firmly believed the saying "walk softly and carry a big stick."

"I thought I told you to stay on that sofa."

He swung around, and his eyes widened as he saw the poker. "You can't keep me here. I didn't steal anything. You can check my backpack."

She glanced around. The crystal inkwell was on the floor. She picked it up and saw the chip on the hinged silver and crystal top. "The inkstand set that was valued at twelve hundred dollars is now worth a fourth of that because of the damage you caused. You owe me eight hundred."

"It's just your word against mine."

Maureen placed the ruined inkwell on her desk. "You might have done something stupid, but you don't look stupid. Whom do you think the police will believe?"

He moistened his mouth. "Call them then. I don't have it on me. They can't do a thing to me."

He sounded tough, but he trembled. If she called the police, would it solve the bigger problem of why he'd stolen from her? Scare him into not doing it again? "For weeks I've given you free rein in my store. You've never taken anything before. Why now? Why this?" She motioned toward the inkwell. "You like paintings."

Folding his arms, he looked away. She wanted to— Heat enveloped her. A shocking wave flushed and dewed her body. She flicked open the fan to cool her face.

The teenager unfolded his arms and looked at her strangely.

"You picked the wrong day to mess with me. Empty the backpack on my desk. Now!"

"I—"

"Do it," she snapped, fanning faster.

His mouth tight, the boy unzipped the serviceable black backpack and removed several books. As the heat wave subsided Maureen noted he didn't just upend the pack. He cared about the contents. She also noted the art books from the library, a social studies book, a school ID badge, and a spiral notebook.

She picked up the notebook. His name, address, and

phone number were written in neat cursive on the inside of the binder. Flipping the pages, she saw the detailed drawings of buildings, furniture pieces, fruit. "Did you do this?"

"No."

"You don't want to mess with me today, Jason."

His hands went into his pockets. "What if I did? It's just something I do."

Maureen could tell he was lying again. He cared about drawing, but was too stubborn to admit it. "I'm going to do something much worse than calling the police."

His gaze snapped to the poker in her hand. He stumbled back.

"I'm calling your mother."

A new kind of fear entered his eyes. "She won't come."

"Why don't we see." Maureen rounded her desk to dial his home number.

The store would close in fifteen minutes, and Jason's mother had yet to show.

After repeatedly calling the house number for over an hour, Maureen had finally reached Jason's mother, Phyllis Payne, who sounded more annoyed to be interrupted on her day off while "conducting business" than concerned about her son stealing. After making sure Maureen knew she would not be responsible for her son's debt, she said she'd be there when she finished. Four hours later, she still hadn't arrived.

"I told you she wouldn't come." Jason, his hands shoved deep into the pockets of his jeans, thin shoulders hunched, did his best to appear unconcerned, but it was clear by the way he refused to look at Maureen that he was hurt.

What kind of mother wouldn't come if her son was in

trouble? Maureen asked herself. After working with the families of the high school students she and the Sisterhood mentored, she'd learned not to judge. A large majority of the parents were single mothers who had their backs against the wall.

A few might not care, but most had their hands full trying to keep a roof over the family's head and food on the table, just trying to keep the family together and survive. "Then we'll just go to her. Get your backpack."

"Let it go, lady, and I'll pay you back."

She folded her arms. "Obviously you don't have a job. Just where do you plan to honestly earn eight hundred dollars?"

"That doesn't mean I can't get one," he said.

She'd heard enough young people speak poorly to realize he came from a home where the mother was educated. The potential was there. He wasn't lost. "The backpack."

Giving her a go-to-hell look he went to her office, stuffed the things back inside and shrugged it over his shoulders. Another thing about Jason, he hadn't cursed her. Even at his angriest. He respected her. He'd learned manners. She was determined to find out why he had been driven to steal.

Maureen rang the doorbell of the neat frame house on a street in an older but well-cared-for neighborhood with clipped lawns.

The door opened and a tall woman with a pretty but unsmiling face answered the door. She was neatly dressed and groomed. Over her shoulder Maureen saw the front room was clean, if sparsely furnished. Beside Maureen, Jason dropped his head. "I'm Maureen Gilmore. I called you about Jason."

The frown on the woman's face didn't clear. "I appreciate

the call, but Jason knows the rules. Get into trouble and he's on his own," she said.

Since the woman didn't invite her inside, Maureen didn't ask. "The cut-crystal inkwell he damaged cost twelve hundred dollars."

"What?" Her face hardened. "Jason," she snapped, and his head jerked up. Her gaze drilled into him. "Don't I have enough trouble with you? First, I have to pay for summer school so you can graduate on time because you were too lazy to check with your counselor about graduation requirements until school was almost out. Now this!" She put one slim hand on her hip. "Why do you want to be like that worthless father of yours?" Her hands flashed out, caught the strap of the backpack, and dragged him into the house.

"How do you propose the debt be paid?" Maureen asked.

"He'll have to work it off," his mother said. "He can come to your store after class until the debt is paid."

Maureen was stunned. "Surely you don't expect me to let him work in a store where he can steal from me again? Besides, he isn't knowledgeable about antiques. I don't need him."

"I'm not handing over my hard-earned money," she said. "I told him if he did the crime, he'd pay the time."

"But he's your son," Maureen said, unable to hide her disbelief.

"That doesn't mean he's going to ruin my life." The door closed in Maureen's face.

Something was wrong.

Simon didn't know why Maureen had canceled, but he hadn't liked hearing the shakiness in her voice. She hadn't sounded that upset when her house was burglarized. Before the night was over he intended to know the reason.

Calling Ryan and asking him was out. One thing Simon did know was that Maureen wouldn't appreciate him going behind her back, and he wasn't so sure she wanted Ryan to know they were attracted to each other.

There was only one thing to do: learn the reason for himself. Getting out of his brother Patrick's truck, Simon went to Maureen's door and rang the bell. Patrick, as usual, was with his fiancée, Brianna, one floor down in her condo. Simon had borrowed the truck because his car was being serviced and they hadn't finished on time. Also, if Ryan and Traci were planning to get together tonight, he didn't want Ryan wondering why he was there.

The door opened and he knew he had made the right decision. The perpetual smile was missing from Maureen's face. She looked miserable. "Simon."

He liked the way his name sounded on her lips. "Good

evening, Maureen." He held up the wicker picnic basket in his hand. "I thought we might have dinner."

"I—"

"Please," he coaxed, knowing he'd have to talk fast. "We can eat, and then I can leave and you can get back to work."

She hesitated, then moved aside. "Please come in."

"Thank you." He stepped into the spacious foyer. The beautiful and gracious house was a reflection of the owner. "It's a nice night. I thought we might eat outside on the terrace, if you don't mind."

She looked relieved. "I have a pitcher of lemonade in the refrigerator. I'll get it and some glasses."

He shook his head. "Everything is in here."

"You seem to have thought of everything," she told him, the corners of her mouth lifting.

"I certainly tried." He took her elbow, watched as she swallowed. Good. He still got to her. He started toward the double glass doors and the lighted terrace. "I even have a tablecloth and napkins."

"You must have done this before," she said, then tensed and bit her lip.

Simon pretended not to notice. Maureen was too well mannered to pry or criticize. He didn't mind if she was a bit jealous, but he wanted her to know how unique and special she was to him. "First time." Releasing her arm, he opened one of the double French doors and followed her outside to a rectangular glass-topped table near the pool, which was complete with a whirlpool. "I wanted this to be fun and effortless." Setting the basket on a padded chair, he opened the top and took out a blue plastic tablecloth. He'd noticed blue and cream were the predominant colors in her house.

"Let me help." She reached for one end of the cloth.

"Thanks." Together, they set the table and put out the food. "Hope fried chicken is all right."

"It's fine. Please sit and I'll prepare our plates."

Simon had planned to do that, but he took his seat. She still appeared a bit nervous. Perhaps keeping her busy was for the best. She served, then he held her chair for her. Once seated, he blessed their food. "Can I ask you a question? Two really."

She tensed immediately, setting her glass of lemonade on the table. "It depends."

"Why do you keep changing your mind about me?"

She looked away.

"I might be putting my foot in my mouth, but I think you wanted to go out with me when we first met. You accepted the other day, then you canceled. Some women don't like dating policemen, but you were hesitant before you knew my profession." He studied her. "You aren't the indecisive type. Do you mind telling me why you are with me?"

"What is the second question?" she asked.

"Why did you sound so shaky this morning?"

She bit her lower lip. "I didn't sleep very well last night."

Immediately sympathetic, his hand covered hers. He'd thought she had gotten over the burglary. "I'm sorry."

She peered down at his hand on hers. Simon didn't even think of moving it. He wanted her to know he cared.

Her head lifted. "It . . . it didn't have anything to do with the burglary."

Instinct told him that her not sleeping and her being upset this morning were related. "Is there anything I can do to help?"

Her thick black lashes flew upward as she pulled her hand

from beneath his. Her cheeks flushed and she lowered her gaze. "No."

Since he didn't want her to be uncomfortable, he changed the subject. "Is tomorrow afternoon around one all right to come by your shop to do the inspection?"

"Yes, but I need to tell you about Jason before then," she said.

He stiffened. Anger shot through him before he could prevent it. "You're seeing someone?"

She looked startled, then pleased. "No. Jason is a high school student I caught trying to steal an inkwell today." She told him everything. "I couldn't call the police. I couldn't ruin his life."

"Maureen, I guess you know what a chance you're taking," he told her.

"Not as much as you might think. He's been to the store many times in the past. This is the first time that he's taken anything," she told him. "Jason can be saved."

His hand swept down her arm, giving in to the desire to touch her; her skin felt as soft as he'd dreamed. "For both your sakes, I hope you're right. There's nothing worse than facing the reality that, no matter what you do, you can't keep a person from going down the wrong road."

"One of your teens?" she asked.

"More than one." He blew out a breath. "I worked with a lot of them in Myrtle Beach. I'm doing the same thing here with another policeman coaching a basketball team. They think they're tough and know all the answers. When reality slaps them in the face, many of them act tough when you can see the fear in their eyes."

"Jason was the same way," she revealed. "He's scared of his mother, yet something stronger than that fear made him take that inkwell. He never even looked at it before. I've watched him. His interest is painting, and he's good at it."

"It would be my guess that he did it for a gang initiation," Simon said. "The more valuable, the higher his standing. He hadn't reckoned on you."

"He picked the wrong day to mess with me," she said, her mouth tight.

"Hopefully the day has gotten better," he said.

She smiled. "It has. Thanks to you."

He smiled back. "Can I press my advantage and ask you to go out with me on my brother's boat this weekend? He and his fiancée might join us; that is, if they aren't doing last-minute preparations for their wedding."

Her face softened. "They must be excited."

Simon chuckled. "That's putting it mildly. They glow when they're together. Her parents and my older brother and his wife are the same way."

"That's how it should be," Maureen said quietly.

"No one has to tell me that you and your husband were happy," he told her.

"Yes, we were. When he first died I didn't think I could go on, until I remembered what he always said to me." Her face grew thoughtful, her voice dropped to barely above a whisper. " 'Remembering me with a smile, living your life to the fullest, is the greatest tribute you could give our love.' "

"Sounds as if he was a wise and unselfish man."

"He was." A sigh fluttered softly over her lips. "Ryan reminds me of him so much."

"Is he spending the night again?"

"No. I refuse to let them make me afraid to live in my own house," she said, her face defiant.

"Glad to hear it." He came to his feet and began cleaning

up the table. "I'd better get out of here and let you get back to work."

Maureen came slowly to her feet. She didn't want him to go. She'd enjoyed talking to him. And not once had she had a HF. "If the offer is still open, I'd like to go out Sunday afternoon."

"Will three be all right?" He paused in putting the lid on the potato salad.

"Perfect." She closed the lid on the container of potato salad for him and put it inside the basket. "I can meet you there."

He gave her the address of the condominium. "I'll give your name to security so you can park your car in the underground parking. From there, you can take the elevator to the first floor and I'll meet you in the lobby."

"I've seen those. They're beautiful. Quite a view of the Ashley River." She closed the top of the wicker basket.

"Patrick bought the condo from our niece because of the marina for his boat. He met Brianna when she was moving in." Simon propped his hand on the hamper. "From the moment they met, he knew she was the one."

Maureen remembered the zip of sexual heat when she first saw Simon. She wanted to blame it on pure sexual attraction, but she knew that wasn't the extent of it. "Sometimes it happens that way."

"Yes, it does." His voice dropped two octaves, the sound arousing her.

Time to end this. "I'll see you to the door."

"Always the perfect hostess." Picking up the hamper, he reached for her arm. "I hope you sleep better tonight."

"I'm sure I will." *If she didn't have erotic dreams about him that left her achy.* Stepping away from him, she unlocked the second lock and opened the front door. "Good night."

"Good night, and thank you." He switched the basket to the hand farthest away from her.

"I should be thanking you," she said. "I wasn't in a very good mood before you arrived."

"Glad to be of help." He leaned over and brushed his lips gently across hers, then straightened. "If you can't sleep and want to talk, call me."

The kiss was incredibly sweet. She wanted more. She swallowed before she could talk. "I-I'll be fine."

He smiled, deepening his dimples. "Good night, Maureen."

She closed the door because she knew he'd want her securely inside before he was off the steps. That point had been one of the lessons for single women. Leaning against the door, she pressed her trembling fingertips to her lips. She knew he'd be a good kisser.

She couldn't wait for Sunday.

The best-laid plans.

After the incident with Maureen in her kitchen, Traci had fully intended to keep the meeting with Ryan strictly business that night. This, in essence, meant she was not going to be moved by his good looks, his smile, or the way his touch made her feel.

She'd failed miserably on all counts, had seen her downfall coming when he'd met her at the restaurant. No man should look that good in a black polo shirt that showed off an impressive set of pecs or sinful jeans that caressed and molded his strong, muscular thighs.

She might have been able to hold it together if he hadn't been in such a sunny mood. Yet, looking back on the time she'd been around him, he was usually easygoing, enjoying life to the fullest. It wasn't likely that a man in his field who specialized in high-risk pregnancies was afraid of risks. Unfortunately, he was also inquisitive.

"Being a lawyer must help out a lot in your business." His elbows propped on the small table, he waited for her answer.

"It does." She picked up a deep-fried onion ring and bit. "How about you? Have you always wanted to go into the medical field?"

"Yes," he answered her. "I didn't know I wanted to specialize in obstetrics until a classmate's mother died in childbirth. People often forget that pregnancy and childbirth carry risks."

Ryan believed in what he did and wouldn't have done anything else. She envied him that certainty. "Because of you, people have lived who might not have."

"I might do the diagnostics, prescriptions, and surgery, but a higher power heals."

She hadn't expected him to be modest. The people she was around had egos the size of Texas . . . which proved she spent too much time around the wrong people. "Maureen said you volunteer at a prenatal clinic for teens one day a week. That must take from your private practice."

He shrugged carelessly. "I became a doctor to help people."

So Ryan was more than handsome; he also cared about his fellow man. He couldn't have been more unlike Dante, who was ruled by his quest for the almighty dollar. He'd chased women, but never allowed them to get in the way of making money.

"We can always use more volunteers." He sipped his tea,

staring at her over the rim of the glass. "The Sisterhood stops by almost every week."

"I don't know." Dante wasn't the only one who'd liked money. But she told herself she wanted it for a different reason . . . to show her mother that she had succeeded in spite of her.

"Think about it," he said. "The clinic isn't going anyplace."

"Hello, Ryan."

Ryan stiffened, then slowly glanced up to the attractive woman standing by their table. She wore a fashionable black suit that fit her slim body perfectly. His mouth flattened into a hard line. The air seemed charged with tension.

The woman turned away from Ryan and extended her hand to Traci. "I'm Elisa Thomas, an old friend of Ryan's."

Traci glanced at the still-silent Ryan, then shook hands with the woman. "Traci Evans. Ryan's mother and I are neighbors."

"Oh." Elisa stared down at Ryan. "Ryan has so many friends. My father is the chief-of-staff at Memorial Hospital, where Ryan sends the majority of his patients."

Traci tried to figure out what was going on. Ryan wasn't the rude or silent type. The friction between them was obvious. An old love gone bad? She was certainly his type: thin, attractive, cultured. Had she cheated? Somehow Traci didn't think Ryan was the cheating type. "Are you in the medical field?" Traci asked.

"I'm a psychiatrist. Ryan sought my consultation for a couple of his patients," she said. "We make a good team."

Ryan's hands on top of the table clenched. "Traci, are you ready to leave?"

Definitely something of a romantic nature. "Yes."

Elisa's smile wavered, but her gaze stayed on Ryan. "I'll see you tomorrow, Ryan. Good-bye, Traci."

Ryan placed enough money on the table to pay their bill plus a very generous tip, then came to his feet as soon as the woman moved away. "Let's get out of here."

"All right." Whatever Elisa had done, Ryan wasn't ready to forgive her. Traci, who until a couple of days ago would have jumped with glee at a woman sticking it to Ryan, found herself annoyed at Elisa and sorry for him.

Ryan was boiling.

Elisa must have an internal tracking system! Almost every time he went out, she was there. Why couldn't she get the message that he didn't want anything to do with her? After they'd gotten into a heated argument in the doctor's lounge at the hospital today, he'd decided the best way to handle her was to ignore her.

She'd latched on to him a month ago after her date had too much to drink at a party of mutual friends. Ryan had taken Elisa home. He didn't think anything about meeting her for lunch the next day as a thank-you.

It was the biggest mistake of his life.

She'd started calling and showing up at his office, wanting to go out again. He'd tried to be nice and told her he just wanted them to be friends. It hadn't worked. She just wouldn't go away.

Walking Traci to her car, he decided he wasn't going to make another mistake. If her marriage had been in trouble when her husband died, the probability was high that trust was an issue. She wouldn't like being lied to.

"Traci." He put his hand on hers on the handle of the door. He felt a slight trembling and moved his away. "I need to tell you something."

"About you and Elisa?" she asked.

"There's nothing between us. But she made me realize that, although we might think we have a good reason for doing something, the other person might not agree," he told her.

"Ryan, I don't understand a thing you just said."

"Sorry." There was patience in her eyes. He just hoped she'd be as understanding after he finished. "I asked you out to help with Mother's birthday party because I wanted your help, but I also wanted to take you out and I didn't think you'd accept otherwise."

He watched helplessly as her eyes hardened, her body stiffened. "I apologize for the deception. I couldn't think of anything else. I wanted to take you out. I still do."

"Sure. Just as soon as hell freezes over, give me a call." Opening the door, she got into the car, then slammed the door.

"Traci!"

She spun out of the parking lot with the tires squealing. Ryan cursed under his breath and ran to his car to follow her home. As he did so, he saw Elisa at the edge of the parking lot, a smile on her face.

Ryan had made a fool out of her.

Traci pressed down on the accelerator and the car answered her request for speed. The speedometer inched toward 80 miles per hour. The only thing she hated worse than being lied to was being made a fool of. She sped through the signal light as it went to yellow.

Her mother had promised she'd only have to stay a few days with her grandparents, that she'd come for her birthday, for her programs at school. Each time it was a lie, but stupid Traci had kept wishing and praying that her mother would finally make the eighteen-mile drive that separated them. Her stepsister, Carla, got all the love, the affection. There was never any left over for Traci.

She thought she had gotten smarter. The next light flashed to red before she could go through. She hit the brakes. The car screeched to a stop.

A car horn blasted next to her. She ignored it.

"Traci. Slow down."

She looked at Ryan in the lane next to her. "Go to hell," she said, then gunned the Benz. Her grandfather had taught her to drive before her legs were long enough to reach the pedals. Why couldn't his daughter have loved and cared for her as much?

Traci turned into her driveway and stopped by the walk-way leading to the house. Jumping out of the car, she rushed to the door and opened it just as Ryan quickly exited his car. She took great pleasure in slamming the front door in his face.

"Traci. Open the door. Traci!"

"Leave, Ryan, or I'm calling the police. Elisa doesn't know how lucky she is." Not waiting for an answer, Traci snapped off the light she'd left on in the foyer and headed for the stairs. She never wanted to see Ryan again.

He'd blown it!

Ryan considered ringing the doorbell again, but knew it would be useless. Traci was pissed at him and she wasn't going to get over it any time soon . . . if ever. No, he had to believe that she'd calm down in a few days and listen to reason.

Hands shoved into the pockets of his slacks, he walked to his car. The lights in the master bedroom were on and he imagined Traci jerking off her jacket and slinging it on her bed, then reaching for the button on her skirt. He grabbed the car's door handle before he let his mind wander further.

Starting the motor, he backed out of the driveway, thought briefly of stopping to see his mother, but kept going. She'd know something was wrong, and although he thought she might be suspicious that something was going on between him and Traci, he wasn't ready to discuss it yet.

If Traci didn't get over being furious with him and forgive him, there might not be anything to discuss . . . except his stupidity. He'd already figured out she had trust issues. Perhaps he should have waited to tell her. Or asked her straight out for a date in the first place. He turned into his condo and parked.

He'd lived in the three-story unit since he'd come back to Charleston to set up private practice seven years ago after completing his residency. There were newer and certainly more expensive condos on the ocean, but he liked it here because everyone knew everybody and they looked out for each other.

Getting out, he walked through the flower-filled courtyard. All fifteen owners paid $25 a month to a lawn service to maintain the grounds.

"Ryan."

He stiffened, then watched Elisa emerge from the shadows of the arbor, which was draped with deep purple clematis. "Why can't you leave me the hell alone?"

"Ryan, please," her voice trembled. "I love you. Don't do this to me."

"You—" He abruptly broke off and tried to calm down. The more he yelled, the more emotional she'd become. "Elisa, you need help."

"I need you." She began unbuttoning her blouse. "I need you to make love to me."

Shocked, appalled, he caught her hands. "Elisa. Don't."

"Why can't you see how good it would be between us?" she said, tears glistening in her eyes.

As angry as she made him, he knew she needed help. "Why don't we call your father, and he can come get you."

"No." She jerked away, stumbling back. "He'd try to keep us apart."

That was the idea. "Elisa, go home."

Anger stole across her face. "You want that overweight sow you were with tonight."

He crossed to her in two long strides and grasped her arm. He trembled with rage. "I want you gone, or I'm calling the police *and* your father."

"I'll make you sorry for choosing her over me," she cried, her eyes cold.

Fear coursed through him. His hands clenched around her arms. "Bother her in any way, and I can guarantee you won't like the consequences."

She trembled, her head lowered. "I just want you to love me."

His hand uncurled and he stepped back. He gave her the only truth he could. "I'm sorry. You have to listen. I could never love you."

"Yes, you will, Ryan. One day you'll love me." Turning, she ran out of the courtyard.

Ryan blew out a breath. He had wanted to handle it discreetly between the two of them, and not involve her father. That wasn't going to happen. Elisa was obviously unstable.

Six months ago he had referred a patient to Elisa, a fashion model who was having difficulty coping with the scars from her C-section. Elisa had helped the woman. She'd been good at what she did. Two months ago when Elisa had taken a medical leave to write a book, he hadn't thought anything about it. Now he considered that might not be the whole story. Since she wasn't seeing patients, he hadn't pushed the issue.

Because of Elisa, time might have run out for him and Traci.

8

Occasionally too much information caused problems.

"Once a thief, always a thief," Henrietta declared.

"Henrietta, that's not true. People can change for the better." Maureen had debated if she should tell Henrietta the full story of why Jason was going to work there, then decided she didn't have a choice.

Maureen had called Jason's mother again the night before to try and tell her how impossible it was for Maureen to hire him. She might as well have saved her breath. His mother wouldn't even entertain paying one cent on the damaged inkwell, let alone the inkstand. Jason would be there after class each weekday until Maureen said otherwise. Maureen had been left listening to a dial tone.

She had come close to forgetting the entire episode. Two things stopped her: Jason's talent and the fact that he had never stolen from her before. If it was possible to steer him in the right direction, Maureen was going to do it. For that, she needed Henrietta's cooperation. There was no way Maureen could get by without explaining why he was there every day. As expected, her sales associate was a hard sell.

"You're too trusting." Henrietta folded her thin arms over her hot pink jacket. She loved bright colors. "On the other hand, I plan to keep an eye on him. If he knows what's good for him, he had better not steal anything again."

Maureen blew out a frustrated breath. Henrietta, like Traci, didn't give her trust easily. Both women's problems stemmed from a man. "He didn't steal anything."

"He wanted to and, in my book, that makes him a thief," she said emphatically. "Speaking of the devil. Well, is he just going to stand there?"

Jason, head bowed, stood with his hand on the door handle. "He's probably embarrassed."

"He should be," Henrietta said without a trace of sympathy.

"Everyone can make a mistake," Maureen said. "I called Principal Hayes at his high school yesterday afternoon and learned Jason has never been in trouble at school."

"With twelve hundred students he might not remember that boy," Henrietta said.

"He'd remember the ones who came to his office," Maureen said. "And Jason wasn't one of them."

"Maybe he was flying low on the radar or had a teacher too tired or overworked to write a referral." Henrietta's eyes narrowed. "I'm watching him now."

Maureen took Henrietta by her thin shoulders and turned her until they faced each other. "That's exactly what we can't do."

"What?"

"If you care about me, you'll give him a chance," Maureen said.

"But—"

"How many times have you been judged harshly because

you were black, a woman, had gray hair?" Maureen talked over Henrietta and pressed her point.

Henrietta's mouth tightened. "This isn't the same."

"Close enough. Give Jason a chance. If he blows it, I'll let you have first crack at him, then it's my turn." Maureen stuck out her hand. "Deal?"

"He'll probably steal us blind," Henrietta said, but she lifted her hand.

"I'm betting he won't. If he ever works up the nerve to come inside." Maureen frowned.

"Are you going to go get him?"

"Nope. He *should* be embarrassed. Let's finish with the inventory." Maureen picked up the clipboard just as the door finally opened and Jason came in. "Good morning, Jason," Maureen greeted.

"Good morning." He glanced at her, then away.

"I'd like you to meet Henrietta Rudley, my friend and assistant," Maureen introduced, unobtrusively nudging Henrietta.

"Good morning, Jason."

"Good morning."

Maureen gave Jason the clipboard. "You can help with inventory."

He sneered. "So you can tell if I steal anything."

"You aren't the first person to take something from here that didn't belong to them and, unfortunately, you won't be the last." Maureen wasn't backing down. She knew better. Teenagers pushed, but this teenager was going to learn as Ryan had that she didn't take crap from anyone. "It's the end of the quarter, and I have to pay taxes on the merchandise I haven't sold."

"You can read, can't you?" Henrietta asked.

Maureen didn't know if she had done it to get him to help, or to annoy him. "Some of the terms are in French and Italian."

"I'm not a dummy."

Henrietta folded her arms. "Could have fooled me."

Maureen groaned inwardly. "Why don't I help you until you get the hang of it."

Jason kept his gaze on Henrietta. "I can do it."

Unfolding her arms, Henrietta went to two chairs shoved together. "*Brisée.*"

Jason looked at the papers attached to the clipboard, then flipped through the pages, first from the front, then from the back.

"They're alphabetical and grouped," Henrietta offered, surprising and pleasing Maureen. She wasn't going to be able to referee them. They had to learn to work together.

Jason flipped more pages. Finally he looked at Maureen. "I don't see it."

Maureen didn't move. "I don't think I heard you correctly."

He frowned. "I said I don't see what she's talking about."

"Is that the way you ask for help?" Maureen asked.

"You wanted to help me before," he reminded her.

"I did, but, as I recall, you said you didn't need my help." Maureen faced Henrietta. "He did say that, didn't he?"

"He did," Henrietta answered dutifully.

He looked angry enough to leave but said, "I need help."

"And what's the magic word?" Maureen asked.

"Please," he said through gritted teeth.

"Not very gracious but, since you did ask, I'll help." Maureen moved her polished nail to halfway down the front page. "Check." His hands clamped on the clipboard. "I traveled extensively, studied for years before I felt comfortable enough to be able to open my own business. There is no harm in not knowing, the harm comes in not knowing and being too proud to ask."

"You want to make a fool of me," he said, rage shimmering in every line of his body.

"Why would I want to do that?" Maureen asked.

"Because I broke the Italian inkwell."

"How do you know that?" Maureen asked; she hadn't mentioned the origin of the inkstand.

"I Googled it on my computer last night." He looked at Henrietta. "There's a society of inkwell collectors. Silver George II inkstands or Napoleon II bronze doré, like the one over there, can cost four to seven thousand. I'm no dummy."

"That had to take hours," Henrietta said, a hint of admiration in her voice.

He shrugged carelessly. "I had the time."

Maureen was unsure if he'd "had the time" because he was grounded or because he didn't have any friends. He'd always been alone when he came to the shop. His inquisitiveness and initiative pleased her. "How did you remember the details?"

Again he shrugged, then looked down at the clipboard. "What's next?"

He didn't like talking about himself, but there was much more to Jason than met the eye. Hopefully, she'd get a chance to find out.

Simon entered Forever Yours ten minutes before his appointment. He wasn't much of a shopper, but there was a welcomeness about the shop. He saw the tall, lanky teenager almost immediately. He closed the coffee-table-size book he had been looking at and watched him. Simon wondered if the kid had enough experience with the police to make him or was he just naturally suspicious.

Simon moved aimlessly around the shop, thinking of the woman who was responsible for this, the woman who helped a teenager who'd stolen from her.

Simon glanced around. Sure enough, the kid was still watching him. This time he was by the doorway leading to the back. Interesting.

Simon heard her voice before he saw her, and he smiled. She sounded happy, mildly distracted. She stepped into the room, saw him, and her face softened.

"Simon."

Just hearing her say his name was pleasurable. "Hello, Maureen. How are you?"

Her smile widened. "Busy, but that's a good thing."

He chuckled. "I imagine."

"Have you met Jason? He's the latest employee," she said, moving to the teenager.

"No." Simon nodded. "Hello, Jason."

Jason nodded, then went back to the book he had been reading, *Antiques of the Eighteenth and Nineteenth Centuries.*

"I'll check out the shop. I'll let you know when I've finished."

"I'll leave you to it then. Jason, I'll be in the back."

Simon watched her leave for the sheer pleasure of looking at her, then took out his pad and went to the front door. Time to go to work.

"What are you doing?" Jason asked.

"Checking out the shop to make it safer," he replied, checking the lock and the beautiful but thin glass on the front door.

"You're with a security firm."

"Sort of. I'm a policeman."

Jason stepped back. His frightened gaze shot to the door.

Simon could read the kid's mind. "She probably wouldn't mind me telling you that her house was recently burglarized. I'm here on loan from the Myrtle Beach PD to cut down on burglaries. Her son asked me to check her shop."

You could almost see the tension ease out of Jason. "They catch who did it?"

"Maureen caught them," Simon said.

Jason made a face. "Figures."

Simon was sure that one word wasn't meant as a compliment. "She's a smart woman. If you'll excuse me, I need to finish. Nice talking to you," Simon said, then paused. "I help coach a boys' basketball team at the Y on Tuesday and Thursday nights at six. You're welcome to come by."

"I've got better things to do with my time."

"Name one."

Jason opened his mouth, then closed it.

"If you change your mind, the invitation stands." Simon started to the back.

Maureen tried to stay out of other people's business, but there were times when it was impossible.

"Traci, what's the matter?" Maureen asked as they sat at the breakfast table in her kitchen Sunday morning. "You haven't been yourself for the past few days. I might be overstepping, but I know you are avoiding Ryan."

"He asked me out and I turned him down," Traci replied.

Maureen smiled. "Good. Women have always been too easy for him."

"And all of them are skinny!" Traci said with disgust.

Maureen overlooked the pique in Traci's voice. "He's been close to getting engaged twice and gotten cold feet."

Traci almost spewed her coffee. "Engaged. Twice?"

"Both were lovely women, and both were certain he was going to propose," Maureen confided.

"What happened?"

"Only Ryan knows. I asked. All he would say was that it hadn't felt right."

"There might be a third," Traci said under her breath.

"What?" Maureen straightened.

"Just that the other evening at the security meeting more than one woman was hanging on him," Traci said.

"I suppose." Maureen picked up her purse. "We'd better be going."

Traci rinsed her cup and put it in the sink. "My turn to drive. The car is out front."

They reached the front door just as the doorbell rang. "I wasn't expecting anyone."

Traci smiled. "Maybe Simon couldn't wait until this afternoon to see you."

Maureen blushed and opened the door. She couldn't hide the disappointment when she saw a young woman she didn't recognize. "Yes."

"I'm Elisa Thomas. I thought it was time we should meet," she said, then stared coldly at Traci. "Ryan refuses to talk to me. I'm having his baby."

Maureen's eyes widened in shock. "What?"

"Perhaps we should discuss this inside," Traci suggested.

"Yes," Maureen said, her gaze sweeping over the woman, centering on her flat abdomen.

"I'm a little over six weeks," Elisa confided on seeing Maureen's questioning gaze.

"Please, won't you come into the great room." Maureen kept glancing at the other woman. Reaching the grouping of antique sofa and chairs, she motioned Elisa to a seat. "Would you like anything? Tea?"

"No, thank you." Elisa glanced down, then pulled a tissue from her purse. "If only Ryan were as gracious and caring."

"Ms. Thomas—"

"Please call me Elisa," she interrupted Maureen. "I'm carrying your grandbaby."

"I-I don't know what to say." Maureen laced her hands together. "Ryan . . . Ryan is so responsible. I can't believe he would turn his back on his child or its mother."

"She'll tell you." Elisa sniffed. "I tried to talk to him the other night when they were out, and he wouldn't even speak to me."

Maureen turned to Traci. "You were out with Ryan?"

"Not exactly," Traci said, not liking it one bit that Elisa had dragged her into this mess with Ryan. "We happened to be at the same restaurant and shared a table."

Elisa sniffed louder. "You can't imagine how much it hurt to see him with another woman, even one I knew he could never be interested in."

Both Maureen and Traci straightened, inwardly bristling at the snide comment.

Either unaware or uncaring, she continued. "I love him so much. I tried to talk to him at his place after he left you and he—" Tears fell faster. "Afterward he ordered me to leave."

Traci wasn't sure if she'd taken Maureen's hand or it was the other way around. He'd made love to that woman after he'd left her? After he'd almost pleaded for her to believe him? *He deserved to roast in hell.*

"I can't believe Ryan would be so callous."

A spark of something flared briefly in Elisa's eyes. "I'm carrying Ryan's child. I didn't think you'd turn your back on me, too."

"No, no," Maureen hastened to say and went to sit beside the other woman. "I'd never do that."

Elisa smiled, smug and satisfied.

In that instant, Traci knew the other woman lied. The tightness in her chest eased. She'd let her emotions get in the way of seeing through the lies. The best had tried to con her and failed.

"Thank you." Elisa laid her head on Maureen's shoulder. "Thank you."

"Excuse me," Traci said. She went to the other room and dialed Ryan's number.

"Hello. Dr. Gilmore speaking."

"Elisa is at your mother's house. I suggest you get over here." Traci hung up, but not before she heard the sharp expletive. Not wanting to leave Maureen alone with the conniving woman, Traci returned and saw her still clinging to Maureen. She also saw Maureen's grateful expression that she hadn't left.

While Elisa's head was bowed, Traci mouthed, "Ryan is on his way." The relief on Maureen's face was instantaneous. Now, all they had to do was wait until Ryan arrived and sent Elisa on her way.

Where is she?" Ryan yelled the instant he entered the house twelve minutes later. The slamming of the front door reverberated through the house.

Traci watched Elisa jump and burrow deeper into Maureen's arms. "Why is he so angry? It's his child."

Ryan stalked into the great room, rage shimmering from him. "Get up and get out of this house before I drag you."

Elisa began crying. "All I want to do is love him."

"Get out!"

"Ryan, please," Maureen pleaded. "We have to think of the baby."

"Baby?"

"Elisa says she's carrying your baby," Maureen told him.

Grim-faced and furious, he started for the woman. Traci hopped up from an armchair and grabbed his arm. "Calm down."

"She's lying," he snarled.

"I don't know why he's treating me this way after—" She started crying again, clinging to Maureen.

"Ryan, please sit down," his mother said.

He shook free of Traci. "If you weren't clinging to my mother, I'd throw you out of here."

She sniffed. "My father is chief-of-staff at the hospital. He won't let you talk to me that way."

"I could give a rip. If you tell anyone else that lie, I'll sue you for slander!"

"Ryan—"

"Mother, she's lying and using your kindness," he said, cutting her off. "She latched on to me for some crazy reason. She's sick."

Elisa began wailing. "You're mean! How could you talk to the mother of your child that way?"

"That does it." He started for Elisa.

The women shrieked. Maureen held up one hand to keep Ryan at bay while trying to hug Elisa with the other. Traci grabbed him by the tail of his jacket. He swung around, his face livid.

"If you hurt Maureen trying to get to Elisa, you'll hate yourself until the day you die. Now, go sit down over there. Or better yet, go to another room and cool off." Her hand flexed on his muscled arm. "You're upsetting Maureen, and we both know she's been through enough this week."

His furious gaze pinned Traci. "You believe her?"

"I can't think of a reason for her to lie," Traci answered, very much aware that Elisa was listening to every word.

Hurt flashed in his eyes. Throwing Elisa one last murderous look, he left the room.

Traci stared after Ryan. She couldn't have seen hurt in his eyes because she didn't believe him. Their opinion of each other didn't matter. She was there to help Maureen and not to hold Ryan's hand.

Traci firmly turned to Elisa. The tears were gone and in her eyes was the look of satisfaction. Mean, spiteful women pissed Traci off almost as much as mean, spiteful men did.

Feigning a sympathetic expression, Traci went to the other woman and hunkered down in front of her. "Please calm down. I can imagine how upsetting this must be, but it's not good for you or the baby."

Elisa sniffed. "I'll try."

"Good. I'll get you a glass of water." Pushing upward, Traci went to the kitchen. Ryan glanced up when she entered. He didn't say a word; his accusing gaze said enough. She told herself she didn't care, quickly got the water, and went back to the living area. "Why don't you sit up?"

Elisa's lashes flickered as if she were trying to determine if that was a wise move, then she did as requested and took the glass. She took a sip, then held the glass firmly with both hands.

"You've already seen that Maureen is willing to help. You

must realize that this has caught her by surprise," Traci said. "She was telling me before you arrived that Ryan wasn't dating anyone."

"We've been dating for six weeks." Elisa took another sip of water. "We met at a hospital function. We hit it off and he took me home. We were happy until he learned about the baby, then he dumped me."

"Heartless bastard," Traci spat, not daring to look at Maureen. "He tried to make a move on me the other night." Elisa's eyes flashed with anger. "You must have been special if he found time to take you out with his busy schedule."

"He said I was. He said he couldn't live without me," Elisa said. "We were together all the time."

Traci patted the woman's hand. "I'm glad I didn't let him talk me into going back to his place. What's it like?"

"I . . . it's sort of like this." Elisa batted her lashes as if embarrassed, then tucked her head. "I don't remember much. I was more interested in Ryan, the same way I thought he was interested in me."

"You must really love him." Traci shuddered. "I saw him early this summer at Maureen's pool, and that hairy chest of his was a turnoff."

Elisa's chin lifted and she looked at Maureen. "I love everything about Ryan. Hairy chest and all."

Maureen didn't say anything for a moment, then said, "Ryan deserves the love of a good woman, a woman who will love him back."

"That he does." Traci came to her feet. "Elisa, why don't you let Maureen talk to Ryan? She'll make him see reason."

"Will you?" Elisa asked hopefully.

"I'll do whatever it takes to resolve this," Maureen said, rising and bringing Elisa with her.

"I'll walk you to your car." Traci took the glass from Elisa, sat it on the table, then reached for Elisa's arm. Together they went to the front door. "I'll help in any way I can."

"Thank you. I thought you wanted him, too, but I could have told you it wouldn't do any good," Elisa said, her tone superior as they went down the sidewalk.

"You have a clear field." Traci stopped by the woman's car, a late-model red Infiniti. "Drive safely and take care."

"I'll go home and wait for Ryan." Getting in the car with a dreamy smile on her face, Elisa drove away.

"That might be a long wait," Traci mumbled, then she went back to the house.

Chapter

9

Traci found Maureen and Ryan in the kitchen.

His accusing gaze stabbed her. "I never touched her."

"I know that," Traci said, stopping a short distance from him.

"How?" he asked, unfolding his arms.

"You don't have a hairy chest," Traci answered. She should know because she had been foolish enough to drool over it.

"That's what I've been trying to tell you, but you were too upset to listen," Maureen told him, then she smiled at Traci. "You were brilliant."

"If either of you know something that will straighten this mess out, please tell me," Ryan asked, his gaze flickering between Traci and his mother.

"Since I was sitting across from her, I was able to watch her." Traci folded her arms. "Her face alternated between smug and hateful when she was talking about being pregnant by you. She wanted to hurt you."

Ryan's mouth tightened. "She said she'd make me sorry."

Unfolding her arms, Traci leaned back against the granite-topped island. "She tripped herself up when she couldn't describe your apartment she claimed to have been in, and said she liked your hairy chest."

"My chest isn't hairy," he said as if insulted by the prospect.

"I know, but apparently Elisa doesn't, which proves she's never seen you with your shirt off," Traci finished, feeling a bit flushed at the thought of Ryan with his shirt off.

Ryan's gaze narrowed. "The first time we met, I'd come over here to swim. You were outside at the pool with Mother. You left soon afterward."

Hot and bothered, if she remembered. "I had business."

"So you said."

Traci didn't fidget under his hot stare, but it was difficult.

"When Traci asked about your apartment, she said she thought it looked like my house," Maureen said. "Your place is sleek and modern, not filled with a mixture of antiques, the way mine is."

"She tripped herself up by that lie." Traci was thankful Maureen had gotten the conversation going again. "My guess is that she's fixated on you. I don't think it just started either."

Clearly anxious, his mother placed her hand on his arm. "Is that true, Ryan?" His hard glare cut to Traci, then went back to his mother. "Ryan, I want to know."

He shoved a hand over his head, then told them everything. "She's starting to show up more and more frequently. Last night when I finished rounds she was in the parking garage, waiting. Luckily, I was with two other people and she didn't approach me."

"Do you think she's dangerous?" Maureen asked.

Ryan hugged his mother to him. "She's not the woman from *Fatal Attraction*."

"How do you plan to stop her from bothering you?" Maureen asked.

"I'll think of something," Ryan answered.

Maureen wasn't satisfied with his response. "Traci, could you help?"

"No," Ryan said before Traci could answer. "I can take care of this myself."

Traci thought of pointing out what a piss-poor job he'd done in the past, but since she was well aware of men's fragile egos, she took a diplomatic approach. "What are your plans?"

"I'm still working on them," he said.

In other words, he didn't know what to do. Traci didn't need Maureen's imploring gaze to offer help. Traci felt sorry for Ryan. Women had tried to pull that scam too many times on men. "You had better speed up your timetable. The media salivates over this type of news. It certainly wouldn't help with the fund-raising efforts for your clinic patients or your private practice, for that matter."

"Oh, Ryan, that would be horrible," Maureen said.

"It won't come to that," he said, but for the first time worry replaced the anger in his face.

Since Traci knew Ryan was still ticked at her for not believing him immediately, she knew he wasn't going to ask for help, so she did something she'd promised herself she'd never do: offer unsolicited advice. "Talk with her father, tell him what's going on. If he can't get her to stop bothering you, get a restraining order. In the meantime, I'll check her past. More than likely, you're not the first man she's fixated on. For now, let's go eat."

"I'll get out of your way," Ryan started from the kitchen.

Traci stepped in front of him. "You too."

"I'm not hungry," he said.

"Then you can watch us eat." She took his arm, trying not to be moved by the hard muscles beneath her fingertips. "You can drive."

"No."

"Ryan, I'd feel better if you came with us." Maureen caught his other arm. "I'd worry that she would get tired of waiting for you at her apartment and go to your condo."

His anger came back in a heated rush. "Let her."

"Be as smart as I know you are," Traci said. "The woman is unstable. Give her an opportunity to slam your butt in jail on an assault charge, and she will. She wants you, but if she can't have you she'll make your life hell. If that happens, guess who will be in hell with you?"

His gaze lowered to his mother, softened. "She makes me so angry."

"Maybe we should ask Sim—Lieutenant Dunlap for—"

"No," Ryan cut his mother off. "I don't want anyone else involved."

There went that fragile-as-a-snowflake ego again. "Have it your way for now. Let's go eat and try to put this incident out of our minds. Ryan, you drive," Traci ordered. Without giving him a chance to protest again, Traci started toward the front door.

How could Traci have believed that lie even for a second?

Almost two hours later, Ryan was still having a difficult time accepting that Traci had believed he was the kind of man who impregnated a woman, then ran out on her. Did she think he was that low?

Of course she did.

And she wasn't going to let him prove differently. No one had to tell him that, if it weren't for his mother, she would have let him spin in the wind. Unable to help himself, he sneaked a look at her as they strolled along the pier. She looked beautiful today in a lime green linen suit, her shoulder-length hair swirling around her shoulders. He would have liked to brush it from her face.

She didn't want his touch. Didn't want him.

As they had been doing since they'd gotten in his car, Traci and Maureen were chatting, laughing, trying to draw him into the conversation. He didn't feel like talking. In fact, he would have left long ago if he hadn't been driving.

"The brunch was wonderful, wasn't it, Ryan?"

"Yes." At his mother's insistence he'd ordered, then picked at the food on his plate. He'd considered asking his waiter to put vodka in his orange juice instead of champagne. He hadn't because he'd seen too many people ruin their lives with alcohol and barbiturates.

"Isn't it a beautiful day, Ryan?" his mother asked. "You can see the lighthouse on Sullivan Island. Remember when your father and I climbed to the top?"

"Yes." He'd been sixteen and raced ahead of them, trying to impress a girl at the time. He'd almost fallen. The girl had laughed harder than anyone.

"I've only been there once," Traci said from beside him. "When they dedicated the monument to the slaves arriving from Africa."

"We were there as well. It was a moving experience." Maureen stopped and leaned on the rail. "To think our paths could have crossed then, but didn't."

Traci laughed. "I couldn't have afforded to buy the house I'm in then."

"You work hard." Maureen brushed her hair out of her face.

"No more than you do." Traci turned to Ryan. "How are the plans coming for the fund-raising?"

"All right." He stared out to sea, his mind on Elisa, wondering if she'd be waiting for him at his place, if he'd have to move. Thank goodness she hadn't been able to get his unlisted phone number.

"The Sisterhood will help," Maureen said.

He nodded absently. How could trying to help a woman lead to such disastrous consequences?

"Will you have to make rounds today at the hospital?" Traci inquired.

"Yes." How could she act as if nothing had happened when she'd cut him to the quick? He knew she had trust issues, but he still couldn't get over her believing Elisa over him. Anger rolled through him again. "Let's go."

"It's such a beautiful day, I thought we'd stay a little longer." Maureen glanced at Traci.

"We could take one of the tour boats out," Traci suggested.

Ryan shook his head. Elisa could be driving to his place now. "Not today."

"We would be back in a couple of hours," Traci told him.

He tried not to think of all the things an obsessed woman like Elisa could do. The scene from *Fatal Attraction*—the boiling pot—popped into his mind. "Let's go."

Traci resisted the tug on her arm. She'd had enough. Ryan had moped the entire time. "Will you stop sulking?"

"I'm thinking."

"Sulking," she repeated. "You haven't said five words together since we left the house."

He stared down at her face. "I'm a deep thinker."

"I'll give you something to think about." Impulsively, she grabbed a fistful of his polo shirt and pulled him to her. She laughed at the startled expression on his face. The laughter died as she became aware of the hard body pressed to hers. The world narrowed to the two of them. Her gaze somehow wandered to his lips. Heat and desire rolled through her.

"I—"

His mouth settled firmly over hers, cutting off what she'd been about to say. Pleasure swept through her as his tongue danced with hers.

He lifted his head, his smoldering gaze holding hers. Air rushed in and out of her lungs. Realizing she still held him, her fingers uncurled. She swallowed, swallowed again. "I-I guess I shocked you out of sulking."

"You certainly did," Ryan said, grinning down at her.

Embarrassed, she stepped away from him completely. "Good, because it won't happen again. I'm ready to go home." Not waiting, Traci started for Ryan's car parked on the street, ignoring Maureen's pleased expression and Ryan's smile.

Please, no personal summers. Please, no personal summers.

Maureen repeated the silent litany to herself over and over as she walked with Simon down the pier of the marina to the *Proud Mary*. The luxury boat was a sleek thirty-footer that rode gently on the waves

She welcomed the cool breeze off the Ashley River and couldn't wait to be on the water, especially since Ryan and Traci had finally stopped circling each other. She couldn't be more pleased or happy for them. "I'm sorry your brother and his fiancée couldn't join us."

Simon threw her a mischievous look. "I'm not."

Maureen couldn't control the blush or the pleasure that spread through her. Neither was she.

"I was afraid this day would never happen." Taking her arm, Simon helped Maureen step onto the deck of the boat.

"I wondered myself." Smiling, she watched him hunker down and untie the boat. "Do you need any help?"

"Got it." Standing, he went to the helm and started the motor. "I thought we'd go where the spirit leads."

"That sounds like a wonderful idea." She was unable to keep from noticing his strong hands, his muscular thighs in shorts, his long, narrow feet. Out of nowhere popped the old adage about the size of a man's feet correlating with another part of his anatomy.

Heat flushed her face. She groaned.

Simon glanced over his shoulder. A frown creased his brow. "Are you all right?"

She smiled despite her embarrassment. "Yes."

He didn't appear convinced. "You're sure? We can put this off."

She went to stand beside him. "No more cancellations for us."

"Right." He opened the throttle of the boat. The craft cut through the water.

Sighing in pleasure as the breeze wafted over her, Maureen closed her eyes. "I'd forgotten how good this felt."

"I'm glad I'm able to share it with you."

"So am I," she told him, enjoying the feel of his body pressed against hers. She glanced around and their gaze caught, clung. His lips touched hers gently, then they were gone, leaving her wanting more.

"If I kiss you the way I want to I might not be able to concentrate on what I'm doing," he confessed. "But later . . ."

Maureen licked her lips, watched his eyes narrow, felt his body harden. Later.

Less than thirty minutes later Simon anchored near a cove and pulled Maureen into his arms.

With a trembling sigh, she came to him, her body aligned with his, her mouth sweet and seductive. He relished the slow building of heat, the way her slender body fit in his arms. She was perfect in every way.

"I don't think I could have waited another second," he breathed against her mouth.

"Me neither."

"Maureen." He kissed her again, he couldn't help it, didn't want to, and from the way she was clinging to him she felt the same way. He was indeed a lucky man.

10

Ryan was putting an end to Elisa stalking him today.

As soon as he arrived at his office Monday morning, he had his secretary contact Elisa's father for an appointment as soon as possible. He was taking Traci's advice. Just thinking about her made him grin as he strode down the hall of the administrative offices in the hospital.

She was as passionate as he'd guessed. Her fire and passion had been hidden behind that wall she'd built around her. No more. Ryan had finally broken through, and he planned on keeping the door opened.

Entering Dr. Thomas's outer office later that day, Ryan spoke to the secretary, who greeted him before she waved him on. Dr. Thomas was a top-notch administrator who was fair and conscientious. Ryan hoped he could continue to say the same thing once he left. He rapped on the door.

"Come in."

Ryan opened the door and saw Dr. Thomas in a white lab coat sitting behind a massive desk covered with several piles of manila folders. "Good afternoon, Dr. Thomas. Thanks for seeing me."

"I always have time for my doctors. Have a seat." Smiling broadly, Dr. Thomas swung away from his computer monitor and laced his long-fingered hands on top of his polished desk. "Especially after Elisa's call last night."

Ryan took the side chair and fought to keep his expression calm. "What did she say?"

"Just that you were dating and having some problems," he answered jovially. "You want me to put in a good word for you, I suppose?"

"No. I want you to tell Elisa to stop stalking me." Ryan watched the smile slide from the doctor's face.

"What?" Dr. Thomas shouted, his broad shoulders pressing against the back of the leather chair.

"I'm sorry to be so blunt, but there is no delicate way to put this," Ryan said.

The older man planted his hands firmly on his desk and came to his full height of six-three. "My daughter would never do such a thing."

Ryan came to his feet as well. "She would and has for the past four weeks. I made the mistake of taking her home from a party we both attended because her date had too much to drink. It was a simple favor but she latched on to me."

"How dare you insult Elisa that way," he said. "She's attractive, successful, and sought after professionally and personally. She doesn't need to chase after any man."

"That's what she's done." Ryan wasn't backing down. "Yesterday she showed up at my mother's house, claiming she was pregnant."

"You bastard." Enraged, Dr. Thomas started around the desk.

"I've never been intimate with her." Ryan didn't want to

deck the chief-of-staff. "She tripped herself up when she was asked to describe where I live and other things."

Dr. Thomas stopped inches from Ryan, his fists clenched. "Elisa wouldn't lie about that."

"She has." Ryan raked his hand over his head. "She's called my office repeatedly, asking to speak to me. She changes her name, but my staff recognizes her voice."

"You can't be sure it's Elisa."

"I trust my staff. Can you trust your daughter?"

Dr. Thomas looked uncertain for just a moment. "She's a brilliant doctor."

"We both know one has nothing to do with the other," Ryan said. "This is going to stop, or I'm getting a restraining order and considering pursuing legal action for defamation of character."

"That would ruin her reputation and career," Dr. Thomas raged. "You can't do that."

"She hasn't left me with any other choice," Ryan told him. "She'll damage my reputation and career if she spreads the lie about carrying my baby. It's her or me. There's nothing in my past that I'm ashamed of. I'm betting that that's not the case with Elisa. Talk to her, or I'll talk to my lawyer."

"No. No," Dr. Thomas said hastily, fear in his eyes. "There is no need for that. I'll talk to her."

"Then I'll leave it in your hands." Ryan went to the door. "If there had been another way to keep you out of it, I would have taken it."

Dr. Thomas sat heavily in his seat. "This stays between us."

Ryan felt sorry for the man he respected. "I don't want this getting out any more than you do."

The older man glanced away. "Good-bye."

"Good-bye." Feeling as if a weight had been lifted from his shoulders, Ryan left the chief-of-staff's office. He knew just whom to thank.

Traci had just checked the pot roast in the Crock-Pot when the doorbell rang.

She frowned and glanced at the clock. Seven thirteen. She wasn't expecting anyone. She and Maureen had talked earlier. Both were in for the night.

The chime rang again. Going to the front door, she pressed her eye to the peephole. Her heart knocked. *Ryan.* He had a large bouquet of fresh cut flowers and he was smiling. She'd always thought she'd be a sucker for flowers, since she'd never received any. She already knew she was a sucker for Ryan's smile, just like she had been for his kiss that tied her in knots and made her want more.

Telling herself to be cautious, to remain professional, that the flowers didn't mean anything, she opened the door. "Hello, Ryan. You look happy."

He came inside and closed the door behind him. "Euphoric would be a better word, and I owe it all to you." He handed her the flowers. "I feel like celebrating."

She smiled in spite of herself. "I can see that."

"You were dead on about speaking with Dr. Thomas. He's going to talk to Elisa, and I have my life back."

"I'm glad." He wore happiness well.

He caught her free hand, twirling her around in a circle, then back into his strong arms. He stared down into her face, inches from his.

She wasn't sure who moved first, but suddenly his hot mouth was on her, igniting the passion of the day before. As before she had no time to gather her defenses against the on-slaught of desire. Whatever his faults, the man could kiss. Her toes actually curled in her thick socks.

Her eyes flew wide and she pushed out of his arms. She'd bet none of the other women he'd dated had worn socks, a black "Eat Dirt" T-shirt, and faded blue jeans.

"Why did you do that?" he asked.

"I . . ." She couldn't think of a lie when he was watching her with such hunger, the same hunger she knew was build-ing within her.

"You think too much." He handed her the flowers she'd dropped, then grabbed her free hand and kissed her knuckles. "On second thought, why don't I go get takeout and we can stay in and neck."

"I thought you were mad at me," she said, trying to clear her brain so she could think. This was not supposed to be happening. "I'm supposed to be mad at you."

"I'd say the kiss yesterday changed things," he said, nib-bling on her fingertips.

It had, but she wasn't willing to take the risk Ryan pre-sented. The fact that she allowed him inside her house after promising herself she wouldn't was proof enough. She started to withdraw her hands.

His hands tightened. "No. You're thinking again."

"That's what keeps me out of trouble," she confessed. It wasn't as if he hadn't already figured out the effect he had on her.

"I'm not out to play games with you, Traci." His thumb grazed across the top of her hand, sending shivers through her. "I'd planned to give you a few days to get over being up-set with me—rightly so," he hastened to add when her eye-brows lifted, then he continued. "I wasn't going to give up."

"I don't like being lied to."

"I get that and I'm sorry. It won't happen again," he told her.

"If it does, I'm walking. No second chances," she said, realizing as she said it what it meant.

Apparently Ryan understood as well. He released her hand and circled her waist with his arms, meshing their bodies from breasts to thighs. "Fair enough."

Standing this way with him shouldn't feel so good, so right. "I'm sorry I didn't believe you at first," she confessed. If she wanted honesty, she had to give it as well. "I wanted to believe the worst about you."

"I don't need two guesses to figure out why. You don't know what it did to me when you believed her," he said, his eyes troubled. "But to be fair, we hadn't developed our relationship enough for you to believe in me. I'd like to change that. Starting tonight."

This was her last chance to make a run for it. He kissed her on the forehead and running became the furthest thing from her mind. "How about pot roast instead of takeout?"

"Lead the way."

Ryan followed Traci into her kitchen, which was obviously designed for someone who liked to cook, but who also liked style and elegance. There was crown molding, heavily carved doors of dark stained oak, inserts of granite in the cabinetry, large canisters of pasta and grains and a huge bowl of fruit on the island, which boasted its own sink. The floor was marble. Ryan could see a family entertaining here or a large party. As far as he knew, Traci didn't entertain.

Traci lifted the glass top of a Crock-Pot and poked whatever was inside with a fork. This was a lot of space for one woman. Under any other circumstances he would say the owner was trying to impress others. Yet, from what he'd observed and what his mother had told him, she wasn't the type.

"Anything I can do to help?"

Replacing the lid, she arched a brow. "You don't look like the domestic type."

He laughed and crossed the room to kiss her on the lips for the sheer pleasure of it. "Mother loved Dad and me, so neither one of us is helpless in the kitchen."

"Smart woman," she said, her voice just the tiniest bit unsteady. "The two drawers at the end have place mats and flatware."

"I'm on it." Reluctantly, he moved away.

Traci popped several rolls into the microwave. "Glasses in the third cabinet. Tea in the fridge, if that's all right."

"Tea is fine." Finished with the place settings, he filled the glasses with ice from the dispenser in the refrigerator and placed them on the table.

Traci placed their plates on the dark chocolate linen place mats. "I'll bet you weren't always this agreeable to helping out in the kitchen."

Ryan returned to the table with the pitcher of tea and filled their glasses. "Nope. I complained, but since I liked my head where it was, I did it out of hearing range."

Traci laughed. "The salad is on the bottom shelf. I'll get the rolls and salad plates. When did it hit you that she might have been right?"

"My first year in medical school when I lived in an apartment." Putting the green salad on the table, he pulled out her chair for her, then took his own seat. "Time became a precious commodity. I didn't want to waste it standing in line to order food or wait for them to prepare it."

Traci said grace and handed him the bread basket. "You mean you couldn't find someone willing to feed you?"

Traci might have said the words playfully, but Ryan knew better. She thought he was a player. "Not my style to use a woman just to cook for me." He served her the salad. "The first year of medical school was pretty intense. For that matter, so was the second and third. I didn't really get to know Dallas until my internship."

Traci sat back in her chair. "I went to SMU Law School."

"What year?"

"Ninety-one to ninety-four," she answered, her fork poised over her salad.

Ryan shook his head. "I guess I should have gotten out more. I was there then. That's twice we could have met."

"You probably wouldn't have noticed me." She picked up a bit of lettuce.

Ryan placed his hand on her free one. "I noticed you the first time I saw you. I don't mind telling you, you kept me up that night with some pretty wild fantasies."

Traci glanced at him out of the corners of her eyes. "Well, I guess I can confess that you did the same to me."

He grinned, then finished his salad and cut into his beef. "You could have surprised me. I couldn't tell if you liked me or wanted my head on a spit."

She made a face. "Both. I didn't *want* to like you."

"Because you thought I was a player?" he asked.

"Something like that," she said. She wouldn't meet his gaze.

Since Traci wasn't the shy type, he knew there was more to it than that. He'd probe later. Now he was just glad she had let down her guard enough to give him a chance. "Good thing I'm persistent." He winked at her. "This is great. Did your mother teach you how to cook?"

Her shoulders jerked, then she went as still as a wall. "My grandfather."

There was more to it than that. There were more layers to Traci than he'd suspected. Instead of eating, she was moving food around on her plate. He couldn't have that. "He did a great job. By the way, are we all set for the party?"

"Yes." She finally looked at him. "I took the liberty of hiring a caterer, one Maureen has used and been very pleased with. They'll take care of the food, flowers, everything. All we have to do is send out the invitations and keep Maureen in the dark."

"You're good at this." His plate empty, he reached for his sweetened iced tea, glad to see that she was eating again.

"I enjoyed doing it," she told him. "I ran our plans by the Invincibles and they all like the ideas we came up with. They're bringing party favors, but want to keep it a secret."

Ryan paused in placing his glass on the table. "Do you think that's wise? They can get pretty risqué at times. I shudder to think about what went on in Vegas."

"Look at it this way, you didn't have to get us out of jail," Traci said, her eyes twinkling.

"But I can still picture what happened when I picked all of you up at the airport and saw Ophelia's face when she was dragging things out of her overnight case looking for her medicine and a man's black thong fell out." He ground his teeth. "Mother threw her big purse on it, you yelled rat, and all of you broke into giggles."

Traci's lips twitched. "What's happens in Vegas stays in Vegas."

"All I can say is that I'm glad we were in the parking lot of the airport and not in the terminal." He braced his arms on the table. "Are you up for another project?"

"Depends." Picking up their plates, she went to the sink.

Ryan hadn't expected it to be easy. Traci was a cautious woman. He followed her with their glasses and salad plates. "We're trying to raise money for baby supplies and, if we have enough, money for the mothers to go to trade school or junior college. Sadly, too many of my clients aren't ready for motherhood emotionally or financially."

Rinsing the plates and glasses, Traci put them in the dishwasher. "All babies and children should know that they're loved."

The sadness in her voice tugged at his heart. He brushed the back of his hand down her cheek. "Unfortunately, that doesn't always happen."

She turned from the sink. "What do you want me to do?"

"For a man who's been thinking about you for several months, that's a loaded question," he told her, half in jest, half serious.

She blinked, then smiled seductively at him. "Let's just stick with the clinic for the moment."

"Pity," he answered, then said, "You know PR and a lot of successful people. Perhaps you can work with the clinic manager and come up with a fund-raising plan. You can drop by the clinic this week and meet her."

"I think that can be arranged."

"Good." Ryan placed his hands on the double sink, blocking her in. "Now that that's settled, it's my turn to tell you what you can do for me." Leaning over, he whispered in her ear, then gently bit the lobe. When he leaned back to see her face, she looked intrigued.

I have a surprise for you, Jason," Maureen said.

Jason's brown eyes widened with suspicion. He pulled his hands out of his pockets, where he kept them most of the time. Maureen didn't know if that was his usual habit or if he didn't want to be accused of stealing anything.

Maureen lifted the oblong-shaped wooden box, which was wrapped in an artist's rendition of a street scene in Paris and tied with a red bow. "Come on. Take it. It won't bite."

His hands curled around the package. He looked from her to the gift.

"Please open it." Maureen linked her fingers, hoping she'd guessed right.

Slowly he slipped the elastic bow aside, then turned the package over and began working on the top. Ryan had always torn into his packages at that age. It was almost as if Jason were savoring the experience.

Head down, he began to pull the paper back, got to the middle where he could see the art set, and stopped. His hand ran over the wooden case, then fisted. Surging to his feet, he laid it on her desk. "I don't want it."

"Do you mind telling me why?" she asked, displaying none of the disappointment she felt.

"What would I do with it?" His hands went into his pockets again. "Henrietta said I shouldn't stay long."

Against the odds, Henrietta and Jason were getting along. She knew a lot about antiques and Jason, like Avery, was willing to learn and share her passion. "I saw the drawings you did in your notebook. You have talent. And talent should never be wasted."

"A black man can make a living painting, but not on a canvas," he tossed out.

Maureen could almost hear the words being carelessly tossed at him. "If you believe that, then why do you still sketch?"

"To pass time. Social studies is boring and there's nothing to do at home," he told her. "I'm probably the only kid on the block without an X-Box or his own TV."

"Ryan, my son, said the same thing to me when he didn't have an Atari video game. He lived through it and is now a doctor." She smiled. "I like to think he turned out all right without it."

"You're rich. He was set for life," Jason sneered. "He didn't have to worry about paying his way."

"We're well off, but that wouldn't have gotten him through years of studying to get where he is today," Maureen said patiently. "His grades, determination, and hard work did that. Nothing was given to him. I'm proud that he worked to make his own way in the world."

"Saying I'm not?"

Patience, Maureen reminded herself. "I'm saying that dreams are possible. No idea was ever manifested without them. Come with me." She went into the main store.

"This was a dream. The past is a gateway to the future." She rubbed her hand over a one-hundred-year-old chest. "Imagine what was stored in here. Perhaps cherished heirlooms, a wedding gown, christening clothes. The past makes us who we are. In Forever Yours I offer treasures from the past at a price that will make the buyer and me happy. I'm able to see that another piece of history isn't lost, but cherished."

"Yeah, right. Are we finished?"

So he was a tough sell. "As soon as I answer your question." He frowned as if trying to remember what question. Maureen opened the front door. "Henrietta, we'll be back shortly."

"It's your time to waste," he said, following her outside.

Maureen's brows arched as she closed the door behind them. "I'd forgotten how difficult teenagers can be." She didn't expect a response and got none. Seeing a break in the traffic, she crossed the busy street and opened the door to a bookstore and art gallery.

Jason balked. "I can't go in there."

Maureen tensed. "You didn't—"

"No," he said, his lips pressed together tightly. "The prune-faced guy in there thought I was going to steal because I never bought anything. Said I was bad for business."

"So you came into my store."

He shrugged carelessly. "You weren't my first choice."

Teenagers, had a group ever been so glib? "Then you already know that black artists are commanding high prices for their work." She moved to stare through the plateglass window to view a painting on a wooden easel out of the direct sun. "That Frazier painting is priced at five thousand. I know because I'm considering purchasing it for my art collection."

His hands came out of his pockets. "You have an art collection!"

Finally, she saw an interest in his eyes. "An extensive one."

"Ah . . ."

"Yes?" she said when he didn't say anything further.

"Maybe I could see it sometime," he said, trying to appear as if it didn't matter in the least.

"I think that can be arranged. Now, let's get back to the store." She crossed the street with him beside her. "I want those packages ready for shipment."

He opened the door for her. "When do you think we could go?"

Maureen recalled Ryan's enthusiasm when a family friend, the man who had delivered him, became his mentor. Minutes were like days, weeks. "Maybe tomorrow. Tonight I'm going to watch Lieutenant Dunlap's team play."

"The po po?"

She stopped in her tracks. "I beg your pardon."

"Po po. The policeman."

"I see." She continued. "Yes, Simon is a policeman. I told him I'd drop by."

"You're busy. I get it."

Maureen stepped on the sidewalk. Probably not very many people had put what he wanted first. "Want to join me? We can grab a pizza afterward."

"Sure. I don't have anything better to do." Jason opened the front door to the store.

Maureen lifted her face to the sky and pressed her hands together beneath her chin. "Please."

"What are you doing?" Jason asked.

She lowered her hands and stated at him. "Asking for patience not to box your ears," she said, then the insidious heat moved over her. Fanning with both hands, she hurried into the store for the fan. She turned in circles, looking for where she might have left it.

"Here it is." Jason held out the paper fan. "You left it on the English library tub chair you showed to the last customer."

Grabbing the fan, she swept it back and forth, blowing out a breath as she did so. "Thank you."

"You . . . you aren't sick, are you?" he asked with genuine concern.

She was touched. "No."

He watched her closely in that serious way of his. "Do you want me to grab you a bottle of water from the fridge?"

"Yes, please."

"Be right back." He took off.

Henrietta came up to Maureen and pulled the switch of the ceiling fan overhead. "Decide how you're going to handle them?"

Maureen fanned faster. She didn't want to take hormones, but she wasn't sure about herbal therapy either. "No."

"Here." Jason unscrewed the cap and handed it to her, waiting until she'd taken several swallows. "Did that help?"

"Yes." Maureen replaced the cap. "Thank you. Now, we'd better get to work. We have a game to go to tonight." She just hoped she didn't have to deal with the hot flashes then.

Why don't you believe me?"

"Elisa, please calm down and listen," her father told her. He was in charge of over a thousand people, yet he couldn't control or help his daughter. She was beautiful with an unlined oval face, impeccably dressed in a gray-and-black designer suit, had finished fourth in her class, yet . . . "Dr. Gilmore threatened legal action. You can't afford that after the last incident."

"I told you that wasn't my fault," Elisa yelled as she paced in her father's study. The large masculine room had break-front bookcases on all the walls. The floor was polished hardwood. Ten-foot windows with Roman shades flanked the desk. The room was masculine and comfortable.

"Elisa, please listen to your father," his wife, Ellen, pleaded, her eyes brimming with tears. Unlike her husband and daughter, her petite frame barely reached five feet. Always neatly groomed as befitting a woman of her status, she wore a prim blue suit. "Think of your career, your reputation."

"You're thinking of your own reputation." Elisa's eyes were wild. "Daddy couldn't wait to leave California and take this position. You deserted me again."

"Elisa, that's enough," Dr. Thomas ordered. "You know we had no choice. It was the only way to save you."

"I don't need saving. All I need is Ryan." As quickly as the anger had come, it disappeared. "He's just playing hard to get."

Dr. Thomas's throat felt tight. He'd give his life to help her. How had they made so many mistakes? "Baby, your mother and I have talked. You and she can take an extended vacation anywhere you want to go. You can work on your book."

"I'm not interested in writing a book." Arms folded over her chest, she glared at her father. "You made that up. I don't see why I can't resume my practice."

"You know why," he said, his gut churning in remembrance.

Elisa waved a careless hand. "He shouldn't have said those hateful things to me."

Her mother went to her. "We could go to London, then take the train over to Paris, the ferry to Italy."

"I'm not leaving Ryan," Elisa said dismissively. "Not while that chubby nothing is after him." Her eyes went cold. "He went to her house last night."

"Oh, Elisa. Please," her father pleaded. "Can't you understand that this will only lead to more trouble, and this time I might not be able to get you out of it?"

"Oh, I understand. You've never been on my side. Never," she said, her voice rising with each word.

"Elisa," her mother said, tears shimmering in her eyes. "We love you."

"No you don't, but that's all right because Ryan does." Elisa ran from the room. She didn't slow when her parents tried to call her back.

She got to him.

Simon would have sworn he had his entire attention on the heated basketball game between his team, the Sharks, who were competing against the Dragons in the thirteen- to seventeen-year-old division, but when Maureen walked into the gym with Jason, he immediately saw her. In a sleeveless white dress, she looked as elegant and as desirable as she had Sunday with her hair tossed by the wind, laughter in her beautiful eyes.

He still found it hard to believe that he'd held her, kissed her, felt her tremble in his arms. She waved and he waved back.

"Dunlap, keep your eyes on the game." There was no heat or accusation in the head coach's request. A twenty-year veteran of the Charleston PD, Bobby Frost had a stocky build with an abdomen that hung over his belt from too many late-night meals, beers at the favorite hangout of his station, and a minimum of exercise.

"Have you ever heard of multitasking?" Simon asked, watching until Maureen and Jason took their seats in the bleachers above them.

"She's out of your class." His eyes on the game, Frost walked the length of his players on the bench.

Initially, Simon hadn't known she was wealthy and, when he had, it hadn't mattered. He was interested in the woman, not her bank account. He had no intention of letting her money get in the way. Thankfully, it didn't bother her that she had more money. He had a sneaky suspicion that her age was the culprit. He didn't think of her as older, he simply thought of her as the woman he wanted. "That shows you don't know very much."

Bobby, being a smart man, let his gaze wander from Maureen's to Simon. "You lucky son-of-a-gun."

"I think so." Simon gave his attention to the game and saw Miguel Williams hogging the ball again. No matter how much they'd talked about sportsmanship, nothing seemed to stick.

The seventeen-year-old had been sent to the program in an attempt by the judge to give him another chance to go straight, to see that the gang he led would only lead to imprisonment or death in a cold, dark alley. Someone was always tougher, more vicious. Gang members would turn on you faster than a rival. "Pass the ball," Simon yelled.

Miguel went for a layup and missed. The other team took possession of the ball. "Stay on your man. Stay on your man!" Simon yelled. They tried, but the Dragons were too fast. Their best scorer faked out Miguel, passing the ball behind him for his teammate to score.

Simon called time-out. "You want to do the honors or do you want me to?"

"I'm tired of talking. You're on," Bobby said. "I hate to say it, but I'm not sure that one can be saved, and I don't want him dragging down the other players who are trying so hard."

Simon agreed to a point, but he wasn't ready to give up on the brash kid just yet. He'd come from a good home. Both parents were hardworking, honest people. Neither could understand why Miguel wanted to be a thug. Miguel was the last player to reach the coaches.

"Miguel, there are five men out there," Simon said.

"None of them were open." Blowing hard, he caught the towel thrown his way and wiped his sweaty dark-chocolate face.

"I saw differently. Take a seat. Will, you're in."

"What?" Miguel protested, throwing his arms out wide. "I'm the best player you have!"

"Not from where I'm sitting," Simon said.

"I've never been benched," Miguel said, his voice carrying.

"Even the best are benched. Take a seat," Simon told him. Miguel slammed his towel to the floor. Simon ignored the tantrum and gave his players instructions. "We're a point behind with less than two minutes remaining. Let's pull together and win this one." Simon stuck his hand out. One by one, the players stacked theirs on top, then they ran back out on the floor.

They played hard and they played as a team. When one of the Dragon players missed a shot, Will was there to grab the ball. He one-armed the basketball to a teammate who was running back up the court. He caught the ball and shot from twenty feet out, hitting nothing but net just as the buzzer went off.

The Sharks went wild, jumping and shouting. The coaches were enveloped with hugs.

"Congratulations, Simon," Maureen said.

The noise around him faded. "Thanks. Glad you could come. You, too, Jason."

"Where are your manners, Dunlap?" Bobby asked.

"Maureen Gilmore, Jason Payne, meet Bobby Frost, the head coach of the Sharks and sergeant in the Burglary division of his precinct," Simon introduced.

"Pleased to meet you," Maureen said. "You had me worried."

Bobby laughed, showing a gap in his front teeth. "That was our first win in three games. What a way to do it." He turned to the grinning young man who had made the pass. "Way to go, Will."

"How about we celebrate with pizza?" the good-looking young man asked with a grin. Cheers went up.

"Sorry, payday is a week off," Bobby said with obvious regret.

"I got it," Simon said. "Before you hit the showers, I want you all to meet Jason Payne. He works part-time in Mrs. Gilmore's antique shop."

Miguel snickered. Jason hunched his shoulders. A look from Simon had Miguel straightening up. There were various calls of "hi" and "man" from the other players.

"Hit the showers," Simon ordered. "We leave in fifteen minutes." All the Sharks except Miguel raced from the court. Bobby followed.

Simon hoped he wouldn't have trouble with Miguel. Chastising him in front of the other players who, unfortunately, thought he had it going on because of his wild rep, would only make the surly teenager more rebellious. "Maureen, do you and Jason want to join us?"

"I don't want to impose," Maureen said.

"You wouldn't be," Simon insisted. "Please."

She turned to Jason. "Would you like to go with them?"

"Not particularly. Some of them go to my school." Jason worked his shoulders. "I don't want them . . ." His head lowered.

Simon realized the teenager was concerned with them learning the reason behind Jason working for Maureen. "When they get a look at Maureen's Beamer, they'll think you're lucky to work for her," Simon said.

"You're an employee, as Simon said." Maureen briefly placed her hand on Jason's thin arm. "That's all. I'd like to go, if you don't mind."

He frowned. "You won't go if I don't want to?"

"No, I won't. I promised you pizza afterward and I always keep my promises," she told him.

"I don't want to go," he said.

"Then we won't." Maureen turned to Simon. "Congratulations again. Good-bye. Let's go get that pizza, Jason."

The youth didn't move. "You meant it."

"I don't lie, and I keep my promises," she told the teenager.

"But you want to go, I can tell," Jason said, obviously puzzled.

"Yes, but what you want takes precedence," she said patiently.

Jason looked from her to Simon. "You're not going to say anything to make her change her mind?"

"I respect Maureen and her decisions," Simon said easily.

"I'd like for the both of you to join us, but the decision isn't mine."

"It's mine," he said slowly, as if finally realizing he had power. His shoulders straightened. "I guess we can go."

"Thank you, Jason," Maureen told him. "Do you need to call your mother and let her know you'll be later than we expected?"

He shook his head. "She just started her shift. Unless my head is severed, I can't disturb her."

Maureen sensed his hurt behind the carefree words. "That's because I told her I'd take care of you."

"I guess." He didn't sound or look convinced.

"We're ready," one of the players yelled, as the team raced back.

"That has to be the shortest shower in history." Simon held up his cell phone. "Who needs to call home?" Three hands went up. "A ride? My car can carry four more." Seven hands went up.

"I can take two in my truck," Bobby said.

"The other one can ride with us," Maureen volunteered.

Simon shook his head as the players quickly called to ride with him or Bobby. "You guys are going to kick yourself when you see her car."

Simon's prediction proved true.

Maureen ended up taking three players. Two of them were in the same grade as Jason and taking summer courses. Arriving at the pizza parlor, Jason stayed with her, staring longingly at the other boys.

"Why don't you join them?" Maureen asked as they went inside.

"They didn't ask me. I'll get us a table."

There was nothing she could say as she watched him walk away. A warm hand on her shoulder had her lifting her head. She stared into Simon's beautiful eyes.

"He'll get there."

"I'm more hopeful than I was last week," she said, watching Jason spin a cheese shaker. "I just wish the road wasn't so difficult or long."

"It's called growing up. Now, what kind of pizza do you want?"

"I forgot to ask." She crossed to Jason. "What kind of pizza?"

"Doesn't matter." He spun the shaker again.

Maureen's heart went out to Jason. The other boys were across the way, laughing at something Miguel said. He seemed to be the leader. She opened her purse and handed Jason a five-dollar bill. "Why don't you select us some dinner music? Perhaps the others would like to help select."

She didn't look to see if Jason had taken her suggestion until she was at the counter. Jason and two other boys were flipping through the charts. Soon the booming sound of rap splintered the air.

"I might regret that decision," she said softly. She ordered an extra-large beef pizza with a pan crust.

Simon looked at the blaring jukebox. "Your doing?"

"Afraid so." As soon as their orders were taken, they went to sit in the booth Jason had picked out. Bobby sat on the other side. When the pizza was served, Jason and the two boys he'd been talking with sat at a table near the jukebox.

And he was grinning.

12

Midway up the walk of Traci's house Tuesday night, Ryan stopped. The hair on the nape of his neck prickled. He tensed, peering into the shadows surrounding the house. Was Elisa or another threat skulking in the bushes?

A cat ran out of the boxwoods hugging Traci's house and ran across the street. Ryan relaxed, then continued. Traci answered the door wearing an ivory silk halter dress that lovingly cupped her lush breasts and made his blood run hot.

His breath snagged. His mouth dried. It took a moment or two to work up enough moisture in his mouth to whistle.

She smiled. "Hello. Glad you like."

"I like." His arms went around her waist, pulling her to him for a heated kiss.

"Hmmm. You're certainly doing a good job of making a believer out of me."

He grinned like a fool. "About time. You ready to go?"

"Let me grab my purse."

Ryan closed the door, enjoying watching the easy sway of Traci's hips, her great legs. She got to him, and he was glad he didn't have to hide it any longer.

Picking up the purse, she came back. "Are you going to tell me where we're going?"

"It's a surprise." He quickly discovered that he enjoyed keeping her a bit off balance, enjoyed seeing her eyes light up with happiness. He had a gut feeling that she'd had some tough times growing up and it hadn't gotten any better after she married.

On the porch, he took her key and secured both locks. Curving his arm back around her waist, they stepped off the porch. They were midway to his car when the sensation of being watched hit again. He halted, scanning the street and shrubbery around them.

"What is it?"

"Nothing." The last thing he wanted to do was worry Traci. This was his mess.

Placing one finger on his cheek, she turned his face to hers. "Ryan, what did I tell you about trust and honesty?"

"Get in the car and we'll talk." He quickly hustled her inside the automobile, then went around to the other side and got in.

"Well?"

"It's probably nothing, but I feel uneasy," he admitted and started the motor. A tire symbol appeared on the dash.

Muttering an expletive, he got out of the car. On the passenger's side he saw the low tire. He resisted the urge to kick it. "This has got to stop."

Traci joined him. Her gaze flickered from the tire to his angry face. "I don't suppose the flat could have been a coincidence?"

"It could, but I don't think so." He turned in a full circle. "She's probably watching."

When he faced Traci again she wrapped her arms around his neck, sank seductively against him. "Don't let her get to you or ruin our evening. Call car service to fix the flat, then we're going out as planned."

With her warm, lush body pressed against him it was difficult to remain angry. "Did I tell you how incredible you are?"

"No. I would have remembered."

"You're incredible," he said, then kissed her, thinking only of the woman in his arms.

Simon had been thinking about a good-night kiss ever since he'd seen Maureen's tongue flick a bit of crust from the corner of her mouth.

He wasn't letting Maureen get away from him without a kiss. Offering to follow her as she dropped off the players and Jason had removed any suspicion from the boys at least. Bobby had nudged him in the side when no one was looking.

He hadn't counted on seeing Ryan standing beside his car in front of Traci's house as a mechanic changed a flat. Maureen stopped in front of her house, then hurriedly crossed the lawn to where Ryan waited by his car. Simon was glad he didn't have to think of a plausible explanation for being there.

"What happened to your car?" Maureen asked.

"Just a flat," Ryan answered, his gaze going beyond her to Simon. "Is everything all right?"

"Yes," Simon replied easily. "Maureen brought Jason to witness the first win of the basketball team I coach. They joined us for pizza. I followed her home to make sure she arrived safely."

"Thanks," Ryan said.

Traci came out of her house to join them. "Hello, Maureen. Simon."

"Hi, Traci. Were you two going out?" Maureen asked, a smile on her face.

"As soon as the tire is fixed," Ryan told her.

"He won't tell me where." Traci smiled, folding her arms. "He also insisted I wait inside."

Simon didn't see any way he could hang around until they left on their date. He'd have to get that kiss another night. The mechanic shoved on the repaired tire. "I'd better be going. Good night."

The disappointment on Maureen's face went a long way to soothing his own. "Thank you for the pizza."

"I'll walk you to your car," Ryan said.

"All right." Simon had been a policeman too long not to know something was wrong. "What's up?" he asked when they reached his car.

"I need the name of a discreet top-notch security firm."

Simon tensed. "Is Maureen in danger?"

"No." Ryan looked toward the chatting women. "I'm not sure about Traci."

"You want to tell me what's going on?" Simon asked.

Ryan blew out a breath and told him everything about Elisa. "The mechanic didn't see anything off with the flat. Traci laughed, and thinks I'm being paranoid."

"But you don't?" Simon asked.

"No," Ryan answered. "I'd feel better if I knew where Elisa was at all times."

Simon gave Ryan the information he'd requested. "I'd seriously think about the restraining order."

"I was going to go in the morning and take Traci with

me, but since the mechanic found nothing out of the ordi-
nary with the flat, I changed my mind," Ryan said. "Traci's
determined that we not let Elisa ruin this or any other evening."

Finished, the mechanic waved to them, then got in his
truck and drove away. "You two go on your date," Simon
said quietly. "I'll stick around for a while with Maureen."

"Thanks. I'd rather Mother not know about the security
firm," Ryan said. "She's worried enough."

"Your mother is a strong woman. It would be my guess
that the information would reassure rather than upset her,"
Simon said as they started back toward the women.

"She is, and you're right. Mother was dead on when she
said we were fortunate you were in Charleston."

Simon just hoped Ryan continued to feel that way when
he found out Simon was attracted to his mother.

Maureen couldn't relax.

"Don't worry. They'll be fine," Simon said.

Maureen looked up at Simon. His arm was around her
shoulder. It had been there since Ryan and Traci had left
moments ago. Despite her fear for Ryan, she took comfort
from Simon being with her.

"Come on. Let's get you inside." Simon started for her
front door.

Maureen's gaze searched around her. "You didn't see her.
Although I know Ryan, for a moment, just a moment, she
had me thinking there was some validity to her accusations."

Simon kissed her forehead as they continued up the walk.
"Don't blame yourself." Stopping at the front door, Simon
opened the door with the key she handed him.

Maureen placed her keys back in her purse. "I can't get over the feeling that her supposed love for Ryan runs as deep as her hatred for him."

"You're probably right." Inside the house Simon sat on the sofa, drawing her down beside him. "But, as of tomorrow, her every move will be shadowed. She won't get a chance to hurt Ryan or Traci. Hopefully, her father will get her the help she needs."

Maureen placed her head on Simon's shoulder. "It might sound strange, but I almost feel sorry for her. She's unbalanced, and her perception of love is warped. Love shouldn't cause pain."

"No, it shouldn't."

The soft drawl of his voice had her tilting her head upward. She saw the sensual curve of his lips, the proud nose, the mesmerizing eyes. Then things blurred as his head lowered, his warm lips finding hers.

His lips brushed once, twice, across hers before settling firmly. Gently his tongue slipped into her waiting mouth. She sighed with pleasure. Her hand tunneled through his thick black hair, relishing the feel on her fingers.

As with his other kisses, her body woke from sexual slumber and quickly remembered and relished this duel of tongues, the sweet pleasure, being content to let the passion build. Her breasts tautened, her nipples hardened. She wanted to feel his hands on them.

As if attuned to her, his large, calloused hands cupped her breasts. The soft moan was impossible to hold back even if she had wanted to. She wanted to know his touch, wanted more of his kisses that heated her blood, want—

Heat flashed through her in one mood-altering moment, dewing her skin. Frantic, Maureen scrambled out of Simon's·

arms before he could feel the moisture on her skin. Embarrassed, she couldn't look at him. Oh, Lord.

"I'm sorry." Her head lifted at the contriteness in his tone. "I'm moving too fast. It's just—" His cell phone rang. For a moment she thought he was going to ignore it. "It's Patrick, or I wouldn't answer."

She barely managed to nod that she understood. How could she tell him he wasn't going too fast at all?

"Patrick, I'm—" Simon came to his feet. "Slow down. Just slow down so I can understand you."

Maureen went to him, her own problems forgotten. "What is it?"

Simon held up his hand for her to wait a moment. "How long has she been cramping?" Then, "Did you call the doc— Can't the service understand she wants her own doctor, not a substitute? This is her first baby!"

Maureen finally understood a little of what was going on. Ryan was very well respected in his specialty. Doctors did favors all the time for each other. She tugged Simon's sleeve.

He held up his hand again. "I'll meet you at the hospital. You drive carefully and tell Brianna to hang in there with my niece or nephew."

Maureen realized he was going to hang up if she didn't talk fast. "What's the doctor's name? Perhaps Ryan can persuade him to come in."

Gratitude flashed in Simon's dark eyes. "What's the doctor's name?" Stunned, he turned to stare down at her. "Ryan Gilmore."

Traci was having a wonderful evening with Ryan.

He was amazing. He made her feel like a woman, not a

cold reject. The surprise was dining and dancing at a posh restaurant where the prices weren't listed on the menu. The room was lavish, the staff attentive. But the best part was being with Ryan.

Now, on the dance floor in his arms, she didn't feel frigid or lonely or overweight. She felt alive, desirable, seductive. Curled into his arms, their bodies close together as they moved on the polished hardwood floor to the music of a four-piece band, she felt as if she were coming out of a cocoon.

"This is wonderful." Her head lifted. "Thank you."

"Thank you." His hand cupped her cheek. "Your skin is so soft. Like velvet silk."

She did something that would have been unthinkable before tonight, before Ryan. She twisted her head and kissed his palm. He made her think of things, sexual things that she wouldn't have dared before. She was definitely blossoming.

Ryan's sharp intake of breath made her feel powerful. His eyes stared into hers. A silent signal seemed to pass between them. "Are you ready to leave?"

"Yes." Her voice was breathy, husky. She realized the sound was due to her arousal. He led her off the dance floor, stopping only long enough to pay their bill. On the way to the front door, Ryan's phone rang.

"I hope that's not your answering service," she said. She had plans for him.

"Not to worry. Another doctor is on call." Outside, he pulled his cell phone from his inside coat pocket. "Hello, Mother. What—"

Handing the claim ticket to the valet, Ryan's gaze went to Traci. "Simon, give the phone back to Mother and call your brother and let him know that I'm on my way to the hospital." He disconnected the call.

"Traci, I'm sorry, but I have to go to the hospital," Ryan told her, hoping she'd understand. "I couldn't turn Mother or Simon down."

"You wouldn't be the man I care about if you did. Let's hurry." Traci recalled her suspicion about the reason behind Brianna's rushed marriage as Ryan's car pulled up. "Did Simon call for his brother's fiancée, Brianna Ireland?"

"How did you know?" Ryan asked, his brow puckered into a frown.

"Woman's intuition."

Brianna Ireland's family had come out in full force.

The moment Ryan entered the waiting area for the maternity ward, he was swamped by people he didn't know, but who apparently knew and cared about Brianna. There was an attractive elderly couple he assumed were her parents. They had their arms wrapped around the other, their faces pinched with fear.

As long as he'd practiced medicine, he'd never get used to the anxious faces of friends and relatives, each one expecting him to make things right. The responsibility was awesome, but he'd never shirk that responsibility, never wanted to do anything else.

Simon quieted everyone. "Thanks, Ryan. Patrick is with her."

"I'll let you know something as soon as I can." He saw his mother in the background and nodded at her. She knew the answer wasn't always the one those waiting wanted to hear.

Traci squeezed his arm and stepped back.

He went to the double door, pulling off his dinner jacket.

He'd already ordered stat blood work. Brianna was three months pregnant and miscarriages weren't uncommon in the first trimester. But Ryan wouldn't borrow trouble until he'd done a thorough exam.

"Dr. Gilmore, Ms. Ireland is in room nine." Head Nurse Simmons matched his steps, taking the coat, handing him a lab coat and a chart. "The lab results are all normal. Litmus test reveals no amniotic fluid. The pains are high, spasmodic. No uterine contractions. Her B/P spiked until her fiancé joined her. Fetal monitor good."

So far. So good. "What would I do without you?" An astute OB-GYN head nurse was worth her weight in gold.

"Luckily, you won't have to find out," she quipped, smiling at him.

He pushed open the door to Brianna's room. Patrick whirled, still gripping Brianna's hand. Tears pooled in her eyes.

"I don't want to lose our baby," she cried.

"You're not, honey. Our baby is fine." Patrick brushed her hair back from her damp forehead. Ryan saw the fear in Patrick's eyes, which he desperately hid from Brianna. "Dr. Gilmore is here. Just relax."

"Good advice. I don't see anything for us to worry about at the moment." Ryan went to the sink, washed his hands, and gloved. "Now, let's see what's going on."

Gas pains."

There was stunned silence at Ryan's announcement, then joyous laughter. Traci breathed a sigh of relief and thanked God. She and Brianna might be on opposite sides because Traci's client was Andrew Crandall, and his soon-to-be ex-wife was Justine Crandall, Brianna's best friend, but Traci wished Brianna no ill. She saw Brianna's father kiss her mother. Brianna was fortunate in more ways than one.

"One word, beneath her elation is a little embarrassment. But, as I told her, I'd rather us know than guess in a pregnancy, especially in the first trimester," Ryan told them. "She's lucky to have so many people care about her."

"She's lucky to have you as her doctor. So are we." Simon shook Ryan's hand, then slapped Ryan on the back. "If you'll excuse me, I need to call my other brothers."

Traci stood with Maureen in the back of the waiting area as the people there introduced themselves to Ryan. Her parents, Mr. and Mrs. Ireland, were first. Next came one of the three owners of Bliss and her husband. Patrick and Simon's niece, Brooke, was part owner of the bath and body shop.

"Hello, Justine,' Ryan said. "I figured you'd be here with Brianna since you've been friends for so long."

"We've always been there for each other. This is another friend of ours, Dalton Ramsey," Justine introduced, and the two men shook hands. "We understand you were out on a date." Tall, elegantly shaped, she smiled warmly. "Thank you *and* your date."

"You can do that personally." Ryan turned to Traci and held out his hand for her to join them. Every person centered their attention on Traci.

Traci had never felt so exposed or unworthy. Justine wouldn't want to meet her once she learned she was the one who had helped her cheating husband.

"Traci?" Ryan called, a frown marring his face.

A hand in her back nudged her forward. It was Maureen, who knew Traci at her worst and was her friend anyway.

Her head up, she joined Ryan, felt his arm circle her waist. "This is Traci Evans. She understood and insisted we hurry."

Justine's eyes cooled. "Did she?"

Traci saw Dalton's arm around Justine's shoulder tighten. Another man who protected a woman. They were more than friends; they were lovers. Once she might have had that with Ryan. Not now, not ever. The people surrounding her thought she was no better than the cheating people she represented, just as Justine did.

They were right.

"Brianna!" her mother cried.

People converged on Brianna in a wheelchair with Patrick beside her, holding her hand while an attendant pushed. Usually impeccably groomed, her hair was spiked on her head. "I'm so embarrassed."

"Nonsense." Her mother hugged her. "Dr. Gilmore is right. The thing to do was check."

"Is he still here, or did he rush off with his date?" Brianna quipped in her playful way.

"He's here," Justine said. The crowd parted.

Traci tensed and waited. She didn't have to wait long.

The happy expression vanished from Brianna's face. "Dr. Gilmore, I thought you had better taste."

A hush fell over the waiting area.

Ryan felt Traci tense. Out of the corner of his eye, he saw her chin lift. To other people she might appear invincible. He knew differently. She hurt.

"Brianna," Patrick hushed.

"If you'll excuse me." Traci started to leave, but Ryan had no intention of letting her go. He was grateful that his mother moved to stand beside Traci.

"Brianna, you might be more cordial to the person who told me to hurry," he told her softly.

"That was before she knew who I was," she said, her gaze angry.

"You're wrong, and you're wrong about Traci," Ryan replied. "She's a gracious, caring woman. You could learn from her."

Brianna's eyes fired. "I—"

"Brianna," Patrick and her mother said at the same time.

"In view of the events, I feel it is in your best interest if I assign you to another doctor. Good night." There was a babble of voices. The wide-eyed wheelchair attendant heard every word. Ryan left, knowing that before morning the altercation would be all over the hospital.

He didn't care. All he cared about was the trembling woman in his arms.

13

What could she say?

How could she expect a man like Ryan to understand why she represented clients she detested? If she tried, the reason would only make him run from her. She was a mercenary and merciless, without conscience or pity. If you had enough money, you could hire her.

"Are you all right?" he asked as soon as they entered her house.

"Why shouldn't I be?" she said, continuing to the great room and tossing her purse on the sofa.

He caught her, turning her to him. "You asked for honesty and trust. Your rules."

"You mean, do I feel as if I should take a hot bath to scrub off the dirt I've helped my clients wade through, then yes," she said tightly.

His hold tightened. "You did a job. Brianna was in corporate law before she came back to Charleston to take over her father's law practice. You can't tell me all the clients she represented were always squeaky clean."

She pushed out of his arms. "I'm tired. I want to go to bed."

"Great idea." He scooped her up into his arms.

Her eyes widened in alarm. "What are you doing?"

"That should be obvious." His feet pounded on the stairs.

"This is not funny," she told him as he reached the landing. She tried to keep her body stiff when all she wanted to do was press closer, weep in his arms.

"Who's laughing? Which way?"

"The front door is back down the stairs," she said, trying to keep the tears of self-pity at bay. She'd made her choice long ago.

"Now who's being funny?" He sniffed the air.

Alarmed, she asked, "What are you doing?"

"Searching for your room." He started down the hall to the left. "I have an excellent sense of smell. The perfume you're wearing is exotic, seductive." He stopped outside her bedroom door. "You wore it for me."

It was a statement, not a question. One she couldn't lie about. "Yes."

He kissed her briefly on the lips and pushed open her bedroom door. She wanted to hide her face. She'd thought tonight might be the night they made love and had left the bedroom neat and clean, changed the sheets, pulled down the duvet and set candles on the dresser ready to be lit.

He looked at her, his eyes darkening. Her body tingled. Her nipples tightened.

"Ryan," her voice trembled.

"I'm here, and I'm not going anyplace." He set her on the bed, then hunkered down to remove her high heels and thigh-high stockings. Air stuck in her lungs as he slowly rolled them down her legs.

"You are so beautifully made." Still kneeling, he looked up at her. "One day I'm going to take great pleasure in kissing you in all the places I've fantasized about." Slipping off his shoes, he pushed upright, then removed his tie and belt. He unbuttoned his shirt, tossed it aside. Picking her up again, he lay down with her, tucking her back against him.

"Ryan."

He pulled the covers over her shoulder. "I'm here, honey. Go to sleep."

Her throat felt tight. She'd never felt so cherished. He cared about her despite what she did for a living, despite what others thought of her.

"Thank you."

He kissed her bare shoulder. "You need to sleep."

She shook her head. "I mean about Brianna. Justine is her client and her best friend. I—" She bit her lower lip. "I was the PR person for Justine's adulterous husband. I helped him skirt the major part of the blame. The woman Andrew had the affair with is married and pregnant. He might be the father. The husband of the woman was once Andrew's closest friend and confidant. The man was crushed, but he's standing by his wife . . . at least until the baby is born and the paternity is established. It's anybody's guess what will happen if the baby is Andrew's. I hope it's not, or Andrew can add another victim to his list."

His hand under her chin turned her toward him. "Did you enjoy helping him?"

"No. His mother wanted me to go after Justine. I refused. I knew she was living with Dalton." She sighed. "I set things up for Andrew to appear remorseful, although I knew he wasn't." Her gaze lowered for an instant, waiting for Ryan's condemnation.

"You did your job. You can't control people's actions."

He was certainly right about the last part. No matter how

much she'd tried not to care, she did, and the feeling grew each time they were together. "Ryan, I can't sleep with my dress on."

He scooped her up, set her on her feet with her back to him and slowly inched down the zipper that stopped in the middle of her back. Reverently he parted the ivory material.

"You're not wearing a bra?" he said, his voice husky, strained.

"No."

She felt his lips warm and tender on her naked skin. She shivered.

"Traci, I'm not sure I can do this."

She turned in his arms, then reached down and pulled her dress over her head. If she had any doubts about how he felt about her or what she was doing, the awed expression on his face made them fade away. He stared as if mesmerized at the breasts that had always embarrassed her.

"You're beautiful."

"You make me believe," she confessed.

"Traci," he sighed her name, his mouth fastening on hers.

Heat and desire enveloped her. She reached between them, fumbling to unfasten his slacks, push them down, but they snagged and wouldn't fall. Her hands trembled when she saw the reason. My, oh, my. Now she was the one mesmerized.

Ryan grabbed the condom out of his pants pocket before he shucked them and his silk briefs off. Then she was in his arms and on the bed with his powerful body over hers. "We'll light the candles next time."

She licked her lips and nodded. "Next time."

His mouth took hers again, his long-fingered hand found

her wet and hungry. Their eyes met, held. He gripped her hips and surged into her, filled her. The fit was exquisite. She moaned, locked her legs around his waist.

"A fantasy fulfilled," she murmured.

"Not yet." He rode her fast and well.

That was—" Traci began.

"Magnificent. Incredible," Ryan finished.

Ryan grinned at Traci. She grinned back. Satisfied and content for the moment, they faced each other on the bed, his arm draped over her. "I told you you could do it."

He kissed her on the forehead. "You bring out the best in me."

She tenderly traced the curve of his lower lip with her fingertip. "You have a beautifully shaped mouth."

He snorted and dropped a kiss on her shoulder. "It has its uses. Like fulfilling fantasy number five." His hot, fantastic mouth kept going lower and lower.

"Oh, my," Traci moaned, and her toes curled just before she grabbed his head and screamed her pleasure.

Standing at the hallway window on the second floor of her house, Maureen watched the lights go out on the second floor of Traci's house.

Smiling to herself, Maureen went to her bedroom. Ryan finally saw what a wonderful woman Traci was, and Traci had stopped living in the past. She'd opened her eyes and arms to love again.

Maureen's thoughts immediately went to Simon. Her

gaze was drawn to her wide bed. Her body stirred. She blew out a breath and pulled aside the down comforter. The phone on the bedside rang.

Hoping it was Simon, she quickly picked up the receiver. "Hello."

"Did I wake you?" Simon asked.

"No." Her body trembling the tiniest bit, she sat on her bed.

"Thanks again for your help tonight," he said.

Her fingers tightened. "Too bad it wasn't appreciated. Your future sister-in-law needs a lesson in manners. Brianna's attack on Traci was uncalled for."

"Believe me, she's heard that from Patrick, me, and her parents," Simon told her. "It was pointed out that she had clients she hadn't wanted to represent. Patrick told her that he agreed with Ryan about removing himself as her doctor. For the record, so do I."

Relief swept through Maureen. It was nice to know she hadn't been wrong about Simon. He was a fair and understanding man. "Thank you."

"How is Traci?"

Maureen's lips curved. "I think she's fine."

"Good. I hate to ask, but I need your support to help Brianna get her foot out of her mouth."

"She's going to apologize?" Brianna hadn't struck Maureen as the apologizing type.

"She's certainly going to try."

"I'm in. What do you want me to do?"

Maureen and Traci usually left for work between 9:25 and 9:30 to be at work by 10:00.

It was 9:32 and Ryan's car was still in Traci's drive. Maureen wasn't snooping. She knew Ryan was in his office no later than 10:00 each morning. He certainly couldn't wear his dinner jacket to work. He'd have to go home or come over to her house to change. She glanced at her wristwatch. She didn't know if she should call and see if they were awake or let them both be late.

On some mornings Traci would call or Maureen would call and invite the other over for breakfast. She hadn't thought that would happen and had fixed a simple breakfast of toast and juice for herself. Both Ryan and Traci enjoyed starting the day off with substantially more. Indecision held Maureen immobile.

Nine thirty-six. Just as Maureen decided she'd phone, Ryan came out the front door of Traci's house. He went a few steps, then went back to grab Traci's hand. She balked. It was obvious she was reluctant to go with him. Ryan wasn't having it. He tugged her down the steps, then started toward Maureen's house.

Letting the curtain fall, Maureen went to the kitchen. She didn't want them to think she'd been spying on them. Well, she had, but in a caring way.

She heard the front door open and picked up her forgotten cup of coffee.

"Hi, Mother. I'm going upstairs to change. Traci's here."

She heard a "sheee," then Ryan's laughter, followed by a long silence. He was kissing her. She was happy for them. Some people could do without love but none of them could. Thank heavens they didn't have to. She had no idea if it was the lasting, forever kind between Ryan and Traci. Time would tell. For herself, she knew it was for a short while and then Simon would move on.

No one had to tell her that a man who volunteered his time to help young people would want children of his own. And she could never give them to him.

The sounds of Ryan's feet pounding up the stairs pulled her from her unhappy thoughts. She'd just enjoy the time they had together, be grateful for that, and not ask for more.

Traci, appearing uncertain, walked into the kitchen. "Good morning."

"Good morning. Would you like some coffee?"

"No, thanks. We—" She looked at the floor, out the window.

"Traci," Maureen went to her. "I'm glad you're my friend. I'm glad about you and Ryan, but if it's going to ruin our friendship, I might think differently."

Her head finally came up. "I really like him, you know."

"I know," Ruth said. "He likes you, too."

A radiant smile came over Traci's face. "I still can't believe it. He's wonderful."

"I happen to think so." Maureen went to pick up her purse on the counter. "I'd better get going. Ryan can set the alarm. Tell him good-bye for me."

"I will." Traci went to her and hugged her. "Thanks. I don't know what I would have done if you had acted differently toward me."

Maureen shook her head. "Never. But I do need a favor."

"Ask."

"Can you please stop by the shop around eleven this morning? I'd like you to talk to Jason," Maureen requested. "He needs to know that hard work and determination pay off."

"Still mouthy?"

"He's a teenager," Maureen quipped, and they both laughed.

Traci called her grandfather as soon as she reached her office.

"Hi, Granddaddy. Sorry I couldn't talk this morning," she said, flushing in remembrance of the reason why.

"You sure you're all right?" Ezekiel Hightower asked. "You sounded out of breath."

Her granddaddy might be seventy-eight, but he was nobody's fool. Traci twisted uncomfortably in her seat. "Exercising."

"I thought you didn't believe in that?" he reminded her.

"Something changed my mind," she said, and smiled to herself. A gorgeous man. "Enough about me. How's your garden?"

"I have cucumbers a foot long. Tomatoes so big it's a good thing they're staked," he said proudly. "If those blasted post office people knew what they were doing, I'd send you some, but they'd bang them up like the other times."

Her granddaddy hated bruised fruit and vegetables. "I might be able to break away and fly down in a month or so."

"If you had your business here, you wouldn't have to wait."

It was an old argument. They both knew why she would never return permanently to Macon. "My client base is here, Granddaddy." Her buzzer went off. "My appointment is here. Love you. 'Bye."

"I love you, too, Scamp. Be careful with that exercise. You don't want to get hurt."

So she hadn't thrown him off track. "I won't. 'Bye."

" 'Bye."

Traci hung up the phone and buzzed her secretary to send the next client in. She was still a bit embarrassed with Maureen knowing that Ryan and she were sleeping together, but it proved to her that he wasn't playing with her feelings. He cared and respected his mother, and letting her know he and Traci were an item showed Traci he cared for and respected her, too. Where it might lead, she didn't know, but she had every intention of finding out.

The door opened and Dee Dee Walker came in. She had dyed blond hair, a seven-thousand-dollar Loro Piana ostrich handbag, and a black eye. Traci could guess how she'd gotten it. Her husband, Craig Walker, was slime. "The appointment says Darlene Smith."

Dressed in an Armani pantsuit that Traci couldn't fit over any part of her body, Dee Dee took a seat in the wing chair in front of Traci's desk. "My maiden name."

Traci folded her hands on top of her desk. "I told Craig I wouldn't represent him any longer. I meant it."

"I know. That's why I came." She gingerly touched her eye. "That bastard did this to me, and he's going to pay and pay good. You can help me."

Traci had experienced the impotent rage Dee Dee felt. Dante had hit her once and ended up with more bruises than she had. He hadn't tried again, but that hadn't stopped him from degrading her every chance he got. "I'm sorry. I can't divulge confidential information about a client."

"I figured as much." The other woman scooted forward. "But you can tell me the best way to ensure, when the time comes to file for divorce, that me and my three children will get what we deserve for putting up with his crap for all these years, not what's left over."

The idea intrigued Traci and it would hit Craig where he would feel it the most. "Essentially, you want to protect your children's financial future and your assets."

"And fry his ass in the process," Dee Dee said, her hand touching her eye again.

Traci smiled. "That, Ms. Smith, I can do."

It felt good to be on the other side.

Traci strolled down the street toward Forever Yours with a smile. Dee Dee had left Traci's office on her way to her doctor, who would record the black eye. She would need ammunition for the divorce. Although the other advice she'd given Dee Dee was a bit shady, Traci's conscience was clear.

Entering Forever Yours, she was greeted by a pleasant hello from Henrietta and a stare from Jason. "Hi, Henrietta. I see you have more beautiful things in."

"Business has been good," she said. "How are things with you?"

"Couldn't be better." Traci grinned like a fool. Having the right man in your life sure made living more interesting.

Henrietta folded her arms. "I've seen that look before. And it's about time I saw it on your face."

"Thank you."

"I was just about to go in the back to check on an order. Excuse me."

"Sure." Apparently Henrietta already knew why Traci was there. "Hi, you must be Jason."

"Mrs. Gilmore tell you about me?" he asked, his tone accusatory.

"That you were a talented artist and were working for her? Yes."

Interest piqued where there'd been suspicion in his eyes. "She said that?"

"She did, and Maureen is as honest as they come." Traci crossed to him, pretending to examine an eighteenth-century highboy. "What do you enjoy drawing most?"

"Everything," he said after a moment's silence. "I like seeing it form on the page. It's almost as if I created it."

"You did." She faced him and saw the yearning in his face. "You took a blank sheet of paper or a canvas and gave it purpose."

"Do you draw?" he asked, taking a step toward her.

"Hardly," she laughed, then sobered. "My grandfather taught me that philosophy about life. Your future is blank. It's up to you to give it purpose and not waste a day of it. To draw on it, so to speak."

"He must be rich, too?" Jason said, the thawing of moments ago gone.

"Very," she replied. "But not in the way you might think. He's worked on a farm that his father and his grandfather worked before him. In all of his life, he's never slept past five in the morning, never owed a debt that he didn't repay, never turned his back on his fellow man, never gotten up in the morning or gone to sleep at night without thanking God. His hands are calloused from doing backbreaking work from dawn to dusk and often into the night. His shoulders are a little stooped, but he's the tallest man I know. No matter what, I know he'll always be there for me."

Jason's hands went into his pockets. "It's just me and my mother. We moved here from Detroit when her job transferred her here six months ago."

The yearning, the loneliness in his voice for someone else to be there for him was almost tangible. Traci knew what that felt like. She loved her grandfather, would do anything for him, but until a few years ago she'd desperately tried to get her mother to welcome her back into her life. Traci had finally accepted that that would never happen. "You also have Maureen."

"She's all right, but she'll forget me when I leave." He glanced out the window. "I just work here."

"Maureen is not that type of person. If you're blessed enough to be her friend, she'll be there no matter what," Traci told him. "When I moved next door to her, I tried to keep her at arm's length, but she wouldn't let me. She can be stubborn, but it's for the other person's own good."

"She bought me a drawing set," he murmured as if he still couldn't believe it.

"Sounds like her. She believes in you." Traci folded her arms. "So what or who is going to be the subject of your first sketch?"

"I didn't take it. She probably returned it," he said, regret in his voice, on his face.

"Without a doubt, I can say you're wrong. She still has it. All you have to do is ask for it, then be sensible enough to take the gift and start writing on your life's canvas," she declared.

"You make it sound easy," he grumbled.

"Reaching out to a person who is trying to help you is easy. The hard part is not letting other people keep you down," she replied. "Becoming an artist won't be easy. Some of your friends might call you sissy or stupid. You can listen or ignore them. Your choice and your life, but you only get one chance."

He frowned. "Why are you telling me all this? Why should you care?"

"Because Maureen cares. Because I once stood in your shoes," she confessed. "Don't waste your life; live it."

He stared at her a long time. Slowly his hands came out of his pockets. "I think I'll go ask Mrs. Gilmore for the art set."

"Good idea," she responded. "I think I'll browse for a bit longer."

He hesitated. "Mrs. Gilmore likes for one of us to be in the front of the store at all times."

Even in his wanting, he was being responsible. Maureen was right. He had potential. "I'll watch things."

"Thanks." He was off.

He'd barely disappeared into the back when the front door opened. The smile on Traci's face disappeared. In strode Brianna Ireland.

Sometimes you have to dance with the devil.

Traci recalled one of her grandfather's favorite sayings and went to greet Brianna. As usual she was stylishly dressed in a magenta-colored pantsuit. Instead of the high heels she wore flats. She had the kind of elegant figure and beautiful face that Traci had always wanted. As soon as that thought came, there came another: Ryan liked her the way she was.

"Good morning, Brianna. I'll get someone to help you."

"Traci, could you please wait?" Brianna asked. "I'd like to speak with you."

"There's more you didn't say last night?" Traci's words dripped with sarcasm.

"I'd like to talk to you about that," Brianna said.

Traci folded her arms. "You want me to ask Ryan to take you back as a patient."

"I can do that myself," Brianna told her. "I'm here to ask you to forgive me."

Traci couldn't hide her surprise. Her arms dropped to her sides. "What?"

"I'd like to blame it on the hormones, but I can't. I was so scared last night. I just wanted Dr. Gilmore, and when I saw you with him, my fear turned to anger that you might have kept him away from me and my baby," she confessed.

"I think I understand," Traci said slowly.

"Patrick and my parents weren't happy with me." She made a face and blew out a breath. "Nothing like the man you love and the parents you adore on your case to make you see reason."

"You aren't known for backing down," Traci said. "Are you sure this isn't to get Ryan back as your doctor or keep me quiet about your pregnancy?"

Brianna's face softened, her hand tenderly cupped her flat abdomen. "Although I don't want my pregnancy fodder for gossip, it's not likely that I will be able to keep my condition hidden much longer."

"I would never divulge information about Ryan's patients, and that includes Justine," Traci said, and watched Brianna's gaze sharpen.

"What do you mean?" she asked.

"Merely that I always investigate all the parties involved when doing PR work. It can be . . . useful," Traci said.

"If you hurt Jus—"

"If I had wanted to do that, I would have released the information," Traci interrupted. "Her husband might have been my client, but that doesn't mean I approved of him or what he did. You're right. She deserves happiness, but so do I. If things had gone badly last night for me, I'd like to think I would have forgiven you, but I'm not sure."

"If anyone turned Patrick against me, I'd make their life hell," Brianna hissed.

"So we understand each other."

"We do." Brianna adjusted the shoulder strap of her

bag. "Good-bye, and thanks for listening and accepting the apology."

"Believe it or not, I admire you and never wanted you as an enemy, but if it came to that, so be it," Traci told her truthfully. "Obviously, someone wanted us to at least be civil to each other."

Brianna smiled for the first time. "Simon put in his two cents, and he arrived with Maureen. You and Maureen are friends. Maureen is Ryan's mother. You're dating Ryan."

"And Ryan is both Justine's and your doctor."

"Justine's at least." Brianna started for the door. "Depends on how well I can grovel."

"You aren't the groveling type," Traci said.

"For my baby, I am. Good-bye." The door closed after her.

Traci stared after her, then pulled out her cell phone and dialed. "Dr. Gilmore. Traci Evans calling."

I thought you said you and Ryan were dating?" Cicely Andrews practically cooed the question. Model thin with an emaciated look, dyed blond hair, and dreadful taste in clothes, she sat across the restaurant table from Elisa. "Word is he's seeing a PR guru."

Elisa's fingers gripped the salad fork, anger sweeping through her. She detested Cicely. She was as false as her boob job, which still couldn't help her keep a man. Elisa had accepted the luncheon invitation only because it was near the hospital and she'd have an excuse for dropping by to see her father and possibly Ryan.

But she detested even more being made a fool. Ryan would pay for his disloyalty. She knew the perfect way. Her fingers relaxed. "You know how men are. They take what sluttish women offer."

Cicely gasped. She'd been passed around more times than a party tray and all of their associates and friends knew it. She was a pediatrician, which was a fitting profession because like her patients who, because of their age, moved on to another doctor, men in her life eventually moved on as well.

"Why don't you bring Ryan over to the party next week at my house?" Cicely asked.

"I'll ask, but we like just staying in." Elisa placed her fork on her plate and picked up her glass of wine. "Perhaps next time."

"No one has ever seen you together." Cicely twirled her wineglass by the stem. "He's been seen with this woman. People are beginning to wonder, but you know I defended you."

The bitch was asking to be slapped, but she wasn't to blame. Elisa knew who those people were and they'd pay dearly. "People are always talking about something. You remember the gossip and the nasty divorce that followed when the Doubleday Hotel had the false fire alarm at two in the morning and you were seen with the father of one of your patients?"

Cicely's fingers pressed so hard on the stem Elisa expected it to break. Cicely could dish it out, but she couldn't take it. She should have remembered that no one messed with Elisa.

No one.

Simon called just as Forever Yours was about to close.

"How about an early dinner and a movie tonight?"

"I'd love to." Please, no hot flashes, she prayed. "I can be ready by seven."

"Sounds good. I'll bring the movie guide and we can select what we want to see."

"That's a wonderful idea," she said. "See you then."

"I thought you might show me your art collection this evening." Jason gripped the box of art supplies.

Maureen hung up the phone and glanced at her watch. It was five minutes after six. In traffic, it would take twenty minutes to reach her house. Jason's house was another twenty minutes away.

He shrugged and turned to go. "It doesn't matter."

Rounding the desk, she grabbed his arm. Traci had told her about his recent move. He was lonely and didn't have much faith in people. "You're not being fair. Or are you trying to test me again?"

"You said you'd show me."

"If I don't have time to get ready for my date with Simon, I'm going to be very difficult to work for tomorrow."

Jason didn't appear the least afraid. "I can handle it."

She grabbed her purse. "Remember that."

I can't believe it."

She'd been right about him.

The awe in Jason's voice made up for the smirk he'd worn just before they left Forever Yours. He went from one painting to the other, his fingertips inches from the paint of some of the best African-American painters of the eighteenth through the twentieth century.

"You have Tanner, Pippin, Wells, Motley, White." He shook his head as if it were too much for him to take in.

"James, my late husband, collected African-American paintings." Maureen moved to a bronze sculpture by Fuller, a marble by Lewis. "I collected sculptures and bronzes. We started with an artful entry. When our collection outgrew that area, we decided on an art room that connected to his study and my office."

Jason looked at her. "That's good or the thieves might have—" His voice trailed off, his head bowed. "I'm no better than they are. I'm sorry."

She went to him. "Apology accepted."

His head lifted; regret shone in his eyes. "Why do you put up with me?"

Teenagers. Blunt. Maddening. And didn't have a clue. "Because I believe in you. Because people helped me, helped my son. No one goes through this life and achieves anything without the help of someone else," she said. "I might have grown up with more money than you, but James didn't. He worked hard to be successful. It's what's inside that counts."

"Mama said people are out for themselves," he said, but he didn't sound convinced.

"Some people are, but when you find those people, you cut them out of your life and move on. You find people who believe in you, who want the best for you," she said with quiet emphasis.

"Because I only get one chance," he said slowly, as if the words finally had meaning and were sinking in.

"If you live it right, once is enough," she said.

The doorbell rang. She glanced at her watch and barely kept from groaning. "Simon."

"I'm sorry. I can get myself home." He hurried out of the room and down the hallway, which was lined with African-American artwork.

"Jason. Come back here," Maureen yelled, going after him.

"It's all right. I'm used to taking care of myself." He opened the front door to leave.

"Simon, please stop him," Maureen called on seeing Simon in the doorway.

Simon caught Jason by the arm as he rushed by. "What's the hurry?"

"I didn't take anything," Jason told him, trying to free his arm.

"I don't recall saying you did." Simon stepped into the foyer and released Jason.

"Of course you didn't. But it's miles to your house, and I don't want you walking," Maureen told him. "If Simon doesn't mind, we can drop you off at your house on the way to the restaurant."

"I told you, I can get home by myself." He hunched his thin shoulders, the standoffish kid again. "I just need my art set and backpack out of your car."

Maureen pulled her car keys from the pocket of her jacket. "If you promise me you'll come back inside and let us take you home, you can go get them."

"You trust me with your car keys?" he asked, incredulously.

"Yes." She picked up his hand and placed the keys in his palm. "Hello, Simon. Please have a seat. I won't be but a few minutes. Jason and I lost track of time." She hurried up the staircase.

"I don't understand her," Jason said, his voice barely above a whisper.

Simon gave him a gentle pat on the back. "Join the men-without-a-clue club."

"She's late because I asked to see her art collection. She

could have made me wait—" He shook his head. "She's different."

"And she cares a lot about you."

Jason's hand clenched around the keys. "You want to go with me to the car?"

"I believe my instruction was to have a seat. Don't forget to lock it back up." Simon went to the great room, leaving the teenager in the foyer.

You took a chance giving Jason your keys," Simon told Maureen as they watched Jason let himself inside his house, trying to balance a pizza box and his art set. True to her word, Maureen had come back downstairs ten minutes later and they'd left.

"Who stopped for pizza?" Maureen asked.

Simon pulled off when the front door closed and the lights came on in the house. "After he kept hinting that he was hungry, but he didn't want us to be late, what could I do?"

"He got me the same way. He's testing us to see how far he can push us." She turned in the seat as much as she could. "He wouldn't have dared pull that on his mother. He's afraid of her."

Simon stopped at a signal light. "In a good or bad way?"

"Bad, I'd say, but I don't think she sees it that way. He tries to pretend it doesn't bother him, but he wants her love." Maureen shook her head. "She wants to get him out of her life as soon as possible. It will always amaze me that a woman can carry a baby for nine months and not love it, not do everything possible to see that the baby is happy and loved."

"Sometimes things simply go wrong." Simon pulled

through the light. "Miguel has great parents. His older sister has a 4.0 grade point average in college and his younger brother is on the honor roll in high school. Neither has even been to the principal's office. Miguel is just as smart, but he chooses to use his intelligence in a destructive way. Wish I knew what it was about some middle children that get them so mixed up."

"Being a parent is scary, but there's nothing like it," she said, feeling her way. She wanted Simon to know she didn't expect forever, that she didn't want to deprive him of being a father.

"You met my niece, Brooke, and her husband at the hospital last night." Simon pulled into the parking lot of the restaurant. "She became an instant mother to two wonderful children. She says she wouldn't trade the experience for anything. Her little girl is a tomboy and her son is neat and studious, although Brooke is working on him to loosen up a bit."

"You like working with children. You'll make a great father," she said, trying not to look at him.

"At the moment, I'm just trying to be a great uncle." Opening his door, he came around and opened hers.

Maureen didn't say anything. There was nothing to say. Inside the restaurant the hostess greeted Simon by name. On the way to their table, several of the waitstaff waved. "You must be a regular."

"I guess it shows." Simon held the chair for Maureen, then sat next to her in a quiet area of the restaurant. "Patrick and Brianna introduced me to the place. It's a favorite of her parents." He picked up the menu. "I've never eaten anything here that wasn't good."

"Hi, Simon," the waitress greeted warmly. Her gaze

flickered briefly over Maureen. "Glad to see you back. What can I start you out with? Appetizers? Drinks?"

"Thanks, Casey." He turned to Maureen. "What will you have?"

Maureen started at Simon's question. She had been paying more attention to the waitress. The attractive young woman stood very close to Simon, and had only glanced at Maureen, dismissing her as a threat. "Sweetened iced tea."

"Make that two," Simon said. "Please give us a few minutes."

"Sure." Casey placed her hand on Simon's shoulder before leaving.

Maureen simply stared at the brazen, disrespectful woman. In her day— Her thoughts stumbled. It wasn't her day. That was the point. Women were allowed to show men they were interested in them. They were even praised for their boldness. She was out of her element here.

"What's the matter?"

"I'm old," she blurted, and could have crawled under the table. She slapped her hand over her mouth, but, as her mother always said, once the cows were out, it was too late to lock the gate.

"By whose standards?" Laying the menu aside, he propped his arms on the table. "Certainly not mine or anyone who has been around you longer than a few minutes. You're vibrant and beautiful. Not too many people could run up or down your stairs the way you do and not get winded."

Hearing him call her vibrant and beautiful helped, but she had to face facts. "How old are you?"

He hesitated, then, "Forty-nine. Fifty in five months."

Maureen barely managed not to groan. It was as bad as she'd thought. More than ten years separated them.

"Age doesn't matter. It's the person," he said, as if reading her thoughts.

Casey appeared at the table. "Ready?"

Maureen glanced at the menu and ordered the first thing she saw. "The shrimp platter, please."

"Make mine oysters on the half shell."

Casey took both menus, and grinned down at Simon. "I'll take care of it myself," she practically purred.

Maureen frowned at the departing woman's back. "She certainly isn't the shy type, is she?"

Simon scooted his chair closer. "Brianna almost went off on her the last time we were here when she made a play for Patrick. He and I ignore her. We know what we want."

With Simon so close to her, his eyes gazing into hers, Maureen's heart hammered foolishly and she almost forgot about their age difference. Almost. "You were fourteen when I had Ryan."

"I fail to see the relevance," he said quietly. "If I hadn't had strong parents, I could have been a father at that age like a few boys in my class. One has nothing to do with the other. Only what we feel."

"Here you are." The smile on Casey's face slipped when she noticed how close Simon was sitting to Maureen. If the waitress didn't get it, his arm on the back of Maureen's chair stated they were there as a couple.

"Thanks, Casey."

"You're welcome," she mumbled, but with none of the earlier warmth.

Simon tucked his head to say grace, then picked up an oyster. "You want to share?"

Maureen remembered oysters were considered aphrodisiacs. With Simon's strong body, she didn't think he'd need

any inducers. Neither did she. "No, thanks." She picked up
her fork, but simply held it as Simon ate. Her body heated as
she recalled his lips on her, his tongue mating with hers.

"Change your mind?"

He caught her staring. His eyes were dark, smoldering.
He wanted her. Desired her. Her age didn't matter. Nothing
mattered but how they felt. "I think I have." She opened her
mouth for him to feed her, and couldn't wait for them to be
home so they could do to each other what their eyes were
saying.

Are we cool?" Jason asked the moment he saw Maureen the
next morning in her office at Forever Yours.

"Yes." Maureen hoped she didn't blush. She and Simon
had skipped the movie and gone back to her house to neck.
She could still feel the imprint of his upper body on hers.

"You need your fan or your water?" he asked.

"Neither, thank you." Maureen tucked her head. The
heat flushing her cheeks wasn't due to a HF. "I'm fine. You
want to go with me to watch the Sharks play . . . if your
mother says it's all right?"

"There's a free art exhibit at Avery's college. She invited
me, and I'm going over there." There was pride in his voice
that Maureen hadn't heard before.

"How do you plan to get there, then home?"

"The bus. I got it covered. I'd better get back outside."
He started to leave, then turned back. "Thanks for taking
me to see your art collection."

"You're welcome." Maureen folded her hands on her
desk. Jason was a much different boy than he'd been when
he'd first walked into her store. It just went to show you that

you never knew what a seemingly insignificant thing could do to change the course of your life.

Like her meeting a client and seeing Simon for the first time. Life held a lot of surprises if you were open to them. She was up to them, and to seeing where her and Simon's relationship went.

Simon and Maureen saw each other every night that week, and they always ended up on her sofa driving each other almost to the brink of no return.

Simon had never thought of wanting in degrees . . . until he'd held and kissed Maureen. She was a fire that burned hotly in his blood. Yet, indecisiveness kept him from taking that final step.

"Simon," she moaned into his mouth, her hand under his shirt—one of them had jerked it out of his pants. Her touch set him on fire.

She made him tremble. She was precious to him. She deserved better than making love on the sofa, but he wasn't sure how she'd feel about making love in the bedroom she'd shared with her husband. She still had his picture on her night chest. He'd seen it the night her home had been burglarized.

He broke off the kiss and held her tightly to him. He was holding it together by sheer will. He'd like nothing better than to strip her down to her soft, velvet skin and surge into her moist heat, feel her clench around him. Air hissed through his gritted teeth.

"Simon, what's the matter?"

He thought of evading for all of two seconds. Instead he lifted her chin until their eyes met. "I want us to make love in a bed and I want you to be comfortable. I'm not sure how you feel about that."

She tucked her head. "I thought of us together in my bed."

His body jerked, hardened. "You have?"

Her head lifted. "I have."

He kissed her gently on the lips. "Thank you." Standing, he extended his hand.

Without hesitation she stood and placed her hand in his. He picked her up in his arms, dropped a kiss on her lips. "Thank you."

Chapter

15

Simon had never been so glad that he'd worked out as when he climbed the stairs. He didn't stop until he placed Maureen on her feet by her bed. Grabbing his shirt and T-shirt, he pulled both over his head and tossed them aside.

His muscles rippled under Maureen's fingertips as she ran her fingers across his upper torso. He sucked in his breath. "You're so strong," she murmured.

"I want to see you." He turned her around and unzipped the black sheath she wore, marveling as more and more of her skin was revealed. He dropped tiny kisses on each shoulder, felt her tremble beneath his lips. He shoved the dress over her hips, then turned her to him.

Air became harder for him to draw in. Her breasts were barely covered with lace. His gaze went further to the tiny scrap of lace panty and the thigh-high stockings. He was indeed a lucky man.

His mouth took hers in a tender kiss that quickly built in intensity and need. When she reached for his belt, he reached in his pocket for the condoms he thought he might one day get to use. Wrapping one hand around her, he tumbled them into bed, shoving the condoms under her pillow.

"I'm hot."

"Me, too. I want you so bad."

"No!" She pushed out of his arms and ran to the bathroom, shutting the door behind her.

Confused, feeling like a heel, he followed. Twisting the doorknob, he found it locked. "Maureen, I'm sorry." His hand flattened on the closed door. "I shouldn't have pushed. Come on out. Nothing will happen."

"Just leave."

Simon's gut clenched when he heard the catch in her voice. It worsened as he heard her sobs. "Please, honey, don't cry. Yell at me. Anything. But please don't cry."

"Please, just go."

"No, I'm not leaving with you upset." He tried the door again. He could jimmy it, but it wouldn't be fair. "We can wait to make love until you're ready. Being with you is enough."

"If you care at all about me, you'll leave."

How could she not know he cared? Was that it? Did she need the words? "I do care about you, more than I have any other woman. That's why I can't leave when you're upset."

Silence and sobs were his answer.

"Talk to me, Maureen." He'd been sure she'd been with him all the way. Had she gotten cold feet as he'd expected or had she suddenly thought of her dead husband? "We can get through this, I know we can, but we have to talk."

Utter condemning silence. At least he didn't hear her sobbing. Hearing her cry, and knowing he was the cause, was like a knife through his heart.

"Maureen." His hand slid down from the door. Obviously, she wasn't coming out, but he had no intention of leaving until he fixed whatever the problem was between them. His body ached for release that wasn't going to happen. Maureen came first.

"We're going to talk about this." He picked up his discarded shoes and clothes and put them on, then moved to the far side of the door to wait. Sooner or later she'd come out and he'd be there. Folding his arms, he leaned back against the silk wallpaper. Everywhere his eyes looked, there was elegance and beauty, just like the woman who lived there.

There were fresh cut flowers on the night chest by her bed. He'd given them to her tonight and been pleased when she'd held them lovingly to her chest, then taken them to her room before they had gone to the theater. A group of shells surrounded a vanilla candle next to a book with a brass bookmark. The chandelier in the ceiling was shaped like leaves and brimming with crystals. There was also a ceiling fan. Beneath his feet was a polished hardwood floor. A few feet away was an Oriental rug with the rich blues and subtle stone colors that were carried throughout the room.

He tried not to let his gaze drift to the four-poster bed, but it was impossible. The sheets felt like velvet against his skin, but it hadn't held a candle to the softness of Maureen's skin, the sensual scent she wore. She was temptation personified. He wanted to make love to her, but he also enjoyed her company, her laughter, her sharp intelligence. He wasn't giving that up.

In a flash, he recalled the condoms he'd slipped under her pillow. He unfolded his arms to retrieve them.

"Simon?"

He stopped. Too late. The bathroom door cracked open. There was an unimpeded view of the bed. After a few moments, the door swung open wider and Maureen came out wearing a short white cotton robe belted at the waist.

She sniffed. Dabbed at her eyes with a tissue. Simon was about to go to her when she mumbled, "Why did I have to have that stupid hot flash?"

Stunned, Simon remained immobile. Of all the reasons that had run through his head, menopause had never been one of them. Perhaps because, when he looked at her, she didn't look any older than he was. She certainly didn't kiss and make his body zing as if she were older.

He knew he had a problem as she continued to the bed. She'd turn and see him. And be embarrassed. He knew there was no way to leave without her seeing him. Perhaps if—

She tensed as if sensing someone there, then swung around. Clearly embarrassed, she palmed the lower half of her face with both hands.

Simon quickly strode to her, taking her hands from her face. He could treat this seriously or lightly, and he had better get it right. If he didn't, Maureen was lost to him, and he didn't think he could stand that.

"It must be rotten to deal with hot flashes. Would you like to take a swim? Take the boat out? Take a cold shower together?"

Her sweet mouth trembled.

"Oh, honey." He kissed her softly on the lips, moved to the curve of her jaw. "We'll work through this." He kissed the tears from her eyes. "You just tell me if we need to stop."

His hand cupped her cheek, found her skin cool, not flushed or moist. Simon's oldest brother had once confided in him about his wife's hot flashes. Simon had witnessed them a time or two on his own. A fine sheen of moisture suddenly dampened Maureen's skin.

"I'll be right back." Quickly crossing the room, he turned on the ceiling fan and then lowered the thermostat, glad he'd inspected her house and knew where things were. When he turned, he saw her hands were palming her face again. He couldn't have that.

"Guess none of my suggestions sounded good right now." He pulled off his shirt and slacks and toed off his loafers. "If you change your mind, all you have to do is tell me."

Her eyes widened when she saw the arousal he was unable to hide in his silk briefs. "Simon," she said when his hands covered hers, bringing them to her sides.

He kissed her forehead. Soft and dry. "Yes?"

"I—"

"I know, honey. It's all right." Curving his arms around her slim waist, he tilted her head up, smiled into her uncertain face, then settled his lips on hers, slipping his tongue into her mouth. She remained immobile for all of two very long seconds, then she melted into his arms.

He kissed her thoroughly. When she was straining against him, he untied her belt and slipped his hand inside. He shuddered. There was nothing underneath except warm, fragrant skin.

He nipped her lip. "You have incredible skin." His hand swept up to cover her breast, relishing the hard nipple pushing against his palm. Her breast was firm and filled his hand. He wanted to see all of her.

Catching her around her slight waist, he lifted her off her feet and didn't put her down until they were by the bed. Raising his head, he slipped her robe slowly from her shoulders. Inch by incredible inch, her body was revealed to him. "There is nothing about you that doesn't please me."

"Simon." Her hands rested gently on his chest. "I—thank you."

"Thank you for trusting me." He pulled her into his

arms, relishing the feel of her naked body against his. "You're all that I desire. All that I ever could have hoped to desire. Let me show you."

Picking her up, he placed her on the bed and came down on top of her. Lacing their fingers together, he planted nibbling kisses on her face, her shoulders. When she sighed, he released her hands and moved to take the tempting peak of one breast into his mouth. She gasped, arching upward.

He suckled and laved the point in his mouth, then moved to the other one. His hands reached down to the junction of her thighs and found her wet and hot. She whimpered, her body moving restlessly against him.

His head moved down, kissing the valley between her breasts, her quivering abdomen, as his hands pleasured her.

"Simon." His name came in a heated rush.

Moving back up, he captured her mouth with his, kissing her deeply. Beneath her pillow, he found the condom. Releasing her, he removed his briefs and sheathed himself.

He joined them, filling her completely. She closed around him like a tight fist. Pleasure coursed through him. He stared down into her passion-filled eyes and knew she felt the same exquisite joining.

He began to move. She met him thrust for thrust. He felt her stiffen beneath him, felt his own body coiling tighter. He quickened the pace, pumping, driving. She shattered first. He quickly followed. His body quivered; he felt hers do the same.

His breath coming in spurts, he gathered her to him and rolled over on his back. When he thought he could move again, he tilted her chin up. Relief and gratitude swept through him when he saw the contented smile on her face. "Are you all right?"

She smiled. "I don't know. Maybe we should try that again, and I could tell you."

Laughing, he rolled over on top of her. "My pleasure."

Maureen couldn't keep the grin off her face.

Walking Simon to her door a little before seven the next morning, she couldn't have been happier. Her hot flashes didn't faze Simon. She'd had a couple of bouts last night, rolling away from Simon, flushing with heat and embarrassment. He'd gotten her a bottle of water, a cool washcloth, and turned back on the ceiling fan he'd turned off earlier because she'd become chilled.

He'd taken them so matter-of-factly that when she'd had one while they were eating breakfast together, she'd dared to say out loud that she didn't know how women stood them. He'd loosened her robe and kissed her on each shoulder. With his eyes twinkling, he'd suggested she might feel better if she took the robe off. She'd batted his hand and laughed as he'd expected, but the thought had been tempting.

Thank goodness they didn't dampen her sexual desire. They'd made love that morning when they'd woken up.

"I'll pick you up at eight thirty," Simon said.

"I'll be waiting."

"I'll miss you, miss this." Curling his finger through her belt, he pulled her to him, kissing her long and thoroughly.

Her eyelashes slowly fluttered upward. "Then you won't be late."

"No way." He dropped a kiss on her lips, then started down the walkway that would lead him to the garage where his car was parked. He didn't get two feet.

"You bastard!"

Simon jerked his head around to see Ryan charging toward him, his fists balled and fire in his eyes. Traci, in a robe, raced after him.

"Ryan, no!" Maureen rushed to intercept Ryan.

Simon cursed under his breath. He'd planned to leave early to prevent Ryan finding out. Not for anything would he want to hurt, embarrass, or do anything to jeopardize Maureen and Ryan's relationship. He certainly didn't plan to fight Ryan.

"Ryan, no!" Maureen spread both hands against her son's heaving chest.

"I thought you were my friend!" Ryan yelled, blowing from anger, not exertion. "I trusted you!"

"Ryan, calm down, and let's go into the house." Traci caught his arm.

"I'm not going a step with that bastard!" Ryan yelled. "You took advantage of my mother."

Simon had been considering walking off and letting Ryan cool down until Ryan slung that accusation. He closed the distance between them. "I care about Maureen."

"That's a pile of crap." Ryan bristled. "She's almost ten years older than you. She'll be sixty soon and you're not even fifty."

Maureen dropped her head. Simon's own fists clenched. "Age has nothing to do with the way we feel."

"Oh, give me a break!" Ryan sneered. "I've heard of your rep with women, and it's certainly not with women my mother's age. She's feeling vulnerable since the burglary, and you cashed in on that."

"Stop it, Ryan!" Traci shook his arm. "Can't you see you're hurting Maureen?"

"He doesn't want her, Traci. He couldn't."

With a whimper, Maureen ran into the house. Simon took a step toward her, but Ryan jerked away from Traci and blocked his path. "You've done enough. Get your sorry behind off this property, and don't come back."

Simon's fists clenched and unclenched. "If you weren't Maureen's son . . ." Whirling sharply, he started toward his car.

"Oh, Ryan," Traci said in an exasperated voice, then she went after Maureen.

Not finding her downstairs, Traci went to Maureen's bedroom and knocked. "Maureen. Ryan is wrong."

"I just want to be alone."

"All right. I'll call you later." Traci met Ryan at the top of the landing. "You upset her. She's locked herself in her room."

"Me?" he shouted. "This is Simon's doing. I never thought he'd be so underhanded."

"Simon is not the one who made her feel old and stupid."

"She'll be sixty soon!" Ryan bellowed. "We're planning her birthday party!"

"So what!" Traci yelled just as loud. "She's still attractive and has desires. Simon is your fraternity brother and your friend. He's a good man."

Ryan slumped in a chair on the landing and closed his eyes. "I don't want to think about her being—"

Hunkering down in front of him, Traci rested her hands on his thighs and waited until he opened his eyes. "You're an OB-GYN doctor, surely you have female patients who are older and remain sexually active."

"They're not my mother," he muttered stubbornly.

Traci palmed his cheek. "Exactly. Don't punish her because you're unwilling to see her the way Simon does."

He shook his head. "I don't know. I want to see her happy, but—" He stood, bringing Traci with him. Releasing her, he went to his mother's door and knocked. "I love you."

"I love you, too," came his mother's faint reply through the door.

Traci hugged him. "I'm proud of you."

He hugged her back. "I'm not promising anything."

"I know, and I'm still proud of you. Maureen needed to know you haven't changed toward her."

He frowned. "That would never happen." He looked at the closed door. "Check on her today, will you?"

"You know you don't have to ask." Taking his arm, they went back down the stairs and out the door, locking it after them. "Now you'd better go, or you'll be late for the lecture."

He sighed. "Good thing I'm not in surgery. 'Bye." Kissing her on the cheek, he was gone.

Traci was worried about Maureen.

Arriving at her office that morning, the first thing she did was call Forever Yours. Henrietta answered the phone and said Maureen had called in ill. Traci called Maureen and got her answering machine. A call to Ryan revealed he had gotten the machine as well.

A little after eleven, Traci finally reached the maid, who said Maureen was in her room resting. Crying her eyes out was more like it, but Traci was already working on the cure.

Sudden loud voices and curses outside her office had Traci reaching for the phone to call security. The door burst open and Elisa tumbled in, wrestling with a man Traci had never seen before. Behind her was Traci's secretary.

"I've alerted security."

"You lied to me, you conniving bitch!" Elisa screamed, attempting to free herself from the man holding both her arms behind her. "You want Ryan for yourself, but you'll never have him!"

"Are you with her?" Traci asked the muscled man, who appeared to be in his mid-thirties. He wore a lightweight sports jacket and jeans.

"Sam Bledsoe. Dr. Gilmore hired me."

Elisa stopped struggling. "Ryan sent you to get me?"

"You'll have to ask him about that," the man answered.

"He sent you to spy on me?" Elisa raged, starting to struggle once again. "It's too late. I saw him with Porky."

Traci lifted a brow. There was no doubt who "Porky" was. "Ryan doesn't think so."

"You bitch!" Elisa screamed, struggling ineffectually against the man's superior strength.

"Ms. Evans, I wouldn't aggravate her," the man suggested softly.

Traci folded her arms. "But she can aggravate me?"

Two men in building security uniforms rushed into the room.

"Please take this woman to your office and hold her there," Traci suggested.

Each burly officer grabbed an arm. Elisa's screams became louder. "Maybe we should call the police," one suggested.

"No." Elisa needed psychiatric help. A police record might jeopardize her chance to practice psychiatry again. Never had the saying "physician, heal thyself" been more appropriate. "Just take her to your office."

"If you say so." They left with the man Ryan had hired following them.

Traci picked up the phone and dialed. "Ryan, Elisa is here

and she's out of control. You need to get over here and bring her father with you."

Ryan's temper was on a short leash.

Elisa, in restraints in a chair, called him every foul name he'd ever heard of, and he had heard a lot. Strangely, the more she ranted, the more he felt sorry for her. He wouldn't wish mental illness on his worst enemy.

Dr. Thomas saw the restraints and became angry. "Take them off her. She's not a criminal!"

"Only because charges haven't been filed, but that doesn't mean that they won't be," Ryan said.

"For what? Barging into an office?" Dr. Thomas questioned.

"Vandalism," Traci answered. "She damaged Ryan's tire," Traci guessed.

"He shouldn't have been at your house," Elisa spat. "He's mine."

Dr. Thomas briefly hung his head. "I don't want to see her treated this way."

"Then help her," Ryan snapped. "You had to know she had a problem. Stop enabling her. Get her the help she needs."

"We tried." Elisa's father turned on Ryan. "Nothing gets through to her. Sending her away only makes it worse instead of better. She thinks we abandoned her."

"So you checked her out early?" Traci theorized.

Dr. Thomas seemed to age ten years in front of their eyes. "We love her. She's our only child."

"Greg." Ryan clasped the older man's shoulder. "Tough love isn't easy. My guess is that each episode gets more violent. What if she'd taken a knife to a person?" He flinched and Ryan knew she had. "I realize it's not her fault she's ill, but I won't jeopardize the people I care about. Either you check her into a facility within eight hours or I'm filing charges and notifying the medical board."

Dr. Thomas's head snapped up. "They might take her license."

"Do you think she could help anyone in her present condition?" Traci asked.

"No," he admitted. "There's a facility, but it's a five-hour drive from here. There is no way I could get her on a plane."

"Bledsoe, can you accompany them in a car?" Ryan asked.

"Not a problem," the private investigator answered. "I can have a driver here within fifteen minutes, ready to go. Dr. Thomas, his daughter, and I can sit in the backseat."

"Make the call." To Elisa's father, Ryan said, "Don't ruin this chance for her. If you do and she comes after any of us, I won't hesitate to handle things in my own way."

"I won't." Dr. Thomas went to Elisa. "We're going on a little trip."

"You can't fool me." Tears streamed down her cheeks. "I'll be good. I promise. Ryan, help me. Please help me."

He went to her. "I am."

"No, you're not! Nobody loves me. Nobody!" she cried.

Traci glanced away from the other woman's suffering. She'd once felt the same way. She didn't wish that hell on anyone.

It might sound crazy, but—"

"You feel sorry for her," Ryan finished for Traci. They stood with their arms around each other, watching Elisa get into the car. All the way to the car she had looked at Ryan, silently begging him to save her. One day, he hoped she'd realize that he had.

Bledsoe got in after her and closed the back door to the big black Lincoln, and the car pulled away from the curb.

"You talked to Mother yet?" he asked, not liking one bit that she was hurting and there was nothing he could do to help her. Worse, that he might have caused the pain.

"No, but I've contacted the Sisterhood, and we're going over there tonight to cheer her up," Traci told him.

"I guess that means I won't see you tonight." He swept her hair back from her face.

"Afraid not. Maureen needs us."

"She does. Tell her I love her."

"She knows, but I'll remind her." Traci placed her hands on his chest. "Just think about what I said. Let her live her own life."

"Men aren't honest the way they used to be."

"Oh," Traci said mildly. "So I can't trust you?"

"Of course you can," he quickly told her, then sighed. "I get your point."

"Good, because I don't like repeating myself."

"It's a good thing I know you care." He kissed her briefly on the forehead. "Call me as soon as you leave Mother's."

"It might be late."

"Doesn't matter. I want to know how she's doing."

M aureen was miserable.

There was nothing like your own son throwing your age into the face of your lover to kill a budding affair. Drawing her feet under her, Maureen curled up in the window seat overlooking the back gardens and leaned her head back against the wall. Misery ate at her.

She knew she was in bad shape when she'd missed work for the first time since she'd taken off a week for James's funeral. She'd felt lost until she remembered his words of encouragement. Now, all she seemed to be able to remember was Ryan shouting her age.

She swallowed the lump in her throat and fought tears. She hadn't even gotten dressed. If her mother were alive, she would have been scandalized. No decent woman kept her robe on past seven in the morning. Perhaps that was it.

Maureen wasn't a decent woman. Her eyes clamped shut.

A knock sounded on her door. Karen, the maid, was probably coming to tell her she was leaving. Maureen didn't want to face anyone.

The knock came again. Maureen pulled her feet from under her and stood. Another thing her mother said—and Lillian Louise Canfield had always had a lot to say whether you wanted to hear it or not—was that the world didn't care how you felt, so don't waste their time or yours telling them about it.

Maureen opened the door. Her bottom lip began to tremble. Tears she'd been trying to hold at bay all day streamed unheeded down her cheeks.

"There, there, dear." Nettie drew Maureen gently into her arms. That Nettie was several inches shorter didn't seem to matter to either of them. "We're here now."

"And we're staying until you're better." Ophelia wheeled a loaded serving cart into the room. Serving dishes, stemware, and plates rattled. Behind her was Donna, carrying a wine bucket and four bottles of wine.

"Traci called and thought we ought to come earlier than planned." Betsy carried a bouquet of canna lilies, Maureen's favorite flowers. "She's coming as soon as she leaves work."

Nettie dried Maureen's tears with a white handkerchief that had a two-inch border of lace. "What do you want to do first, talk, drink, or eat?"

Maureen bit her lower lip. "Talking won't do any good."

"Pour her a drink, Donna," Ophelia suggested.

"Pour all of us one." Betsy set the flowers beside the other bouquet. "Simon's doing?"

Maureen sniffed and nodded. "He said his mother always said flowers and not cooking makes a woman feel better. That and shopping."

"Smart woman," Nettie said, drying another tear from Maureen's cheek. "Smart son, too, to know a good woman and go after her."

"I'm too old for him, just as Ryan said." Maureen accepted the drink Donna gave her and stared down into her glass of pinot noir.

"And here I always thought he was smart." Ophelia snorted. "Before Ryan put his unwanted two cents in, what were you feeling?"

"I was happy," Maureen admitted. "Simon didn't even seem to mind my hot flashes."

Betsy nodded her head emphatically. "I knew, with a strong name like Simon, he had it in him to rise to the top."

"And now he's gone." Maureen began to tear up again.

Ophelia guided Maureen's glass to her lips. "Take a swallow."

"It won't help," Maureen protested.

"It won't hurt," Betsy said, taking a sip of the wine, then setting the glass aside to remove the tops from various chafing dishes. "I'll bet you haven't eaten."

"I'm not hungry." Maureen took a sip of wine to appease them.

"You can't drink too much on an empty stomach." Betsy took the glass. Nettie gently nudged Maureen into a chair and pushed a small table in front of her. Donna placed a plate of soul food in front of her. Ophelia spread a napkin in her lap and gave her a fork.

"I'm not hungry," Maureen repeated.

"Eat," Nettie said, preparing her own plate. "Afterward, and perhaps after a few more glasses of wine, you'll realize that Simon is still yours if you want him."

"I'm too old," Maureen insisted, reclaiming her glass and taking a sip without being coerced.

Ophelia leaned down to whisper loud enough for all of them to hear. "Last night, when it counted, did you feel old or feel good?"

Maureen flushed, remembered, gave the only possible answer. "Good. I felt good."

All of the women moved in closer. Maureen took another sip as her body stirred, hungered.

"Fill her up again, Donna," Betsy ordered with a laugh. "Maybe if we get her drunk enough, she'll jog my memory."

"She'll have to do more than jog mine," Nettie said. "However, I'm willing to let her try."

The women laughed and, wonder of wonders, Maureen laughed with them.

The party was in full swing when Traci arrived.

The temperature of the room was a cool sixty-eight, the ceiling fan was whirring, and three empty bottles of wine were lined up like soldiers on the small table in the sitting area of Maureen's bedroom. Maureen, Nettie, and Donna were on the bed: Ophelia and Betsy on the love seat in the sitting area.

"It's a good thing I brought reinforcements." Traci held up the cardboard box in her hands.

Ophelia chuckled. "Traci, we're not lushes."

Traci grinned, trying not to stare at Maureen, but she'd noted the tissue clamped in her hand, the misery in her eyes. She could shake Ryan. Might still do it. "Good thing I know that."

Sitting the box on the floor, she removed a two-gallon jar with a spigot. Lemon slices, cherries, and raspberries floated on top.

"Raspberry lemonade," Betsy said. "Maureen's favorite."

"Heck," Donna said from the bed. "Just when I was hoping she was drunk enough to spill more about last night."

Traci whirled, a thermos of coffee in her hand. "Then perhaps I should pour this out."

"Don't you dare." Nettie gracefully sat up from reclining

against the headboard and got out of bed. "Perhaps it's for the best. My heart probably couldn't take the excitement."

"Your heart is in better shape than any of ours," Maureen said, then bit her lip. "Especially mine."

Traci frowned. It wasn't like Maureen to feel sorry for herself. Traci looked at the other women in the room. All almost imperceptibly shook their heads. Setting the thermos aside, she picked up two bottles of alcoholic lemonade from inside the box. "Perhaps we should stick to the hard stuff."

"If we do, we'll be zonked out of our minds." Donna reached for the half-full glass in Maureen's hand.

Maureen moved her hand away and downed the contents. "Anything would be better than this ache."

"Ryan is dead meat when I see him," Traci declared.

"Save a piece of him for me," Donna said. Her cry was taken up by all of the women.

"He-he meant well." Maureen sniffed.

Traci went to her, took the glass. "Remember what your mother always said: A braying jackass is loud, but that doesn't make him important or right. All it makes him is loud."

Maureen blinked. "Did I tell you that?"

"You did, dear," Nettie confirmed. "It was at the Chippendales review we snuck—er, went to when that loud man tried to pick you up."

"Mama didn't like people to know she knew curse words," Maureen said, pulling her lower lip into her mouth. "We were too genteel for that."

"What do you think your mother would have said if one of her children would have tried to tell her what to do?" Traci asked.

"None of us would have dared." Maureen gingerly shook her head. "Even Papa knew when to back down. No one messed with Mama. If one of us had sassed her, she would have knocked us silly. She always said she'd forgotten more than we would ever learn."

"Brenda and Carolyn know better than to tell me how to run my life," Nettie said. "I'm small, so I fight dirty."

All the women laughed.

"My five tried, especially when they started smelling themselves, as the old people used to say. I set them straight," Donna said. "When they could afford the mortgage, food, car note, and all the other things they were getting, then they could come back and talk to me. Until then, I didn't want to hear it. Now, they all have teenagers who are giving them the blues. It's payback time."

"Isn't it something how history repeats itself?" Ophelia turned the spigot on the raspberry lemonade. "My four boys were always in and out of the house, leaving the door open and letting the cool air out. No matter how many times I'd tell them to close the door, they'd forget. Now they live in Texas and their electric bill is enormous. It's not the door these days, but the lights. My grandchildren complain that they're put on rations for electricity."

"History repeating itself isn't always good." Betsy's hands curved around her empty wineglass. "Errol and David." She paused, lowered her head. "I worry about my sons."

"We're here," Nettie said, going to her. "If we can help, you know we will."

Betsy blew out a breath. "I took them to church, to their Boy Scouts meetings, their games. I never missed a PTA meeting or parent conference night. Yet . . ." Her voice trailed off. She lifted her glass, then frowned on seeing that it was empty.

Ophelia took it, filled it with raspberry lemonade. "You're

a good woman, a good mother. Don't ever blame yourself. You were there for them."

"And Rudolph wasn't." Betsy sipped. "His success came first. I'm not sure where the boys or I came in. He thought a generous allowance and loose discipline was the answer. They looked at me as the ogre because I didn't want them to have so much."

Traci crossed to Betsy and hunkered down. "Maureen knows and now I'll tell you. Due to unforeseeable circumstances, I went to live with my grandfather when I was four. It was hard when other children had their parents and I didn't. I didn't really learn to appreciate him always being there for me until I was an adult. He just loved me until I could love him and myself back."

Betsy reached out her hand and Traci took it. "Thank you."

"You're a great woman, Betsy." Traci released her hand and stared at Maureen on the bed. "That goes for you, too, Maureen. I don't have any children, haven't really thought about it, but if and when the time comes, I hope and pray I can be there for them as you were there for your child, love them as much."

"And not let them control your lives." Ophelia drained her glass and reached for the strong stuff. "As if childbirth isn't bad enough. Betsy, you're not alone in your doubts. There were times when I didn't know if I was loving them too much or not enough."

"They think you're the bad guy when they can't do what the others are doing," Donna said.

"Or don't get the latest games or toys," Maureen put in.

"That's why I don't dye my gray hair." Nettie took the bottle of alcoholic lemonade and filled her glass. "I earned every last one of those gray hairs raising the girls."

"And you never stop thinking of them as your babies," Betsy said. "They're just in grown-up bodies."

"And think they know everything." Traci poured herself a glass of the strong stuff.

"We know they don't." Ophelia filled all their glasses. "To the Invincible Sisterhood and our honorary member, strong women who have loved incredible men." She looked at Maureen and Traci, and continued, "And two who might be blessed to love again."

They all toasted. Traci and Maureen were slow to drink. Traci didn't know about Maureen, but she wasn't willing to say her desire for Ryan went deeper than lustful caring.

There had been few times in Simon's life when he hadn't known what to do.

Like a besotted teenager, he'd driven by Maureen's house four times. He was worried about her. He'd called her store and learned she wasn't coming in. No one had to tell him that was unusual. Calls to her house had been picked up by the answering machine.

He pulled up behind a 1978 Buick in mint condition. Nettie's late husband's car. The matronly woman didn't drive so someone must have driven her. In the driveway was a late-model Chevrolet and a five-year-old Benz. They'd been there when he'd driven by a little after four that afternoon. It was a little past seven and the cars were still there.

He had no way of knowing what that signified. He just hoped it didn't mean that Maureen was still embarrassed over what had happened. Or worse, thinking about listening to Ryan and not seeing Simon again.

The flat of Simon's hand hit the steering wheel. Ryan

needed to mind his own business. Simon had no doubt he wouldn't take kindly to his mother telling him to give up Traci. He'd blow a gasket.

Simon straightened as a white panel van pulled into Maureen's drive. Anthony's Catering was scrawled in elegant black script on the side. The driver, a clean-shaven man in his mid-twenties, got out, opened the back doors, and hopped inside. He quickly emerged carrying several containers.

The front door of Maureen's house opened. Simon leaned forward, hoping he'd see Maureen. Instead, it was Traci and Betsy. Betsy took the containers from the delivery man and went back inside the house. Traci waited for the man to return with several trays. She stuffed something into the driver's pocket and took the trays. The driver closed the door, unfolded the paper from his pocket, then shot a fist into the air. Grinning, he ran back to the van, backed up, and drove off.

That was a lot of food for no more than six women. Or maybe the others had picked up some women he didn't know. Perhaps they were having some kind of party. He hoped so. Starting the car, he pulled around Nettie's Buick. He'd call Maureen tomorrow. Meanwhile, it would be a long, miserable night, just as it had been a long, miserable day.

Ryan drove straight to Maureen's house once he left rounds at the hospital that night.

The cars of the Sisterhood gave him pause and made him feel even worse than he had all day. He loved his mother. Not for anything would he want to hurt her. She had to know that. Even if he hadn't promised his father to watch over her and take care of her, he'd never let a man use her.

He rubbed his face with his hand. He did not want to think of his mother in that context.

He also didn't think trying to call either his mother or Traci again would do any good. His mother's answering machine was full. Traci had called around seven to tell him she'd talk to him tomorrow, then hung up. She hadn't sounded too pleased with him.

It wasn't enough that his mother was upset with him; his girlfriend was, too. He rolled his eyes, worked his shoulders at such an antiquated term. Yet somehow it fit whatever was going on between them. It was more than an affair. It wasn't just the great sex, they really liked being with each other. He liked knowing he'd see her at the end of the day, and knew she felt the same way.

Until today. Until he'd hurt his mother.

Lights blazed in the house. There was no telling what the adventurous ladies were doing. He'd secretly nicknamed them the Bawdy Broads after they'd spent a wild weekend in Vegas at the Bellagio Hotel. Thankfully, what was done in Vegas stayed in Vegas, as Traci had said.

Ryan started the engine. He'd decided against going in. If Traci and his mother were miffed at him, all the Invincibles would be as well. His presence wouldn't help the situation. They were as close as sisters.

His mother wasn't alone, and that was the important thing. If he had to spend the night without Traci, perhaps it was fitting. Shifting the car into gear, he drove off.

Replete with good food, the best vintage wine and spirits, the most decadent chocolates in the world, the women reclined on Maureen's bed late that night.

"I think we're all in agreement, then," Nettie said, her back pressed against Maureen's headboard.

A chorus of agreements and the nodding of heads accompanied by a few groans came from all the women.

"It makes perfect sense to me." Betsy massaged her temple.

"I'm not sure why it took us so long to reach this conclusion." Donna lay crosswise on the bed with her head propped on her hand, but her head kept slipping off. "Stop moving the bed."

"The bed is fine. It's the ceiling." Ophelia, on her back near Donna, squinted up at the gathered silk fabric of the canopied bed.

"I'm going to live my own life," Maureen said. Her words of conviction might have sounded stronger if she hadn't hiccupped in the middle.

"Damn straight," Traci slurred. "If Ryan can have a woman in his bed, there is no reason why you can't have a man in yours."

"Well said, and gracious, I might add." Nettie, the soberest of the women, added, "Especially considering you're the woman." When there was no comment, Nettie leaned around Maureen to look at Traci, who was lying on the other side. Her eyes were closed, her lips slightly parted in sleep. In fact, most of the other women were sleeping.

Folding her linked hands over her stomach, Nettie closed her eyes. It wouldn't be the first time nor the last that they'd stayed over. Although she couldn't remember if they'd ever all slept in the same bed.

17

Ryan couldn't believe his eyes.

He'd come over early to his mother's house because he had become increasingly worried about her. And to save his thumb. He'd accessed his cell phone address book so many times, it was sore. He stared at the women, their eyes red, their hair barely combed, their clothes rumpled as if they'd slept in them, each clutching a cup of coffee.

"You're all hungover."

To a woman, they shuddered, put down their cups, and covered their ears. He was instantly contrite and concerned. They liked their wine, had even organized a trip to the wineries in Napa Valley, but they had never drunk to this point. At least as far as he knew.

He went to his mother, purposefully keeping his steps soft on the tile floor. His voice was soft when he spoke. "Mother."

She slowly opened one bloodshot eye, then the other. Her breath smelled of spearmint mouthwash. He smoothed the spiked hair on top of her head. "Are you all right?"

"No thanks to you," Traci snapped.

Ryan tensed and slowly turned to see her coming inside

through the back kitchen door. She had on a snappy black suit that fit her lush body perfectly. He knew every luscious hidden curve and planned to get her out of the outfit before the day was over.

Unlike the others, Traci's shoulder-length hair was neatly combed, but the sunglasses at nine in the morning gave her away. Her eyes probably matched the others in the room.

Her unfair and harsh words loosened the tongues of the other women. They weren't shy about letting him have it.

"You should be ashamed of yourself, Ryan," Nettie admonished.

"Never thought you were selfish," Donna snarled, then winced and gulped coffee.

"Your mother deserves happiness," Ophelia barked.

"Shame on you." Betsy poked him in the chest.

"Yeah," Traci cried. "You have double standards."

Ryan felt his face heat. They all knew he and Traci were sleeping together, but it wasn't the same as having it discussed in the open.

"Traci," he cautioned, tugging at his suddenly too tight tie.

"Don't you Traci me, Ryan Gilmore." She advanced on him and took over Betsy's job of digging a hole in his chest. "You were wrong."

"I won't—"

"It's not your decision to make." Traci talked over him. Thankfully, she'd stopped poking him and put her hands on her hips. "Until you come to your senses and apologize, you're on lockdown."

If his face was flushed before, it was fiery red now. "Traci . . ."

She flung up her hand dismissively in the air and went to Maureen. "Be strong. I have an appointment or I'd stay and watch you chew a hole in him." She hugged Maureen, then marched past him without a look.

"Ryan," his mother called as he started after Traci.

He was torn as to which woman to go to. The back kitchen door closed, making the decision for him. "Yes, Mother."

"I love you, but you don't run my life. I'm seeing Simon, and there's nothing you can do about it." She folded her arms.

"Nothing," the other women repeated and went to stand beside Maureen in a show of strength.

That's what you think, he thought. Kissing her on the cheek, he left. If Maureen wouldn't listen, Simon had better.

Maureen was grateful only one drum was left beating in her skull as she walked down the street toward Forever Yours.

Her fault, and she was paying the price. But at least she knew what she wanted: Simon. Just reminding herself of that fact caused her to smile. Ryan would just have to accept it. The smile faded. She didn't want dating Simon to drive a wedge between her and her son. She just hoped that he'd eventually see that Simon was a good man.

Rounding the corner to her shop, she abruptly halted. Jason and Miguel were standing in front of her store. After the way Miguel had teased Jason, she wouldn't have thought they would be friendly. She couldn't hear what they were saying, but their body language and angry hand gestures were enough.

Despite her headache, she increased her pace. Several feet from them, she called his name. "Jason."

Both boys whirled. Miguel said something she couldn't hear and hurried away.

"Jason," Maureen said, staring after the other boy. "Are you all right?"

He shrugged his thin shoulders. "Sure."

"It looked like you two were arguing."

"Just stuff." He frowned at her. "You all right today?"

"Fine, thank you." Unlocking the door, she let him inside. "How did things go yesterday? Did Avery come by?" The sudden smile on Jason's face said she had.

"Yes."

"She's a wonderful young woman and smart. And pretty," Maureen said.

"Yeah," he agreed, grinning for all he was worth.

For once Jason didn't tuck his head or stick his hands into his pockets. Maureen continued to the back. The right person could do wonders for a person's morale. Just as Simon continued to do for her.

Ryan had a plan.

His mother wouldn't dare contact Simon until she was less shaky on her feet and her eyes were clear. There was no way she would want Simon to see her until she was at her best.

Ryan was counting on her waiting until after the store closed at 6:00 to call and probably invite Simon to her house. Ryan planned to nix Simon accepting that invitation. By 5:30, Ryan was knocking on Simon's door. If his mother wouldn't listen, then he intended to ensure that Simon would.

The door swung open. Simon filled the doorway. His face hard, he had on black jeans and a black polo shirt that delineated hard muscles. He had a dangerous look about him that probably drew women like shavings to a magnet. Ryan vowed that he would not let his mother be one of them any longer.

"What do you want?" Simon practically snarled.

"One guess." Ryan brushed past him to enter the condo.

Simon shoved the door shut. "Make it fast."

"Stay away from my mother," Ryan told him.

"You know what you can do with that advice." Simon headed to another room.

Ryan caught his arm as he passed, felt Simon's muscles flex. "I'm talking to you."

"Not for long if you don't remove your hand," Simon threatened.

"Stay away from my mother," Ryan repeated.

"Two seconds," Simon said.

"You probably can take me but, if you hurt my mother, I'll keep coming back again and again," Ryan promised. He wasn't backing down on this.

The hardness vanished from Simon's face so quickly that Ryan's fingers uncurled. "Hurt her? I'd walk through fire before I'd do that. You did that all by yourself."

It was too close to what Traci had said. "I love my mother. This is for her own good."

Simon propped his hands on his hips. "That's a pile of crap. You don't want to think of your mother having a relationship."

"We aren't going there," Ryan hastily told him.

Simon threw his hands in the air, walked away, then walked back. "Maureen is an intelligent, wonderful woman. I wanted to ask her out the first time I saw her. She turned me down. Kept turning me down. I kept asking."

It was as Ryan had expected. "You should have taken the 'no' and walked away. She was probably feeling vulnerable because her sixtieth birthday is coming up."

"The only one who keeps harping on her age is you!" Simon yelled. "I can count. I knew how old she probably was, and it didn't make one bit of difference. She's caring, beautiful, vibrant, fun to be with."

"Maybe for now, but then you'll move on to a younger woman," Ryan retorted. Yet, even as he said the words, they bothered him as if he were being disloyal to his mother.

"Why would I want another woman when I have Maureen?" Simon snapped. "I just told you how much trouble I had trying to get her to go out with me. I had just gotten her not to worry about those hot flash—" Simon snapped his mouth shut.

Stunned, Ryan stared at Simon. Ryan had seen his mother fanning herself lately, the sudden flush of her skin, and figured she was having hot flashes. He hadn't mentioned them because he hadn't wanted to embarrass her. His patients her age discussed the problem with his nurse instead of him.

"You discussed her hot flashes?"

"What Maureen and I discuss is none of your business." Simon went to the door and opened it. "This conversation is over."

Ryan didn't move. Instead, he studied the man he'd been proud to call his frat brother and friend until yesterday morning. Simon had distinguished himself in the police force that had almost killed his younger brother, and had several community service awards for working with youth and the elderly. Users didn't go out of their way to help others, unless there was something in it for them.

"Perhaps I was a bit hasty," Ryan said.

"You think?" Simon's voice seethed with sarcasm.

The unrelenting stare convinced Ryan further. "All right. I apologize. Mother had never looked at another man since we lost Dad. I guess I didn't think she ever would."

Simon swung the door closed. "She loved him with all she had."

"I probably shouldn't ask, but I have to know, how do you feel about that?"

"He made her happy, then made sure she'd remain that way once he was gone," Simon answered. "I'm not in competition with him."

Ryan couldn't hide his surprise. "You must have talked a lot."

"We did. I respect and admire Maureen a great deal. She's not just about herself."

Ryan folded his arms. "Was that last bit a dig at me?"

"If the shoe fits." Simon went to the sofa and picked up a basketball on the floor. "Are we straight?"

"Yeah."

"Good." Simon shot the basketball to him.

Ryan grunted as he caught the fast ball. He eyed Simon. He'd done that on purpose.

Simon picked up his gym bag. "Want to follow me over to the Y and help me coach the team? The head coach can't make it. It's his daughter's birthday."

"Sure." Ryan accepted the offered olive branch. Besides, he'd once been pretty good on the basketball court. If he couldn't beat Simon one way, he'd beat him another way.

It was time.

Maureen had alternated using ice packs and cucumbers

on her eyes when possible all day until the redness and puffiness were gone. Once home she'd put on a fitted ice-blue dress she'd purchased during a lull at the store, and then she'd called Simon. The call had gone into voice mail at his home and on his cell.

"He's not answering." Maureen hung up the phone on the side table in the great room and sat back in the sofa.

"He'll get one of the messages and call you back," Traci assured her from her seat across from Maureen.

Maureen nibbled on her lip. "I might have gotten dressed for nothing."

"Not a chance. As soon as he shows up, I'm history."

Before she could answer, the doorbell rang. Traci grinned at her. "My cue to leave."

Maureen's heart thumped as she came to her feet. "It could be Ryan."

Traci stood with her. "You know as well as I do that lately Ryan has been using his key. Besides, he knows we're upset with him."

"You know you didn't have to do that." Maureen moved to the door with Traci close behind.

"Of course I did. He needs to learn to let you live your own life." Traci screwed up her face. "Although I really miss him."

Maureen's heels clicked on the marble tile in the foyer. "If this is Simon, you could call Ryan and put both of you out of your misery."

Traci shook her head. "No. It's a matter of principle, and it's the right thing to do."

Maureen leaned over to peer through the peephole, blinked, then leaned over again. "I don't believe it."

"What?" Traci asked.

"Take a look for yourself," Maureen advised.

Traci planted her hands on the door and lifted herself up on her tiptoes. "Looks like we'll both be smiling later tonight."

Maureen giggled. "You are so bad."

Traci palmed her face. "I can't believe I said that."

"You notice I didn't disagree." The chime came again. "I guess we'd better let them in." She opened the door and stepped aside. Both men looked handsome in sports coats and white shirts. "I'm glad you two worked things out."

"I want you to be happy." Ryan came inside with Simon close behind.

"Hello, Maureen." Simon's gaze swept her in one encompassing sweep. "You look breathtaking."

Ryan frowned. Traci elbowed him. "What?" he mouthed.

"Thank you." Maureen closed the door, glanced at Simon, then away.

"I was about to leave." Traci hooked her arm through Ryan's. "Walk me home."

"Only if you need to get your purse or something." Ryan looked at his mother. "If you ladies are in agreement, Simon and I would like to take you out to dinner."

"You mean like a double date?" Traci asked, grinning broadly.

A pained look crossed Ryan's face. "In a matter of speaking."

"Maureen and I accept." Traci dragged Ryan to the door. "We'll be back in a jiff."

Outside, Ryan looked back at the door. "I hope this is the right thing to do."

"It is." Traci curved her arms around his neck, pressed her body to his. "I'm proud of you."

He let his forehead rest against hers. "Don't paint any medals on me yet. For a crazy moment, when Simon was looking at Mother and she was looking at him, I wanted to punch him and make her go to her room."

"Then I'll just have to give you something else to think about." She pulled his head down, pressing her lips against his, thrusting her tongue into his hot mouth, her pelvis against the junction of his thighs.

He groaned. One hand palmed her hips, holding her to him, the other swept up and down the smooth curve of her back. A long while later they broke apart, breathing heavily.

"Let's go get what you need so we can eat and go back to your place," he rasped.

"I didn't need anything," she confessed. "I thought they deserved some time alone just as we did."

Ryan's head snapped around to the door. Hanging his head, he closed his eyes for a moment. "Too much information."

Traci thought his protectiveness was sweet, now that it wasn't excessive. "They're probably just talking."

Ryan didn't look as if he believed her. Traci smiled innocently. Simon probably had Maureen in a lip lock before the door closed. Looks like both men were off lockdown.

Ryan let Simon win the argument to drive his car.

Ryan knew he probably would have paid more attention to what was going on in the backseat than the traffic. As it was, he found himself studying his mother, listening to the happiness in her voice, the way she occasionally touched Simon on the arm when she was talking to him. She was comfortable with him. The telling moment came when she stopped talking and began fanning her face.

Moments later the air conditioner in Simon's Ford kicked up, and Maureen had a fan in her hand that wouldn't have fit in her purse and a bottle of water. Without words, Simon showed he cared. He hadn't lied about the hot flashes.

"How did the practice go?" Maureen asked.

"Great." Simon looked at Ryan in the rearview mirror. "My team beat Ryan's by four points."

"Only because Miguel wouldn't pass," Ryan pointed out.

Simon flicked on his signal and pulled into the restaurant's parking lot. "I tried to tell you to let me have him on my team."

"I might have if I hadn't seen him shoot baskets first," Ryan admitted. "He has talent, but he's a little high on his own abilities."

"*A little* is putting it mildly." Simon parked, emerged to open Maureen's door, then took her arm. "It's his way or no way. He doesn't know it, but he won't start for tomorrow night's game."

"Good luck with that." Ryan helped Traci out and slid his arm around her waist.

"I saw him talking with Jason near the shop today, but he left when he saw me." Maureen entered the restaurant door Simon held open for all of them. "It looked as if they were arguing."

Simon frowned. "Are you sure?"

Maureen's frown matched Simon's. "I can't be sure. I asked Jason, of course, because I didn't want Miguel to tease him as he had the other night. Jason said they were just talking."

"Don't worry. It's probably just that," Simon told her.

"Table for four, please," Ryan requested of the hostess.

"This way." Plucking four menus from a slot, the young woman led them to a table on the far side of the room, which was decorated with an underwater sea theme. "Your server will be here shortly," she said with a smile and left.

Seated, Maureen picked up the conversation. "Jason drew me a bouquet of flowers since he couldn't afford real ones. The detailing was perfect. He has a future ahead as an artist if he works and studies hard."

Simon gazed at Maureen, not even attempting to hide his feelings. "He's lucky to have you pulling for him."

"So are the young men you coach," she said.

"I think they're all lucky," Traci said.

"So do I," Ryan agreed, his mother's obvious happiness going a long way to help him accept her and Simon dating. "It's nice to know I was wrong about you."

"Well, I was right about you," Simon paused dramatically. "You might be hardheaded, but you're fair."

Ryan hadn't said three words since they left the restaurant and Traci knew why.

No matter how he tried to put it out of his mind, a part of him knew that Simon and Maureen were going upstairs to that big bed of hers to make love. A part of him rebelled at the idea. Maureen had to be feeling just as awkward.

Simon parked by the walk leading to Maureen's house. The sudden quietness was telling. Traci took matters into her own hands. "Oh, my goodness! I left my purse at the restaurant."

"You're sure?" Ryan peered around the backseat.

"Positive," she answered.

"I'll take you back to get it." Simon started the engine again.

"No." Traci opened her door and got out. "Ryan can take me, if he doesn't mind."

"Of course not." Getting out of the car, he pulled out his cell phone and handed it to her. "Call and ask them to look for it, and tell them we're on our way back."

Traci took the phone, but didn't dial. "Good night, Maureen, Simon. I had a wonderful time."

"Good night," they both said.

"We'd better get back to the restaurant. Good night." Ryan took Traci's arm and hurried her to his car, which was parked on the street. "Traci, what are you waiting for? Get the number from information." Opening the door, he seated her, then went around and got inside and pulled away from the curb. "Your ID and house keys were in your purse. That's too dangerous. Why are you waiting?"

"Perhaps because I didn't have a purse. Just my keys, and they're in my pocket."

"What?" Ryan stopped in the middle of the street. A horn blared behind them. Signaling, he pulled to the curb. "Explain."

She leaned so close their breaths mingled. "I figured I'd finally get a chance to see your apartment."

"You also figured out it would drive me crazy knowing Simon and Mother were together next door." His forehead touched hers. "It's still driving me crazy."

"Only until I get you in bed, and then you're going to be too busy to think about anything except breathing." She nipped his bottom lip. "That and all the wicked things I'm going to do to you."

He quickly put the car in gear and drove off. "What time do you have to be at work?"

"Nine."

His hand landed on her knee, then swept upward. "That should be enough time."

It was half past ten. She licked her lips in anticipation.

Alone again at last."

Maureen sighed in pleasure as Simon pulled her against his hard length. Her body tingled in that pleasant way whenever she was near him. "And what do you plan to do?"

Simon's beautiful eyes narrowed. "What I'm *not* going to do might be a better question." His hands cupped her firm buttocks, squeezed.

"Simon." His name trembled over her lips.

"I love the breathy way you say my name." His lips brushed across hers, then followed the curve of her neck.

"I love how you touch me, equal parts greed and reverence."

"I'm going to make you a happy woman tonight." Hand in hand, they started for the stairs.

I might have been wrong," Traci said, staring up at Ryan. He was propped up on his elbow, staring down at her.

"About what?" His hand made a lazy circle around her nipple, causing her stomach muscles to clench.

"Elisa said she didn't remember much of your apartment because she was too busy with other things." Her hand glided over his chest and downward. "Although she wasn't telling the truth, I can understand how a woman might not pay attention to her surroundings with the right man. An hour ago I was too busy trying to get your clothes off to notice anything else. All I wanted was for us to be together. Nothing else mattered."

The hard frown forming on Ryan's face softened. "The same for me. If I hadn't gotten inside you, I would have whimpered like a baby."

The back of her hand brushed across his semi-erection, felt it surge to life. "I never knew it could be this shattering. Or that I could be this greedy."

"Neither did I," he confessed, his hand sweeping down to her stomach as he leaned over.

The phone on the bedside rang. Ryan groaned and let his forehead fall against Traci's.

"I take it you're on call tonight."

"Yeah." Rolling over, he picked up the phone. "Dr. Gilmore."

"This is Dr. Thomas. We never made it to the hospital with Elisa."

"What!" Ryan came off the bed and hit the floor. "What do you mean she didn't make it to the hospital? What happened?"

Wrapping the black sheet around her breasts, Traci got out of bed and held her ear to the phone so she could hear.

"She started hyperventilating. We pulled into a service station. There was a police car, and she yelled she was being kidnapped. By the time things were sorted out, she was gone."

Ryan cursed under his breath. "When?"

"Shortly after we left," her father confessed. "We thought we could find her by now."

Ryan shoved his hand over his head. "Did you tell the police where you were headed with her and why?"

The long pause was Ryan's answer. "I've hired Bledsoe to look for her. He is also going to put his men on the case to visibly watch your place as well as your mother's and

Ms. Evans's. He thinks she will go underground for a while, then resurface."

"She'll need money for that," Ryan said.

"She has it. Four thousand dollars is missing from my home safe," Dr. Thomas said. "I'm sorry."

"You—" Ryan began.

"He's feeling bad enough, Ryan," Traci said from beside him. "She's mentally ill, and there's nothing he can do to help her."

"Thanks for the call," Ryan amended.

"I'm sorry," Dr. Thomas said. The line went dead.

Ryan hung up the phone. "You really are incredible."

She hugged him. "I just know what it feels like to think no one cares about you."

Frowning, he tilted her chin up. "I wish I could have been there for you."

"You're here now." Stepping back, she dropped the sheet.

It wasn't a pretty sight.

Simon had anticipated Miguel's anger at being benched but it went much further.

"Just because you want to make yourself look good in front of that old bi—"

Simon grabbed Miguel by the jersey before he thought. When the kid's eyes widened, Simon's hand clenched tighter. He knew he had crossed the line. Perhaps it was the only thing that might help Miguel. "You have a foul mouth. If you don't want it washed out with soap, I'd advise you to re-think whatever you were about to say."

Fear and then defiance flashed in the teenager's eyes. He

clawed at Simon's hand. "Turn me loose! My lawyer will have you up on charges," he threatened.

"You can hide behind the law when it suits you, can't you?" Simon pushed his face closer. "I've had all of your attitude I'm going to take. You go down again, and it's no longer juvie, it's the big time. Is that what you want in life?"

"Like you care," he snarled, pushing ineffectually at Simon's hands.

"Do you give anyone a chance to care? You want your way no matter what." Simon uncurled his fingers. "You're selfish and mean-spirited, but you're young. You can change."

The teenager straightened his jersey. "I'm doing just fine."

"Yeah, your parents kicked you out the other day because they're tired of you stealing from them and, since you won't keep a job, you're crashing wherever you can. You come here not because you want to or because the judge orders you to, but because you don't have any other place to go since your gang fell apart."

Miguel's eyes darkened. "You don't know nothing."

"I know you're sinking fast. You can save yourself. You can be something, be a man. The first step is up to you," Simon told him. "Don't throw your life away trying to swagger and be a badass. You'll end up with all the other swaggerers and badasses—in jail—and you'll find out what hell is really like."

Fear flashed in the teenager's eyes. "I'm nobody's punk."

"Miguel." Simon put his hand on the boy's shoulder, but it was shrugged off. He didn't want to push too hard, but he wanted Miguel to understand that unless he changed, he was heading for disaster. "Team sport is just like life. It teaches you to rely on others. It lets others know they can rely on you. Bullying or thinking only of yourself won't get you very far in life or in the game."

"I've heard enough of the psychology crap. If you want to bench me, go ahead. I don't need a sermon." Miguel jerked off his jersey and threw it on the floor. "I'm outta here."

"No, you're not," Simon said quietly. "Part of your probation orders are for you to participate with the Sharks at practice and games."

"Sitting on the bench is for sissies."

"The other team members haven't had a problem with it. Now, put on that jersey and let's get out there."

They stared at each other. Miguel snatched up the jersey. "One day I'll pay you back for this."

"Miguel, threatening a police officer isn't smart," Simon said calmly.

The young man feigned innocence and slipped on his jersey. "Just blowing off, man, I mean Lieutenant Dunlap, sir."

Simon didn't believe him for a second. "It's one game, Miguel. Learn from this. Don't let your anger get you in deeper trouble."

"I don't plan to get in no trouble. Not me. Not me at all." Without another word, he turned and left.

Simon followed him out. Talk and reasoning hadn't helped. Miguel was full of pride, and tonight it would be bruised a bit. But it was better than a bullet or hard time in the pen. Blowing out a breath, Simon followed the teenager onto the court.

He shook his head on seeing Miguel limping. Then Simon looked in the stands and saw Maureen sitting between Traci and Jason. Ryan sat on the other side of Traci.

Simon's heart got that crazy feeling it always did when he

saw Maureen. He waved, grinned when she waved back. No woman in his life had ever affected him as strongly. He thought about her when he wasn't with her and, when he was with her, he dreaded the time he'd have to leave her.

She was important to him.

"Dunlap."

Simon hadn't realized he'd stopped and stared at Maureen until Bobby called his name. Apparently she had been just as caught up because she'd palmed her face, then laughed when Traci leaned over, spoke into her ear, and nudged her. Yep, they were definitely in this together.

"Dunlap," Bobby called, teasing laughter in his voice. He'd been married fifteen years and said he couldn't have wished for a happier life with a more loving woman. With the right woman, living took on an entirely new meaning.

Simon got his feet moving, his gaze moving to Traci, Jason, and Ryan. He waved to them. Jason, his head down, appeared more interested in sketching. Traci wiggled her fingers. Ryan shook his head, then laughed. At least her son finally realized Simon really cared for Maureen.

"Dunlap, keep your mind on the game." Bobby grinned. "This is the first time my family has been able to come to a game in a while. Let's not blow it."

"Wouldn't dream of it." Simon had won the woman and would win the game. Clapping his hands, he went to his team and called out the starting players. To a man they looked at Miguel, his leg stretched out in front of him while he massaged his thigh.

"Cramps." Miguel grimaced. "You'll have to win this one without me."

The teammates traded suspicious glances. They all knew Miguel would crawl to the court if necessary. He was that arrogant and cocky. The team looked at Simon to confirm what they already suspected. Miguel was lying.

Simon wasn't out to crush Miguel's dignity; he wanted to save him. He didn't even glance at Miguel. "You heard the head coach. His family is here and so are some friends of mine. Let's win this game."

Simon and Bobby stuck out their hands, palm down. The team members, including those not starting, crowded around the coaches, trying to join hands. All except Miguel. When Simon turned, the benched player stared at him with hatred in his dark eyes.

The Sharks won in a nail-biting double overtime by a free throw.

At the sound of the buzzer, Maureen surged to her feet, applauding loudly, then she turned to hug Jason. She ignored the tensing of his body and was rewarded when he awkwardly hugged her back.

"What a finish." Traci hooked her arm through Ryan's. "You and Simon did a good job."

Ryan chuckled and kissed her on the cheek. "Thanks, sweetheart, but all the credit goes to Simon and the coach."

"I'm going down to congratulate them." Maureen looked at Jason. "You want to go with me and show Simon what you drew?"

Panic raced across Jason's young face. He clutched the sketch pad to him. "It's nothing."

"Not from what I saw." Traci shrugged when the teenager stared at her. "I admit I peeked. You're good. Just like the flowers you drew for Maureen. You have a way of putting more than just strokes on paper."

"He does, doesn't he? That's why I'm having my drawing framed," Maureen said.

Jason gaped, swallowed. "I-I thought you were just kidding."

"My mother isn't the type to kid. Although I'm not sure how I feel about the competition. Your drawing will really make mine look awful." Ryan rubbed the back of his neck. "Some of my friends tease me that she has my drawings and poems from grade school in her office at Forever Yours."

"And a copy of your medical diploma," Maureen said proudly. "They show the progression of the man you were destined to be." Beaming, Maureen faced Jason. "Just like the drawing of the camellias will. I'll have your earliest rendition. It will be priceless, but I'll keep it and tell everyone I knew you when."

Jason swallowed, blinked, and uncurled his arms. He looked at the top sketch of several players racing down the court. "Do you really think he'll like them?"

"He will." Maureen went down the bleachers to the gym floor. People still crowded around the team and coaches, congratulating them. She waited until Bobby and Simon were free. "Congratulations."

Bobby, with his arm around a young girl who looked to be in her midteens, introduced Maureen and Jason to his wife and daughter. "We've been winning since Maureen started coming. Please don't stop."

"I'm working on that." Simon stepped up beside her, the look in his eyes saying he wished they were alone.

Maureen moistened her lips, tried to swallow to ease her dry throat so she could speak. "To commemorate tonight, Jason sketched some of the action."

"Can I see?" asked Bobby's daughter.

Maureen held her breath as he slowly handed the pad to her. Her family moved to crowd around her, as did some of the other players. She flipped the pages. The compliments weren't long in coming.

"These are great."

"Can you do one of me for my chick?"

"Do mine without the tire tube around my belly," Bobby said, making people laugh.

"You did a great job, Jason." Simon now held the pad in his hands. "If you ever think of selling these, please let me know. My tenure here isn't permanent and I'd like to have this."

Maureen's heart clutched. How could she have forgotten he would be leaving soon?

"You'd buy them?" Jason asked, surprise and delight on his young face.

"Yes."

"Can I think about it?" Jason asked.

"Sure." Simon handed back the sketch pad. "Maureen knows how to contact me. In the meantime, both teams are going out for burgers. On me."

Several of the Sharks asked to ride in Maureen's car. "We may have to draw straws. Now, hit the shower." Simon turned to her as the team ran to the shower. Miguel followed, no longer limping. "Why the sad face?"

"I'd forgotten you're leaving soon."

"Myrtle Beach is less than two hours away, and I'm here now."

Maureen smiled, but her heart wasn't in it.

H oney, what's the matter?"

Maureen wasn't surprised that Simon knew she was

worried. She'd been quiet during the celebration. Once they were back at her house, she had gone into his arms, almost desperate for his touch. He hadn't questioned her need then, but now he wanted answers. Answers she wasn't sure she wanted to give.

"Maureen, what is it?"

Facing him in the dark, their heads on the same pillow, one of his hands swept languidly up and down her arm, his other hand played with her hair. Simon might not touch much in public, but when they were alone he couldn't seem to stop himself.

"Are you worried about the stalker?"

"No." There was no way she'd have him worry needlessly.

She heard the rustle of the bedding. The bright light on the night chest came on. She saw a magnificent display of Simon's muscled back, the beginning curve of his buttocks before he adjusted the three-way light to its lowest setting.

He sat on the side of the bed. "Then what?"

She reached out to run her hand across the muscled warmth of his chest. At times she couldn't believe he was with her when he could be with another, younger woman.

His hand caught hers, kissed her palm. "I think I've already shown I'm not good at guessing what a woman is thinking. Brooke says I'm a lost cause."

She shivered from his warm breath, the lick of his tongue. "You'll be leaving soon."

"Ah, honey." He came down on the bed, brushing his hand across her face. "I'll be ninety minutes away."

"You'll be busy. Things will come up," she mumbled, glancing away, not wanting him to see how frightened she was that he wouldn't come back to her once he left.

Palming her face, he stared down at her. "Nothing is going to come between us. Nothing."

"But—"

"No buts," he talked over her. "I didn't want to tell you, but I've already asked for a transfer."

Happiness flooded her, then remorse. "You're happy in Myrtle Beach. Your other three brothers are in the police force with you."

"There's a lot for me to do here," he told her. "I won't regret moving here."

She bit her lower lip, tried to keep the question inside, but it was useless. "Are you moving here because of me?" As soon as the words left her mouth, she wished she could recall them. What if—

"Yes."

"Simon." She launched herself in his arms, her mouth seeking and finding his. Heat splintered through her. She welcomed it, embraced it.

He covered her body, surging into her waiting heat. She held him tight as his powerful body surged again and again into hers, taking her higher and higher until her body stiffened and her release came. He dropped his head into the curve of her neck and found his own release.

A long while later he rolled over with her in his arms. He kissed her cheek. "I'd better get going."

Her arms tightened. "If Ryan is with Traci, why can't you stay with me?"

"We both know why." He kissed her again. "He's still getting adjusted to us being together."

"Do you want to leave?"

"No."

She snuggled closer. "Then you don't have to. Traci said they were going straight to her house and both cars were going in the garage."

"That means—"

"Yes." She bit his lower lip. "Let's not waste any more of it."

Insatiable.

She'd been insatiable last night with Simon. Shameless even. And he had been the same way. Smiling to herself, Maureen unlocked the door to Forever Yours. She hadn't let her age interfere and she damn well wasn't going to let the insidious hot flashes interfere. If Elisa would come out of hiding and give herself up, Maureen wouldn't have a care in the world.

Putting her purse away in her office, she heard the opening of the front door. They weren't due to be open for another twenty minutes. Perhaps it was Jason. He'd still been riding high on the praises of his sketches when she'd dropped him at his house last night. He couldn't stop talking. Maureen smiled. People having confidence in you did wonders for self-esteem.

Entering the main store, her heart lurched. It was Jason all right, but a uniformed policeman held him firmly by the arm. Neither was smiling. "What's going on? Let him go."

"You might not be so quick to say that once you learn he's been using this shop as a front to sell drugs."

"You're crazy!" Jason yelled.

"That's impossible," Maureen said. "Jason would never do anything like that."

"He was about to enter the shop when I came up. Why don't we see?" The policeman pulled the backpack from

Jason's back, then emptied the contents on top of a dresser. Besides the books, there were several rolls of notebook paper. His accusing gaze went to Jason.

"That's not mine." The teenager looked wildly at Maureen. "That's not mine!"

"It's just notebook paper, Jason," Maureen said, not understanding why he'd become so upset.

"It's more than that." The policeman used two ballpoint pens to unroll the paper. Inside lay a thin line of a brownish, powdery substance. "It's cheese, a new form of drugs that combines heroine and Tylenol PM. It's very addictive."

Jason bolted for the door. The policeman caught him, easily overpowering Jason's frantic struggles to handcuff him. "Jason Payne, you're under arrest for selling controlled substances. You have the right to remain silent. Anything you say can and will be used against you."

"I didn't do anything!"

Maureen was momentarily stunned, speechless.

"Be thankful you didn't get swept up in this mess, Mrs. Gilmore." The policeman led Jason to the door.

"How? How did you know?" she finally asked.

"We received a tip," the policeman explained. "Unfortunately, the drug is gaining in popularity and, since it's cheap, more and more kids are trying it out. Good-bye."

Maureen stared at the closed door, watched as the policeman put Jason in the police car and people stopped to watch. Her good day had just been shot to hell.

He made his bed, and now he has to lie in it."

Maureen stared at the receiver. Jason's mother had hung up on her.

"Is she going down there?" Henrietta asked. She'd rushed into the shop just as the police drove off.

"No." Maureen hung up the phone.

"What?" Henrietta snapped. "That kid is too scared to do something stupid like that."

"He stole an inkwell," Maureen reminded her.

"For his mother's birthday."

"How did you know that?" Maureen asked.

Henrietta folded her thin arms. "The day you came back from being sick and you made a big fuss over that sketch, he was mumbling that you were trying to fake him out. He'd given a similar sketch to his mother for her birthday and she had washed it in her jeans. He didn't blame her because he thought it was a stupid, worthless gift."

"Oh, Henrietta." Maureen's heart went out to Jason.

"Some women don't deserve children."

Maureen gently placed her hand on the other woman's tense shoulder. Henrietta was childless. "That's why we're here. To help take up the slack."

"Then you're going?" she asked.

"As soon as I can get Traci."

"Why Traci and not Simon?" Henrietta wanted to know.

"Because I don't want Simon mixed up in this. Because Traci is a lawyer and knows her way around a police station." Maureen collected her handbag. "I'll call."

I don't believe Jason did it either."

Traci strode beside Maureen on the way to the holding cell and Jason. "He's too insecure and shy."

"We'll get to the bottom of this," Maureen said.

"That we will," Traci promised. "The cell isn't pretty, so prepare yourself."

"He must be terrified."

"He has a right to be." The words were barely out of Traci's mouth before she saw Jason huddled in a corner. At least he was in a cell by himself. Front-row tickets to ball games did wonders, she thought. "Thanks, Myers. I owe you."

The jailer nodded, then stepped aside.

"Jason."

His head came up and he almost fell in his haste to reach them. He looked down the corridor they'd come from. "Where's Mama?"

"She—she—" Maureen bit her lip.

"We're here," Traci said, realizing Maureen wasn't going to be able to tell Jason the truth. "You want to tell us how those drugs got in your bag?"

Tears rolled down his cheeks and he wiped them away. "I don't know. I— You believe me?"

"I wouldn't walk out on a client like Clint Herd if I didn't," Traci told him. Clint was one of the good guys. With three sons of his own, he'd understood why Traci had to leave.

"The football player?" Jason asked, awe replacing fear in his voice.

"The same. Now, back to you. Maureen said you keep your backpack in her office, so no one could have gotten to it. After work, you two went directly from the store to the game." Traci frowned. "I don't remember seeing it at the game last night."

"It was on the floor of the backseat of Mrs. Gilmore's car," he told her. "There's so much room back there, I didn't think of moving it. I'd already finished my homework assignment so I didn't unload it when I got home last night. Just picked it up and left this morning."

"Then the only time it was out of your sight was in the car to or from the restaurant," Traci said. "Who was in the car that might have it in for you? Who would have a reason to frame you?"

"Miguel," Maureen and Jason said at the same time.

He'd been consulted last.

Simon didn't know how to take that. If there hadn't been a need to fingerprint the notebook paper ASAP, he wasn't sure they would have come to him at all. That hurt.

"What's taking so long?" Maureen asked, her arms wrapped around herself. "He is so scared."

"It's only been five minutes." Simon watched Maureen pace. He went to her and circled her waist with his arms.

She looked up at him. "What?"

"Why didn't you come to me first?" he asked.

"Macho time. I'll be at the vending machine." Traci quickly left.

"Simon, it should be obvious."

"Like I said, I'm slow."

A smile curved her soft mouth as her arms circled his neck. "You're not slow. You're brilliant."

"Then why didn't you call me instead of Traci when this went down?" he asked, unable to keep the bite out of his voice.

Her brow arched. "Simon, surely you don't feel slighted?"

"I'm trying not to," he told her truthfully.

"I didn't want you involved," she told him. "The policeman insinuated that I was lucky not to be dragged into it. Apparently, the tipster insinuated I might be involved."

"What?" His hands tightened. "You didn't mention that before."

"Because I knew you'd worry."

"I care about you, I'm supposed to worry, especially if my association with you had anything to do with this," he told her.

She held up both hands. "Now, wait a minute. If we're right, Miguel's vindictiveness caused this. Don't you dare blame yourself, or I won't tell you anything else."

"There's more?" he asked.

"Well, not now," she said. "I'm talking future tense. I hope you don't, because I like talking to you."

"And apparently trying to protect me," he said.

"It seemed the thing to do."

The phone on his desk rang. He picked it up. "Dunlap. Yeah, what do you have? Thanks." He hung up. "Miguel's prints were the only ones found on the paper."

He's innocent."

Jason's mother didn't react at Maureen's statement. When they'd approached her at the grocery store where she was the assistant manager, her lips had tightened, then she had directed them to an office filled with lockers, a time clock, and cardboard boxes. "So what happened?"

Traci explained about Jason's fingerprints not being on the paper. They belonged to another boy that the police were going to investigate. There was no need to mention that Simon had used his influence to get the arresting officer not to charge Jason with resisting arrest.

"He had better keep it that way," his mother said. "You go straight home, and don't leave the house until I get there."

Jason tucked his head. "Yes, ma'am."

Traci's temper spiked. "What kind of mother are you?"

The other woman unfolded her arms. "You don't question me."

"Tra—" Maureen began.

"Someone should," Traci talked over Maureen. "He's scared to death. If Maureen hadn't been on his side, he'd be looking at a long jail sentence for something he didn't do."

"So you want a pat on the back?" his mother asked sarcastically.

"I want you to act like a mother who loves him," Traci shot back. Jason's mother was too much of a reminder of Traci's uncaring mother. Every child deserved to know they were wanted and loved.

"If I didn't love him, I would have left him at the hospital," she said, her voice shaking. "His daddy had walked. I didn't have a job and my family wouldn't help me because they'd told me not to marry Jason. I wouldn't listen."

Traci figured out what Jason's mother didn't say. "Since you couldn't punish the father you named the son after him and have been punishing his son."

"He's the spitting image of his father," Jason's mother said, not denying Traci's statement. "He's not going to walk over me like his father did."

"But he's had you to raise him, teach him." Maureen stepped forward. "He's courteous, well spoken. I didn't call the police when he took the inkwell, an inkwell he wanted for your birthday, because I sensed something good in him."

Jason's mother's eyes went to him. "You took that for me? You gave me the drawing of the flowers."

"You didn't keep it." His hands went deeper into his pockets. "Just like the other ones I gave you."

"A black man can't make a living drawing. How many times have I told you to stop wasting your time," she said, frustration in her voice.

"He's not wasting his time," Maureen quickly defended. "He has talent."

"And that will get him exactly nowhere," his mother told them. "At eighteen he's out of my hair, so he better make the most of the time left by getting his grades up so he can go to a trade school. I'm not going to support him."

"I love you, Mama. I'm sorry if having me made you unhappy and ruined your life." His head fell.

"Don't you talk to me that way," she said. "I worked two jobs for the pay of one to keep you with me, to feed you so you'd grow up to be somebody. I didn't coddle you. I'm making you a man. This is for your own good."

"Men need love, too," Simon said. "My parents and grandparents always made sure me and my brothers always knew that." He grabbed Maureen and Traci's arms. "We'll take him home."

"You think I'm a bad mother. I could care less what you think," she snapped.

"What about what Jason thinks?" Traci said, resisting Simon's tug on her arm.

"He's never gone hungry or been ashamed of the clothes he's had to wear," his mother told them. "We moved here for a better life."

Neither had Traci, but it hadn't substituted for a mother's love. If not for her grandfather, she wasn't sure how she would have turned out. "Jason, wait outside with Maureen and Simon."

The teenager left without looking back. Maureen looked a bit uneasy, but she left with Simon. Traci waited until the door closed. "Don't let him continue thinking he was a mistake, that raising him is a duty instead of a pleasure, that you can't wait for him to leave, that his dreams don't matter."

"You can stand there and say that with your expensive clothes," she sneered. "I work for everything I have."

Traci got in her face. "So did I. My grandfather worked his farm from the crack of dawn until late at night so I could have an education. He wanted me to go further than the eighth grade, which was all the schooling he had. When I went to college, there was no scholarship or student loans. I carried a full load of courses and worked my butt off. It was the only way."

Traci swallowed. "I worked hard for two reasons: to make my grandfather proud and make my mother finally say she loved me. She never did, and now I wouldn't walk across the street to give her a glass of water if she were dying of thirst."

Jason's mother's eyes widened.

"Keep pushing Jason away and treating him the way you do, and you'll lose him." Traci went to the door. "You have a chance to get to know a shy, sensitive young man, a young man you helped create and mold into the person he is. Blow it and you only have yourself to blame."

Opening the door, she closed it quietly behind her, feeling drained until she saw Jason's hopeful face. It was like looking into a mirror. She'd worn the same look until she'd wised up. Her mother would never love her. She'd survived. If not for her grandfather, she might not have.

Everyone needed someone who believed in them, loved them. She'd finally realized that. "Jason, if Maureen can spare you tomorrow, I'll pick you up and you can meet Clint Herd. You play your cards right, and he might even let you sketch him."

His eyes rounded like saucers. "Really? You aren't kidding me?"

"I never kid. Now, let's get you home." She started from the store. Grinning, he ran to keep up with her. She grinned back.

Cagney and Lacey ride again," Ryan teased.

Traci swatted at him and missed as she finished setting the table for dinner in her kitchen that night. "We simply did what we had to do. I just hope his mother wakes up before it's too late."

"Her loss. But he's got Cagney and Lacey on his side."

She lifted a delicate brow. "Keep that up, and you won't get any supper."

He kissed her on the neck. "I'll just nibble on you."

She sighed with pleasure, and leaned her head over to allow him to continue. "You have a wicked mouth."

"Glad you approve." He dropped another kiss on her bare shoulder. "I like this top." He hooked his finger in the scooped neck and began pulling it down, his warm lips following.

"No." She scooted away, licked her lips. Drawing a calming breath, she went to the stove for the pork loin. "Because of you, I missed breakfast. Because of helping Jason, I missed lunch. I am not missing dinner. I'm starving."

"I'm starving for you, but I'll refrain." He grinned at her. "I don't want you wasting away."

Traci stopped dead still. She hadn't thought about her weight since the night he'd brought flowers. "That's not about to happen."

He frowned. "Traci?"

She placed the dish on the waiting rack on the table. "I'll get the salad."

His hand on her arm stopped her. "We don't sidestep around it."

Her chin jutted. She swallowed the lump in her throat. "You knew I wasn't an Iman clone when we started dating."

"That's right, I did."

The lump in her throat became bigger, but she refused to drop her gaze. "It would take more than a few meals to have me wasting away."

He stared at her hard, then grabbed her hand and started from the kitchen. "I need to show you something."

She tried to pull her hand free, but it didn't do any good. In the powder room off the kitchen, he positioned her in front of the mirror and stepped behind her. She glanced away.

"Look at yourself."

Inside, she was shattering. "I've seen it."

"No, you haven't, so I'll tell you what I see. You have a lush figure that I can't get enough of, hips that get me hot. Breasts that are full and tempting."

Her head came up. Their gaze locked in the mirror.

"Then there's what I can't see." He touched the side of her head with one finger. "The intelligence, the loving, caring nature, the determination to succeed, the insecurity that you try to hide from everyone, but I see it and it makes me care for you more." His hands anchored her waist. "You're beautiful, desirable. I don't ever want to hear you say differently."

She finally got the lump out of her throat. "You're awfully bossy tonight."

"You haven't seen anything yet." Grabbing her hand, he started back to the kitchen. "Wait until we're both naked in bed."

She smiled. She couldn't wait.

Simon didn't like what he'd just been told.

Disconnecting his cell, he went back to the table for two at the quaint little restaurant where he'd taken Maureen for dinner. He'd asked to be notified on the outcome of the police questioning of Miguel.

"Is everything all right?" she asked when he took his seat.

"Depends on how you look at it," he said, then explained. "Miguel's probation was revoked. His were the only set of identifiable prints on the paper. He'll be eighteen by the time his trial starts. He's looking at some serious jail time."

"You'd hoped to save him," Maureen said quietly.

"Yeah. Unfortunately, prison sometimes makes the criminal worse. It certainly won't be easy for him to find a job once he gets out."

"You gave him a chance. He didn't take it." She put her hand on his closed fist. "In life, sometimes we only get one chance."

He kissed her hand. "I'm glad I was presented with two chances to get to know you, but I wished it had been under different circumstances."

"I suppose," she mused and picked up her fork. "But I wonder if I would have kept saying no if I hadn't gotten to see you around people. You have a way that puts them at ease."

"Thank you, but I had an extra incentive." He bit into his red snapper. "I wanted you to feel comfortable enough to go out with me."

"It worked. I guess Patrick and Brianna are getting excited about the wedding this weekend."

Simon chuckled. "They're trying to combine two households and two closets. It's a good thing Patrick doesn't like clothes as well as Rafael."

"Your youngest brother?"

"Yes. He has the pretty boy looks that keep him in hot water trying to juggle the ladies." Simon polished off his fish. "He definitely believes in quantity instead of quality."

"Sounds like the way Ryan used to be before he met Traci."

"The right person will do that to you. Others simply don't exist anymore."

"I know," she said softly.

Simon's body hardened before he took his next breath. Maureen got to him in the best possible way. "What do you say we get out of here?"

"I'd say lead the way."

Traci was sated with good food and good loving, and she had a confession to make.

"Ryan," she said from her position of lying atop him. She didn't think she'd ever get used to being with him this way. He didn't turn purple, his eyes weren't bulging because of her weight. In fact, he looked as contented as she felt.

"Yes?" He threaded his fingers through her hair, which was probably a mess, but he was looking at her as if she were beautiful. She could get used to this, this connection that went beyond the incredible sex.

"I have a confession to make." She traced an imaginary heart on his chest.

He cocked a brow. "What else did you and Mother do?"

Tucking her head, she drew their initials inside the heart before she answered. "It's about me."

Long, elegant fingers moved her chin until he could look her in the eyes. "I'm listening."

That was another thing she liked about Ryan, his patience. Well, in some things at least. "You might have been able to look beyond the surface to the person beneath, but it was your body that caught my attention." She tucked her head again. "I guess I'm shallow."

He hugged her, then rolled until they were facing each other. "Glad it did, but I think you're selling yourself short again. You're around a lot of men better built, better looking, and with more money than I have, yet you didn't go out with any of them."

"A lot of them were married or had egos the size of Texas."

"That still leaves a fair number. And I'll bet they asked."

They had, and she had turned all of them down flat. "Men and dating weren't high on my list."

"Because of your first marriage?" he asked gently.

"I wasn't happy," she confessed. "We both married each other for the wrong reasons. I wanted someone to show off and he wanted a business partner who knew law and had marketing skills. I'd worked for a PR firm before I went to law school. See, I'm shallow."

"I've dated women in the past because they looked good

or were of the same social class or came from the 'right' family," he told her. "We both grew."

He accepted so easily, understood her fears. "Maybe, but I still think you have a hot bod."

"So is yours." Rolling on top of her, he braced his hands beside her shoulders and began trailing kisses over her face, down her neck to her breast. He took the pebbled point into his mouth and suckled. She felt the pull in the core of her body. Restlessly, she twisted beneath him. He answered, joined them with one thrust. Her legs wrapped around his, pulling him deeper into her heat.

Pleasure rolled through her as he stroked her, loved her. They went over together. Sighing, her arms still around him, she drifted to sleep.

His head propped on the palm of his hand, Ryan watched Traci sleep.

Her face was soft. A smile teased her kissable mouth. He wished she could see herself through his eyes. He adored her. The attraction to her had surprised him. But there was an indefinable something about her that tugged at his heart. Perhaps it was the vulnerability she hid behind a tough façade or the loneliness he'd glimpsed in her eyes. Or that she didn't cater to him.

He smiled to himself. More likely than not, she'd chew his butt out on general principle. She let very few people get past the wall she'd put up. Her husband had hurt her deeply, but Ryan had a feeling it had started before that. One day, he hoped she trusted him enough to tell him why she was so skeptical of love and people.

One thing he hoped he had heard the last of was her

thinking he saw her as any way except desirable and beautiful. She was everything he wanted in a woman, and he planned to prove it to her every chance he got.

Reaching over, he turned off the lamp on the nightstand, pulled Traci into his arms, and followed her into slumber.

Traci couldn't believe she had an invitation to the wedding.

"I know this is gauche, but I wanted to ask you in person. Please say you'll come."

Traci stared at Brianna, who had talked her way into seeing her without an appointment, and her fiancé, the handsome man beside her. He, more than Brianna, had gained them entry. Her secretary was a sucker for handsome, well-built men.

"Dr. Gilmore already has his invitation, and we wanted to make sure you knew you were expected and welcomed," Brianna said. "Maureen is coming with Simon."

Traci received few invitations that weren't business related. "You want me to go because of Ryan?"

"Because, despite how dreadful I was to you, you asked Dr. Gilmore to reconsider and be my doctor." Brianna smiled. "I'd like to know the other Traci."

"There's only one." She prided herself on being known as hard-nosed.

"I don't think so," Brianna said thoughtfully. "And I mean this in the nicest way this time, but if you were as heartless as I thought, Dr. Gilmore wouldn't be dating you."

Ryan made her want to be better, for herself, for him. "I accept, and I thank you."

"Thank you." Patrick handed her the invitation. "We'll be looking for you."

Traci came around her desk. "You'll be too busy looking at each other to notice anyone else."

He gazed down at Brianna as she gazed up at him. "There is a distinct possibility you're right. I can't wait for Brianna to be my wife."

"I feel the same," Brianna said. "Coming back to Charleston was one of the best decisions I've ever made."

"The first obviously was saying 'yes' to Patrick's proposal," Traci said, wondering if Brianna realized her slip. She was further along in her pregnancy than the time she had been back in Charleston and met Patrick.

"You have that right." Brianna faced Traci. "Good-bye, and thanks again. By the way, you're receiving a little thank-you today."

"Good-bye." Patrick pulled Brianna into his arms and they left.

Traci stared at the door. There was the distinct possibility that the baby Brianna was carrying wasn't Patrick's, but no one had to tell Traci that Patrick would fight anyone who said differently. He loved the woman, he'd love the baby.

Perhaps everlasting love was possible. Perhaps she'd been wrong. She certainly hoped so because, despite her best intentions, she was falling in love with Ryan.

This was not supposed to be happening.

Sitting between Ryan and Maureen in the beautifully decorated church, listening to Brianna and Patrick exchange their vows, Traci wondered what it would feel like to be loved by a good man. Perhaps, if she didn't feel the heat and hardness of Ryan's body pressed against hers from shoulder to thigh, feel the strength of his hand as he held hers, her mind wouldn't have contemplated such an idiotic thought.

Men cheated.

She knew that as well as she knew her own name. Yet, there was Patrick in a tuxedo, promising to love and honor a woman who carried another man's child—if Traci's theory was correct. His love and devotion to Brianna were obvious. He didn't appear to be the straying type. Brianna wouldn't put up with a phony.

Simon handed Patrick the ring and Traci looked at Maureen out of the corner of her eye. Her friend's face softened with tenderness. Maureen might have told herself that sexual attraction brought her and Simon together, but Traci knew more than that kept them together. She'd been out with Maureen on a number of occasions. Men tried to hit on her all the time. She had never paid any of them any attention until Simon.

Maureen might be in just as much trouble as Traci found herself. The question remained: What, if anything, did they plan to do about it?

"You may kiss the bride."

Traci looked at Ryan instead of the newly married couple. Heat zipped through her. His gaze was trained on her with affection and desire. Emotions tugged at her. What would it feel like to let herself go, to stop guarding her heart?

His smile filled with warmth. Bringing her hand to his mouth, he kissed her before God and anyone who cared to look. He wasn't ashamed to let the world know they were together. He could have his pick of women, yet he was with her. She could worry about the day he would move on or just enjoy.

"Ladies and gentlemen, may I present Mr. and Mrs. Patrick Dunlap."

Smiling broadly, the newlyweds raced back down the isle. Applauding, the audience came to their feet. The radiant happiness of the bride and the groom made Traci say a little prayer that they were one of the lucky couples. As Ryan slipped his arm around her waist, Traci couldn't help saying a little prayer for herself.

For the first time in her life, Maureen was unsure of herself in a social situation.

Simon might not be concerned with her age, but she couldn't believe his family would feel the same way. Walking to her car with Ryan and Traci, Maureen tried not to worry, but she couldn't help herself.

She'd tried on clothes for the past week, trying to decide what to wear. She didn't want to look as if she'd tried too hard to be young—or matronly either. She'd finally settled on an ice-blue suit with a long skirt and a small hat with a touch of lace. The hat was a bit of vanity. A persistent line on her forehead stubbornly refused to yield to any of the antiaging, antiwrinkle creams she'd invested in.

"Maureen."

Her heart skipped a beat. *Simon.* Stopping, her grip on her small purse tightening, she turned to see him racing toward her. In a tux, he moved with a fluid grace and looked gorgeous. Several women obviously thought the same thing as they openly watched his progress. They probably thought she was an aunt or something.

"Hi, Ryan. Traci." He took Maureen's hand. "You can ride to the reception with us."

The shock of him taking her hand in front of Ryan was overshadowed by one word. "Us?"

"My oldest brother and his wife have a car," Simon explained. "They want to meet you."

Panic assailed Maureen. What if they thought she was too old? The entire ride to the downtown hotel where the reception was being held would be awkward for everyone. "We're almost to the car. I'll meet you there."

The smile slid from his face. "I thought you'd enjoy going with us."

Maureen hated seeing the disappointment in his face, but better that than embarrassment. "I'll see you there."

"Yo, Simon. Big bro said for you to grab your lady, and let's ride."

Maureen peeked around Simon's broad shoulder to see a walking angel. Wavy black hair framed an angelically beautiful face, which was in direct contrast to the wicked smile he wore.

"Hello." He extended his manicured hand. "You must be Maureen. I'm Rafael Dunlap."

"Hello." She automatically extended hers, but Simon caught it. She frowned up at him.

"Rafael should have been born a couple of centuries ago. He's a throwback," Simon said. "He thinks it's cool to kiss a woman's hand."

"I happen to admire and adore women." He smiled at Traci. "I'm Rafael."

"Traci Evans," was all Traci got out before Ryan pulled her back to his side.

"She's taken."

"Pity. Every beautiful woman here seems to be," he said with real regret.

"You have enough women after you," Simon told him without heat.

"I don't think that's possible. Big brother is waiting. See you ladies later when you aren't being guarded so closely." Whistling, he strode back up the street.

"If he wasn't such a good kid at heart, I could really dislike him." Simon turned to Maureen. "I'd really want you to go with us. I've told them a lot about you."

"Go on, Maureen. We'll meet you there," Traci urged.

Maureen considered refusing, then realized there was no way she could delay the inevitable. What difference did it make if they met her now or fifteen minutes from now? She might as well get it over with. "All right."

"Great." Simon curved his arm around his waist, his other hand tugging at his tie. "I'll be glad when I can take this thing off. All of the groomsmen have orders from Patrick, who has strict orders from Brianna, that the ties stay until after the first dance. Here we are."

Maureen's mouth gaped. A driver stood by the back door of a black stretch limousine. She thought "car" meant his brother's personal car.

"I got it, thanks," Simon told the driver and opened the back door.

She was trapped. Swallowing her mounting fear, she climbed inside. Several other people were already there. All of them had their eyes trained on her.

Rafael patted the seat beside him. "Sit here so I can tell you stories about Simon that might change your way of thinking about him."

"Ha, ha." Simon closed the door and sat next to the door, putting Maureen between himself and Rafael. "Maureen, I'd like for you to meet my family. John and his wife, Helen.

My younger brother, Alec." Simon grinned. "You already met the baby of the family, Rafael."

Rafael's eyes narrowed. "I'll get you for that."

"Behave, both of you, or you'll have Maureen think Mama didn't raise us right," John said.

Despite her nervousness, a smile tugged at Maureen's mouth. "I can tell you're a close family."

"That's good to know." His oldest brother looked at his petite wife beside him. "Mama might be gone, but Helen will have our heads if we act up."

"They forget that people aren't as fortunate as they are. It's nice meeting you," Helen said. "We've heard a lot about you."

Had he mentioned how much older I am? "He's talked about all of you as well," Maureen said, gauging that Simon's oldest brother and his wife were probably around her age. *This couldn't get any worse.*

"Simon is usually the quiet one," Alec said. He was as handsome as the other brothers, with dark, piercing eyes and a sensual mouth. "After meeting you, I can see why."

Maureen didn't know what to say. Was he kidding with her?

Simon curved his arm around her. "He's almost as bad as Rafael. You can save your breath, Alec."

Alec winked at her. "You can't blame a guy for trying."

"Yes, I can." Simon scooted over and pulled Maureen closer. "That goes for you, too, Rafael."

John smiled. "Forgive my brothers' poor manners. They haven't gotten over the days they used to fight over toys and whose turn it was to drive the car. I didn't let them meet Helen until we were engaged."

"Sneaky," Alec said and smiled at Helen. "But smart."

"All the Dunlap men have good taste," Rafael said just as the car pulled to the curb and stopped. "Even slow Simon. Maureen, save a dance for me."

"Not a chance." Opening the door, Simon helped Maureen out. "She's strictly with me."

Maureen couldn't find her voice until they were several feet away. "My age didn't bother them."

"They're looking at what matters. Your heart," he said. "I have to sit with the wedding party, but as soon as I can, I'm coming for you."

"I'll be waiting," she promised, her fears fading away. Simon was right. What was in their hearts mattered and she was desperately in love with him.

Traci hummed along with the radio on the way home from work Monday afternoon. She was happier than she could ever remember. Elisa remained at large, but Traci seldom thought of the other woman. She owed it all to Ryan. He made each day so much better.

And you love him.

"No," Traci said aloud as if that would make it so. They were great, make that incredible, in bed together. They had just as much fun going out or staying in. As long as they were together, it didn't matter to either of them where they were or what they did. They could differ on subjects, but they still respected the other's point of view. Just seeing him made her heart race.

Stopping at a signal light, Traci closed her eyes and banged her head against the headrest. What had she done? Falling in love was dangerous. One person always loved more than the other. She made her living by that irrefutable fact.

Opening her eyes, she blew out a frustrated breath and continued through the green light. At least, if she had to be foolish and fall in love, it was with a man she admired. But it would be suicidal to let him know.

She saw the black Titan when she turned onto her street. Panic hit her. She gunned the car. From two houses down, she saw him, head bowed, sitting on the front porch. She parked behind the truck in a screech of brakes and raced to him.

"Granddaddy, are you all right?"

Ezekiel Hightower lifted his gray head when she turned into the driveway. By the time she was out of the car he was halfway to her. He carried his seventy-five years well. His shoulders were as straight and proud as they'd been thirty-three years ago when Traci's mother dropped her off for a "visit" and never picked her up.

"Better now that I'm seeing you, Scamp." His arms went around her, holding her close.

"It's Mother, isn't it?" Traci asked.

He set her away from him and stared down into her face, his own troubled. "I can't understand why she can't ever be satisfied."

"Let me get my key out of the car. We'll talk in the house." Traci quickly retrieved her purse and attaché case. "Why didn't you call the office on your cell?"

From the shady part of the porch he picked up a bushel basket filled with vegetables. "I forgot how to turn it on. I figured you'd be home sooner or later."

Her grandfather had to be the most patient man in the world. He had to be to stay married to her shrewish grandmother. Then he'd had a mean-spirited daughter like her mother. "How long have you been here?" she asked once they were inside.

"Doesn't matter." He glanced around the foyer. "This house seems bigger every time I come."

Traci admitted to herself that she'd purchased the house to make a statement that she'd made it. It had been lonely at times, until she'd befriended Maureen, the Invincibles, and then Ryan. "It takes a bit of getting used to."

"I'll bet." He followed her down the hall. "You could fit four of my houses in here with room to spare."

"Probably, but the size didn't matter to me." She placed her things on the island and turned to him. "What mattered was the love you always gave me."

He nodded. "That went both ways. You make me proud."

He'd always said that to her. His belief had sustained her. "Now, stop stalling and tell me how long you've been waiting."

He placed the basket on the counter by the stainless double sink. "I guess since around noon."

"What! Granddaddy, the high today was eighty degrees!"

"I worked in the fields without food or water when it was a hundred degrees," he reminded her.

Her grandmother "forgot" to bring his food and once he'd started plowing he hadn't liked to stop. He had been much younger then, and fussing wouldn't do any good. "Before you leave, you're going to know how to use the cell phone." She washed her hands at the sink, then went to the refrigerator. "Dinner should be ready shortly, and you can eat."

"Smells good." He peeked into the Crock-Pot. "Pot roast. We can make a salad with the cucumber, lettuce, and tomatoes I brought."

Traci handed him a glass of water and their favorite soft drink. "Drink the water first, then you can tell me what Mother is up to now." Traci waited until he had drunk half a glass of water before she began emptying the basket of vegetables into the sink.

"I wish I didn't have to tell you this." He set both glasses on the counter and stared straight ahead. "I considered just driving, seeing the country like I always wanted." He looked down at Traci. "But I didn't want you to worry. I figured, together, we're a good match against Vera."

Panic hit her. The four-hour drive from Macon was bad enough. To think of him driving aimlessly tore at her heart and heated her simmering anger. "Granddaddy, what is it?"

He blew out a breath. "She wants me declared incompetent so she can sell the property that has been in our family for four generations."

Traci kept it together because she knew how much it hurt him to say that. He'd worked all his life in all kinds of weather, just as his father and his father before him had to make sure their families had what they needed. He took pride that his family owned twenty-seven acres, that he could leave a legacy.

"She's reached a new low," Traci spat, no longer able to contain her anger. "She can't get away with that."

"I'd like to think that shyster husband of hers put her up to it since all of his get-rich schemes have ended with them sinking further and further into debt, but she didn't have to listen."

"Her husband can talk her into anything." Including abandoning her young daughter. Traci picked up a cucumber to slice, taking her anger out on it. "How bad is it?"

"Pretty bad," her grandfather told her. "They're in danger of losing their house. I hear they're hiding their car at night to keep it from being repossessed. I'm their ticket. They both know you won't give them a cent."

Traci's hand tightened on the knife handle. "I can't believe she had the gall to ask me for money after she happened to see Dante's obit . . . when she'd ignored me all my life."

Ezekiel placed a calloused hand on her shoulder. "Her loss."

Her hand relaxed. "My good fortune. I got you."

"We got each other."

The doorbell rang. "Expecting company?" he asked.

She blushed. "Yes. I'll be back in a minute."

Her grandfather followed her to the kitchen door. "Would he be the reason you sound different, happier lately?"

Stopping, she looked back at him, a frown marring her forehead. "How do you know it's a man?"

"I know. Now go answer the door," he said as the door chimed again. "He sounds anxious."

Recalling why she never played cards with him, she went to the door. "Hi, Ryan."

He stepped inside the foyer, his sharp gaze roaming over her and then beyond. "Are you all right?"

"Yes. My grandfather is visiting. I won't be able to go to the movies," she said.

"We'll go another day." His hand brushed down the side of her face, sending delicious shivers through her. "Am I still invited to dinner?"

Traci bit her lip. "He figured out you're the reason I sound different, happier. He never liked Dante," she confessed, finding it easier and easier to talk to Ryan about her marriage.

"Shows he's smart." Ryan took her elbow and started for the kitchen. "I promise not to throw you on the floor in front of him."

She playfully swatted him on the shoulder. Both were

laughing when they entered the kitchen. Traci's laughter died as her grandfather's frank gaze sized Ryan up. "Ryan, this is my grandfather, Ezekiel Hightower. Granddaddy, Ryan Gilmore. You've met his mother, Maureen Gilmore."

"Good evening, Mr. Hightower." Ryan extended his hand.

"Evening." The handshake was firm. "I like your mother."

Ryan's mouth twitched. "I'll do everything in my power to ensure that you like her son as well."

"I'll set the table," Traci said. "Granddaddy has been outside waiting for me since noon."

All playfulness left Ryan. "Do you feel all right, sir?"

"I'm fine. Traci, if you were going someplace, I can take care of myself." He took the plate in her hand from her.

"Nothing that can't be changed. We planned to eat before we left in any case." Taking the plate back, she put it on the table with the others.

Ryan opened a drawer and took out the flatware. "I hope you don't mind that I didn't leave. Traci's a great cook."

"Looks like you've been here a time or two," her grandfather said, continuing to watch Ryan closely.

Ryan met the searching gaze head on. "Yes, sir. I'm proud to say I have. Traci is a cautious woman. Took me months to get her to go out with me."

"A woman can't be too careful these days," he said.

"I agree." Ryan finished the last place setting.

"Granddaddy, please sit down." Traci placed his unfinished soft drink on the table.

Ezekiel took the middle seat, separating Traci and Ryan at the round table for four. "What do you do for a living?" He reached for his soft drink.

Traci rolled her eyes and set the salad on the table. Her

grandfather didn't plan for her to be snowed by the wrong man again. "Oh, Granddaddy."

"I'm a doctor. OB-GYN." Ryan held out Traci's chair for her, then took his seat across from her.

Traci bowed her head and said grace. "Ryan also volunteers at a clinic for unwed teenage mothers."

"Is that so?" her grandfather said, with obvious interest.

Ryan picked up his fork. "Traci is helping the clinic put on a fund-raiser to purchase supplies and possibly give scholarships to patients who want to go to college or learn a trade. It's important that they can take care of themselves and their babies."

"In my day, if that would have happened, a man would have been looking down the business end of a shotgun." Ezekiel picked up his fork, his gaze locked on Ryan.

"Sometimes things change, and not for the better." Ryan forked in a bite of pot roast. "Traci tells me you have a farm outside Macon."

"I don't farm much except for my vegetable garden." He plucked a roll from the bread basket. "Brought some with me. Nothing tastes better than homegrown vegetables."

"I agree." Ryan put a generous amount of salad on his plate. "My mother's parents always had a garden. I'd eat tomatoes right off the vine. I didn't care that the juice ran down my chin."

"Done that myself," Granddaddy Hightower mused. "Traci and me have cracked a few watermelons and ate them right then and there."

"I remember," Traci said, biting into her salad. "This takes me back."

"I'll say." Ryan forked in another bite. "Mr. Hightower,

I'm doubly glad you didn't object to me staying for dinner. I agree, nothing tastes as good as fresh garden vegetables."

"There's black-eyed peas, okra, and snap beans," Ezekiel said.

Traci smiled at her grandfather, thanking him without words. He was willing to get to know Ryan better. Five minutes after meeting Dante, her grandfather had taken her aside and begged her to call off her wedding. To her lasting regret, she hadn't listened.

Ryan looked at Traci. "I hope you'll invite me over."

"There's a definite possibility," she teased.

"Ryan, do you play checkers?" Ezekiel asked.

It wasn't lost on Traci or from the pleased look on Ryan's face that her grandfather had called him by his name for the first time. "Not since I was a kid," Ryan answered.

"After dinner, why don't we see how much you remember," he said. "Traci is the worst player in the world."

"Gee, thanks, Granddaddy," she said.

"Ain't no harm in not being good at everything," he said. "You're good at what counts, and I couldn't ask for a better granddaughter."

Traci blinked. "All because of you."

"Well." Ezekiel cleared his throat and came to his feet. "If you'll give me your key, I'll put your car and my truck in the garage and grab my suitcase."

"I'll get it." Traci stood. "We can have dessert when you get back."

"You need any help, Mr. Hightower?" Ryan came to his feet as well.

"No, but Traci might with the dishes," he said, taking the key Traci gave him.

Her lips twitched. "Still hate washing dishes, I see."

"Yep." He left the room.

Ryan caught Traci by the waist, bringing her flush against him. "I think he's warming to me."

"You think?" Smiling, she placed her hands on his wide chest, felt the muscled hardness.

"Yes, and I think something else. I'd better get my kiss before he comes back."

"You read my mind." Lifting herself on her tiptoes, she pressed her mouth against his.

Ryan hadn't won a single game.

He would be disgusted with his poor showing if Traci's grandfather wasn't enjoying trouncing him so much. One game had lasted less than a minute.

"No matter how long you look at the board, Ryan, I still got you," Ezekiel said with relish.

"Granddaddy, it's not polite to gloat," Traci admonished from her position on the arm of her grandfather's easy chair in the great room.

"I'm just stating facts," Ezekiel said with all the innocence of a baby.

Ryan wasn't fooled and, from the indulgent expression on Traci's face, neither was she. "I'm thinking."

Folding his arms, Ezekiel leaned back in his chair. "Putting off the inevitable just makes it worse." He picked up his dessert plate. "I'll just go get another slice of pound cake. Winning gives a man an appetite. Anyone else want any?"

"No, thanks," Ryan mumbled, looking at his single black checker surrounded by four crowned checkers of Ezekiel's.

"No, thank you," Traci said.

"More for me." Chuckling, he strolled off.

"You might have warned me he was such a great player," Ryan said.

"I might have, but I wanted you two to get to know each other better." Traci went to him and hunkered down. Her fingers walked up his thigh. "I'll make it up to you tomorrow night."

Ryan's body stirred. He was grateful his lower half was hidden by the game table. "I'll hold you to that."

"You do that." Standing, she moved back to her perch on the arm of the other chair.

Ryan eyed her rounded buttocks, her shapely legs, and tried not to recall his hands on her hips, her legs locked around his waist. He lost before his next breath. He twisted in his seat. *Down, boy.*

"You move yet?" Ezekiel asked as soon as he entered the great room.

"About to." Ryan reached for his single checker just as the doorbell rang. He tensed, his troubled gaze going to Traci. Without words, he knew they both were thinking of Elisa.

"More company?" Ezekiel asked.

"Maureen might have seen Ryan's car." Traci came to her feet.

Ryan stood. He doubted it was his mother. She would have called first. "I'll go with you then."

"You're just putting it off." Easing down in the chair, Ezekiel forked in another bite of cream cheese pound cake.

In the foyer, Ryan caught Traci's arm. "Look first."

"I'd planned to." She put her eyes to the peephole.

"Good." Glad she remained cautious, Ryan stood by her side. "Well?"

"It's not Elisa." Her hands clenched.

Confused, he turned her to him. "What is it?"

The doorbell sounded again. For a brief moment, panic flared in her eyes. "Just trust me. All right?"

"All right."

She opened the door. Two uniformed policemen stood on the porch. "Yes?"

The officer's gaze went to Ryan and beyond before coming back to Traci. "Are you Traci Evans?"

"I am." She ran a hand through her hair and blew out a disgusted breath. "Which one of my clients is in trouble this time?"

"We're looking for your grandfather, Ezekiel Hightower," the other officer said.

"Granddaddy?" Shock raced across her face. Her hand went to her neck. "Why? Has something happened to him?"

"No, ma'am." The first officer who had spoken told her. "His daughter filed a missing person's report. He has dementia and hasn't been seen since yesterday. We were asked by the Macon police to check here."

Apparently used to estranged families, the police didn't appear to think it strange that his daughter hadn't called to check herself. Ryan might, but he'd keep it to himself.

"I haven't seen him. I've been home since around six." She turned to Ryan and briefly introduced him. "Have you checked with his friends?"

"That's the first thing the Macon authorities did. He didn't have many," the officer said. "His daughter thought he might try to come here."

"As Traci said, we haven't seen him," Ryan said, draping his arm around Traci's shoulder. "If you hear anything, please let us know."

"We will. Good night."

"Good night." Traci closed the door, her eyes and face troubled. "Thanks. You must have questions."

"One." He pulled her to him. "Do you ever think your grandfather will let me win?"

Throwing her arms around him, she kissed him. "You make me believe."

"About time." Catching her hand, Ryan headed for the great room.

Ezekiel, his expression hard, met them at the entrance. "I'm sorry I got you into this mess."

Traci went to him. "If I was in trouble and needed help, would you turn me away?"

"No," he said.

"Neither could I." She faced Ryan. "Sit down and put yourself out of your misery and I might cook a soul food dinner for you tomorrow night complete with a pineapple cake so good you'd slap your grandmother."

Ryan took his seat, wondering what else her grandfather had seen and heard.

Her head on his chest, Maureen snuggled closer to Simon's naked body and sighed with bliss.

"You sleepy?" he asked.

She angled her head up so she could see his face in the dim light of the bedroom. "You couldn't be thinking what I think you're thinking."

He dropped a kiss on her forehead. "You make me insatiable at times, but three times in an hour might just do me in."

"But what a way to go," she said, surprising herself, but holding his gaze. Simon made her feel sexy, decadent even.

He was her dream lover come to life. He fulfilled every fantasy she'd ever had.

His broad, calloused hand swept up and down the gentle slope of her back. "Glad you think so because I agree."

"Good." She placed her head back on his chest and closed her eyes.

"Maureen."

"Yes," she said around a yawn.

"I need to talk to you about us."

All sleepiness vanished. He'd been quiet ever since they'd gotten home from a dinner cruise. Had he grown tired of her?

"It's important."

Her body quaking, her mind screaming at the thought of losing him, she gathered the sheet to her naked breasts and sat up. "I'm listening."

He shoved his hand through his hair. "I rehearsed this a dozen times."

She swallowed the lump in her throat. "Just say it."

"I—" He rolled out of bed and picked up his pants. "Maybe I'll be able to get it out if I'm dressed."

With supreme effort, she managed to remain quiet as he put one leg and then the other in his pants. She desperately wanted to ask him not to leave her. She'd known that their time was limited, but she hadn't known the pain would be so deep.

He came back, kneeled by the bedside, took her hand, and stared at her. Obviously, getting dressed hadn't helped. The waiting was tearing her heart out. "Just say it."

His face lifted. "I love you. Will you marry me?"

"What?" Shock raced through her.

His hand tightened on hers when she would have drawn

it away. "I know the proposal is pitiful. You're everything I've ever wanted in a woman, a wife—loving, intelligent, funny. I love you. Will you marry me?"

Never in a hundred, a thousand years would she have imagined this. She swallowed the lump in her throat, tried to ignore the ache in her heart. "You want to marry me?"

"Yes." His hand grazed over the top of her hand. "I can't imagine my life without you."

"I—" She couldn't think of what to say. Her heart and her head were at war, tugging her emotions in two different directions.

"I know you care about me," Simon said. "You wouldn't have slept with me, gone against Ryan, if you didn't. Our relationship is important to you, just as it is to me."

"Oh, Simon." She closed her eyes, fighting the stinging moisture in them.

"Is that a yes?" he asked, but his usual steady voice was shaky.

Her eyes opened. She stared at the man she had come to love, the man she could never have as her own. "I can't marry you."

His hands tightened on hers. "Is it too soon? Do you need more time?"

"No."

"I know you care," he told her.

"That's why I have to say no," she managed.

"If you're worried about your finances, I'll sign a prenup. Whatever you want. You love this house. If you want to stay here, fine, but I'll take care of the expenses."

She was already shaking her head. "It's not that."

"Then tell me what it is," he said tersely, his patience clearly strained.

She owed him that much. "You want children. I could never give them to you."

"Children don't matter. I want you."

"For now, but what about two or three years from now?" she reasoned. "I've seen your interest in the team you coach and your niece and nephew. You wouldn't be happy without children."

"Maureen, I've already considered that fact and accepted it. You can't tell your heart whom to love," he said gently. "It's you or no one. I'm asking you again. Will you marry me?"

"Don't you understand? I care too much to do that to you," she cried. "Can't we just go on as before?"

His hands uncurled from hers and he stood, staring down at her. "So all you want from me is sex?"

"No," she said, shocked, reaching for his hand. He stepped back.

"It's all or nothing."

Panic assailed her. "Simon, all I can give you is myself. Let that be enough."

"All you're willing to give, you mean." He snatched his shirt from the floor. Worked his feet into his loafers.

"Simon, please, don't go. Try to understand."

He stalked to the door. "I do. You want a stud, and I want a wife."

She gasped at the accusation. "That's not true."

"You know where to find me if you change your mind." Opening the door, he was gone.

"Simon." Curling into a tight ball, she wept.

Ryan jammed on his brakes to keep from hitting Simon's car broadside as it shot out of Maureen's driveway.

Ryan cursed long and hard at Simon's recklessness until he jerked open his door and saw his face, his unbuttoned shirt. Ryan's hand scrubbed over his face. He'd rather eat worms than discuss a lover's spat when one of the people was his mother. But he happened to like Simon. He made his mother happy. Or had until tonight.

"Is Mother all right?"

"She's fine." Simon stared straight ahead, his hands clamped on the steering wheel.

And sheeps flew. His hand on the frame of the car, Ryan asked, "Why don't you park your car and I'll drive you home?"

"I'm fine."

"Simon, I—"

"I asked her to marry me, and she turned me down," he interrupted.

"What!"

"I thought—" Simon stopped abruptly, his hands flexing. "Do you mind?"

Ryan did, but he didn't think he'd get any more out of Simon. "You all right to drive home?"

"I'm getting there." He put the car into gear.

Ryan closed the door and stepped back just in time as Simon pulled away at the posted speed limit. Ryan looked at his mother's darkened house. Considering the way Simon was dressed, Ryan had no intention of using his key to check on her. Moving his car out from the middle of the street, he got out and called his mother on his cell phone.

"Simon," she said.

"No, Mother, it's me," Ryan said, hearing the hope and tears in her voice. "Are you all right?"

"Yes."

She wasn't. She'd never sounded more miserable. "I talked with Simon. He told me he proposed." The muffled sound he heard tore at him. "He's pretty shook up."

"I can't talk now."

"Do you want me to come in?" he asked. "Maybe you shouldn't be alone. I could use my key."

"No," she quickly said. "I'm fine. Good night."

Ryan heard the dial tone and blew out a pent-up breath. She'd hung up on him. His mother was the worst liar in the world. He dialed another number.

"Couldn't wait to get home to talk to me?" Traci said, a smile in her voice.

"Simon asked Maureen to marry her. She turned him down, and they're both in bad shape."

"Where are you?"

"In front of Mother's house."

"I'm on my way."

Ryan clipped the cell phone back on his belt. He'd gone only a few steps before he saw Traci running across the adjoining yards. Before he knew it, he was racing to her. He caught her in his arms.

"She's hurting, and I can't do a damn thing about it," he said.

Traci held him as tightly as he was holding her. "Not now, but tomorrow and the day after, until she stops thinking about her age and goes with her heart."

He held her out in front of him. "What are you saying?"

"She loves him, Ryan."

"Did she say anything to you?" he asked, not sure how he felt about it.

"She didn't have to." Traci looked toward Maureen's

house. "You could just look at her when they were together or when she talked about him."

Ryan considered what she'd said, and wondered if she'd figured out he loved her. "I didn't notice anything different."

He couldn't see her eyes clearly, but imagined her rolling them. "You're excused because you're a man."

He didn't know how to take that either, so he moved on to what was paramount. "How can we help her?"

"Thanks for including me," she said.

"It never crossed my mind to do differently," he said truthfully. "You're the first person I thought of."

Pleasure spread across her face. "We certainly won't let her mope the way she did the last time."

"You're calling the Invincible Sisterhood," he guessed.

"And then I'm playing dirty by inviting myself and Granddaddy over for breakfast since my stove is on the blink," she mused. "Maureen is too good of a friend, too much of a lady, and too Southern to let us go out or tell me to go to McDonald's. I'll casually mention that I wanted to invite the Invincibles over for dinner to meet Granddaddy."

"She'll offer her house."

"You're catching on." She smiled, then she looked at Maureen's house and her smile faded. "I was hoping she would be one of the lucky ones."

"Lucky ones?"

"The ones who find love." She shook her head. "Falling in love is like walking in a minefield. You never know when you're going to make a misstep and the whole thing blows up in your face."

"Not always." Ryan swept his hand up and down her

arm. "My parents were happy, and so are a lot of other couples I know."

"Like I said, the lucky ones. But, for others, that big blast is waiting. I'd better get back to the house. I told Granddaddy I was needed next door."

"You certainly were." Putting his hands on her arms, he stared down at her face. "Thank you for being Mother's friend."

"It's one of the best decisions I ever made." She looped her arms around his neck. "Dating you was another."

He lowered his mouth to her waiting lips. The kiss was sweet and gentle. "Think of me tonight."

"I will and don't worry about Maureen." She started toward the house.

Ryan watched her, smiling as she turned back around to blow him a kiss. He waved, a grin on his face.

Out of the corner of his eye, he caught a movement in the hedges at the corner of Traci's lawn. She'd have to pass that exact spot to get to her front door. Uneasiness moved through him. He took off running. "Traci, look out!"

She stopped, glancing around.

He heard car doors slamming, but none of them could reach her in time. "Run, Traci. Damn it, run!"

"He's mine! Ryan is mine!" screamed Elisa, leaping out of the bushes. Her hands crooked like claws, she went for Traci's face.

He'd never forget what happened next. Traci stood her ground and cold-cocked Elisa. She crumpled like a marionette whose strings had been cut.

"Are you all right?" he asked, still in awe of what had happened.

Traci rubbed her knuckles. "Better than her."

The security Dr. Thomas had hired joined them. "She's out cold," Bledsoe said.

"No thanks to you. Where were you?" Ryan asked. "She could have seriously hurt Traci if she hadn't been able to defend herself."

"We've been here since Ms. Evans returned home," Bledsoe explained. "Elisa must have used the shadows of the houses and the shrubbery to conceal her movements. She was very determined."

"She needs help. She lives in hell daily, and sees it as reality," Traci said.

Ryan gazed down at the unconscious Elisa, who was dressed in a black long-sleeved top and pants. Bits of leaves clung to her clothing and her hair. If she had hurt Traci, he might have felt differently. "She's going to get it."

He pulled out his cell and called her father. "Dr. Thomas. Elisa just tried to attack Traci. The security team will be at your house with her in twenty minutes. She goes tonight to the hospital or else." He slipped the phone back on his belt. "Her father is waiting for you. Call me after she's been admitted."

"You got it." Picking up the unconscious Elisa, Bledsoe started back to the van on the other side of the street.

"Where did you learn to fight like that?" Ryan asked when the van pulled off.

"In grade school," she told him. "It was that or be picked on."

"Why would they pick on you?" he asked. When there was no answer, he prompted her. "Traci?"

"Doesn't matter now. Night." She hurried across the lawn and into the house.

Ryan let her go. He had a vague feeling that it had something to do with her mother, the woman who had wrongly accused her own father of having dementia. It bothered him that Traci didn't trust him completely. He wasn't giving up on that or on teaching her that love meant forever to him and that she was the woman he wanted forever with.

Finally giving up on trying to sleep, Simon pounded out his anger on the punching bag in the exercise room on the ground floor of the condo where he lived.

"You want to talk?"

Simon ignored Rafael standing behind him and kept punching. His youngest brother was spending a few days with Simon so that he could use Patrick's boat. A light sleeper, Rafael had awakened and, seeing Simon was in a foul mood, had followed him.

"Simon?"

If he tried to talk, he wasn't sure what would come out. He loved Maureen, wanted forever with her. Why couldn't he make her see that she was enough?

"All right. I'll talk. You and Maureen had a tiff. Most couples do. You send her flowers, grovel, and it's over."

Simon hit harder, wishing Rafael would just leave him the hell alone. Sweat beaded on his forehead, ran in rivulets down his face. For some idiotic reason, he thought of Maureen's hot flashes and the first night they'd made love. His balled fists shot out faster and faster. He wouldn't settle for sex. He wanted all of her or nothing, and the fear that it would be nothing was tearing him apart.

"So this will take more than flowers and groveling. Since Maureen had on some serious bling at the wedding, maybe jew—"

Simon swung around toward Rafael, anger pouring from

him, his fists upraised. He'd shopped for a ring for the past week, worried about how she'd feel about taking off the two-carat diamond wedding set she wore. He'd finally decided on a diamond and platinum wedding band.

"If it will make you feel better, swing away." Rafael took a step closer. "However, before you do, consider that Helen is going to be annoyed with you, and then big bro will get into it. Although a black eye is sure to elicit sympathy from my date tonight."

Simon closed his eyes and let the anger drain out of him. Rafael had the unique ability to diffuse touchy situations with humor. Was it any wonder he was a top police negotiator in Myrtle Beach?

"Maureen means a lot to you, doesn't she?"

His eyes opened. "I asked her to marry me."

Not a flicker of surprise crossed his baby brother's face. "And she didn't give you the answer you wanted?"

Simon blew out a breath. "No, she didn't."

"Any chance she'll change her mind?"

"No . . . I don't know," he admitted.

"I'm sorry," Rafael said. "What is it about this condo that makes the Dunlaps fall in love? I might have to seriously think of staying in a hotel when I visit."

"I pity the woman who gets you," Simon said.

"On that we agree, so I plan to stay single for a long, long time." Rafael draped his arm around Simon's shoulder. "Let's go get breakfast at the marina. The waitress there likes me."

"I thought you had a date tonight?" Simon asked as they started toward the elevator.

"But I don't have any plans for lunch," Rafael said.

Simon stopped and stared at his younger brother. "You can't be serious."

Rafael punched the elevator button. "I like making women happy."

Simon stepped on the elevator without responding. The woman he wanted to make happy wanted no part of him.

Maureen knew she was being set up, but she was tired of her own thoughts, tired of crying, tired of missing Simon.

"Thank you for inviting us over, Maureen." Ezekiel sipped his coffee at the table in Maureen's kitchen. "Breakfast was delicious."

"It sure was." Traci drained her glass of cranberry juice. "You sure you don't mind the Sisterhood coming over here this evening to meet Granddaddy?"

"You know I don't. You're always welcome." Maureen lifted her coffee cup. She tasted the warmth, but none of the rich flavor. She'd picked at the food on her plate. She felt as if her senses, her body, were barely functioning.

"I'm looking forward to meeting the women." Ezekiel put his cup down. "I've heard so much about them and you. I'm glad Traci has good friends like you and the other women. Especially after what happened last night."

Maureen started, feeling exposed. Traci's presence this morning meant Ryan had told her, but Maureen couldn't believe Traci had shared such personal information with her grandfather.

"We caught Elisa last night," Traci said. "She's finally going to get the help she needs."

Maureen's relief was on two fronts. "What happened?"

Traci quickly explained. "Ryan called this morning to tell me that her father had checked her into a clinic. We don't have to worry about her anymore."

"What a relief," Maureen said, thinking that, before last night, she had thought if Elisa was apprehended, she'd be completely happy. That had happened, but she'd lost Simon. She wasn't happy at all.

"Thanks again for breakfast." Traci gathered the plates and flatware, rinsed and put them in the dishwasher. "I'll come over around six. See you then."

Ezekiel stood and went to the back kitchen door where Traci waited. "It was good to meet you again. Your son takes after his mother."

"Thank you. Good-bye." Maureen wanted nothing more than to sit back down and bawl. Instead, she finished clearing the table. She had to go to work. Staying home and thinking about Simon walking out on her would only make her feel worse.

W ork didn't help. Maureen carried the painful hurt of Simon walking out on her all day. She stayed close to her office so she could hear the phone in case he called.

He never did.

"Do you feel all right, Mrs. Gilmore?" Jason asked, his young face pinched with concern. "Your eyes look sad."

He was dead on and tactful. Her eyelids were puffy, her eyes red from crying off and on since last night. "I've had better days," she answered truthfully. "How are the sketches going?"

His face split into a grin. "Great. Mr. Herd is the best. He even got some of his teammates to pose for me. Traci is drawing up a contract with their licensing agency giving me the rights to sell the sketches on eBay for my college fund. Things would be great if . . ." His voice trailed off, his smile vanished.

"If your mother understood?"

"I showed her the sketches of the players and the ones Mr. Dunlap wants to buy and all she said was 'Don't get your hopes up,'" he disclosed.

Maureen felt for the young man trying to live his dream and gain his mother's respect and love. "I think she's scared for you, Jason. She knows how it feels when dreams shatter."

He swallowed. "You mean like when my daddy walked out on us?"

"Yes. But that's not your fault." There was no way to sugarcoat that horrible fact. "The fault and the loss of knowing you is his. A lot of men would be honored to call you their son," she said.

"Simon lets me shoot balls with the team. He's cool," Jason said. "At the last practice, he gave me his phone number and said I should call if I needed to talk. He even took me out on his brother's boat with Rafael."

Maureen's lips quivered, then firmed. Simon loved children, deserved his own. "He's a wonderful man."

Jason grinned. "He thinks you're pretty neat, too."

That was before last night. The front door opened. She swung around. Rafael, not Simon, entered the shop.

"Hi, Rafael," Jason called. "Is Simon with you?"

"Hello, Jason, Maureen. Sorry. I'm alone." His gaze went to Maureen and stayed. "Can we talk someplace in private?"

She didn't want to talk, but Rafael's carefree expression was gone. In its place was a serious determination that wasn't going to be denied. "My office."

"After you."

Maureen didn't wring her hands, but she wanted to. "Jason, please keep an eye on the front. Henrietta isn't due back from her appointment for another hour."

"I won't let you down, Mrs. Gilmore," he said seriously.

"I know." Maureen went to her office, feeling Rafael's gaze stabbing her in the back. She moved behind her desk, hoping that would make her feel more in charge. It didn't.

"Why?" he snapped out. "And before you tell me it's none of my business, know that I love Simon and that gives me the right."

I love him, too, she almost blurted. Instead, she sank into her chair. "He didn't tell you."

"I wouldn't have asked if he had," he said, impatience in every line of his body.

His smoky black eyes were identical to Simon's, so was the strong chin. There the resemblance ended. Simon's features were sharp, clearly defined. Rafael's were softer, or so she had thought until he stood in front of her desk demanding answers she couldn't give.

"I'm waiting."

Impatience wasn't a trait she would have equated with Rafael, but he loved his brother. "How—how is Simon?"

"His eyes aren't red, but I figure you've both had a rough night and it's not getting any better," he told her.

Her hand lifted to her face, then fell. "I'm sorry."

Rafael placed his hands on the desk. "Your face tells me you care. Why did you turn him down?"

She bit her lower lip. "Does Simon know you're here?"

"No. If he finds out, my— Let's just say it won't be pleasant for me."

"Yet you're here."

"He's my brother," Rafael said. "He loves you and he can't have you."

Tears pooled in her eyes, slid down her cheeks. She glanced away. "Please leave."

Rafael muttered under his breath. "I'm sorry if I upset you. I just wanted to help."

"You can't. There's nothing anyone can do."

"I don't want to believe that, but I'm going." He went to the door. "Before I leave, you should know that Simon has dated a lot of women, but you're the first one he was anxious for the family to meet, the first one he wanted forever with. Good-bye."

The door closed. Maureen put her head on her desk and sobbed.

Ryan knocked on Simon's door with a much different purpose than he had the first time.

The door swung open. Rafael stared at him with a narrowed gaze. "Did you come to dump on him?"

Ryan had a question of his own, and brushed past him. "I saw you leaving Mother's store when I went to visit her. She was upset and left soon afterward. She wouldn't tell me what you said to her. I'm asking you."

Rafael's mouth tightened. "The truth. That she was the first woman he wanted forever with."

"This is hard on both of them," Ryan muttered. "Where is he?"

"On the balcony." Rafael closed the door. "It's a good thing his team doesn't have practice or a game tonight."

Ryan crossed the room and stepped outside. Simon leaned against the wall, his gaze trained in the distance. "If it helps, I'm sorry," Ryan said.

"Wish I could say it did," Simon told him without looking around.

"How about if I said she's hurting just as much."

Simon jerked his head around. Anger and pain flashed in his dark eyes. "She could end it with just one word."

"Mother doesn't do things lightly," Ryan said. "She had her reasons."

"So she said, but I don't accept them," Simon said. "I won't be—" His lips clamped together and he stared out to sea.

Ryan wasn't sure if he wanted to know what Simon had been about to say. Talking about his mother's hot flashes was uncomfortable enough. "I've thought about asking Traci to marry me, but she's not high on marriage. After what happened between you and Mother, I'm not sure I want to rock the boat."

Simon's hard gaze drilled him. "Soon what you have won't be enough. You'll want more, to be there for her, to see her smile, watch her wake up, chase her demons away. If you love her, you won't be able to stop yourself from asking her."

"It's happened already," Ryan said. "But she's not ready."

"Then you accept only part of her or go after all that she is or ever hoped to be," Simon told him quietly. "Just be prepared for the consequences."

Simon didn't have to elaborate on the consequences. Ryan saw them in the bleakness of his gaze, the same bleakness he'd seen in his mother's.

Traci had never seen Maureen look so miserable.

"Maureen, are you sure you made the right decision?" Traci asked as she placed the pan of quiche in the oven.

Sitting at the table in the kitchen with a box of tissues in front of her, Maureen dabbed at her eyes. "Positive. Simon deserves children and I can't give them to him."

Traci took the chair next to Maureen, silently recalling her own miserable childhood with a mother who barely tolerated her. Her salvation had been going to live with her grandfather. At the time, she had seen it as punishment. "Some couples can't have children. Children don't always make a marriage happy."

"How many childless couples have broken up for that very reason?" Maureen folded her arms. "It's hard enough giving him up now. I can't bear to think of him looking at me with hatred."

"Maureen, this is Simon we're talking about. The man is as solid and as steadfast as they come. And I hate to be blunt, but he knew you were through with baby-making the first time you went out," Traci said frankly.

"He thinks he's reconciled, but when Patrick and Brianna's baby arrives, he'll see I was right." Maureen lifted her head. "I'm doing this for him."

Traci sighed aloud. "Falling in love carries too many risks."

"Not for everyone," Maureen told her. "You and Ryan, for example."

Traci's eyes widened. "What!"

"You can't deny that you care about Ryan," Maureen pressed.

"Yes, but I don't want to get married, and neither does he," Traci hastened to add. "We're both happy the way things are."

"I thought Simon and I were too, and look at what happened." Maureen got up as the oven timer went off. "I'll get this while you go get your grandfather. The Invincibles should be here any minute."

"All right." Deep in thought, Traci went out the back kitchen door. Maureen had to be mistaken. Ryan cared about her, but he didn't love her. She might love him, but she was keeping that fact to herself.

Ezekiel Hightower was a hit with the ladies.

Traci couldn't keep from smiling as her grandfather charmed the Invincibles. She hadn't known he was a bit of a flirt. He had Nettie and Donna giggling like schoolgirls. Best of all, Maureen no longer looked shattered.

"I remember going to a Commodores concert one time," Ezekiel said. "When Lionel Ritchie sang 'Brick House,' he could have been talking about any of you."

"Ezekiel," Nettie groaned, but she was smiling.

"Just calling it the way I see it." He smiled at Nettie. "I don't think I ever sat down. I used to love to dance."

Ophelia sighed. "So did I."

"Me too," Nettie admitted.

"I happen to have some old records." Maureen went to the entertainment center on the far side of the room and opened the doors.

Ezekiel walked over to her. "You still have vinyl and forty-fives. Me too. Not sure what I'll do if my old stereo goes on the blink."

"Me either." Maureen picked up a Commodores album and put it on the turntable. The finger-popping "Brick House" came on.

"Come on, Traci. Let's see if your granddaddy still has it!"

Laughing, Traci went to her grandfather. He was as agile on his feet as he had been when she was a teenager and he had taught her how to dance.

"Maureen," he said, holding out his hand. She smiled at him and placed her hand in his. He twirled both women away, then back to him. "This brings back memories."

"Doesn't it?" Ophelia jumped up, working her shoulders and feet.

"You are not going to have all the fun." Donna jumped into the action, bumping hips with the other woman. She was soon joined by Nettie and Betsy, who danced together.

The song ended and was followed by another and a change of dance partners. Nettie and Betsy danced with Ezekiel. Traci kept Maureen on the floor when she would have taken a seat. A James Brown greatest hits album dropped onto the turntable next.

Arms raised to his chest, Ezekiel lifted one foot and shimmied back and forth across the floor in a great James Brown imitation to "I Feel Good." Traci applauded with the other women.

He winked at Traci. "If I wasn't scared I'd break something I'd do a split."

Traci's laughter joined that of the other women. "Granddaddy!"

"Come on, Nettie. You, too, Ophelia." Ezekiel took their hands. "Let's get on the good foot."

Traci had never seen the ladies dance so much, not even when they went to Vegas. Clearly, her grandfather brought out the youthfulness in all of them.

"No one told me there was a party going on."

Traci's heart thumped on hearing Ryan's voice. Her body heated on seeing him, so broad-shouldered, so handsome, with a smile that turned her knees to jelly. How had she ever managed to gain his attention? What would she do if he grew tired of her?

Maureen greeted Ryan, as did the other women. Traci for some reason felt awkward and shy. Then it came to her as she looked at Ryan with his arm around Maureen while he talked quietly to her.

Today she'd finally admitted to herself that it wasn't just great sex and someone to talk with. It was the real thing. She was smack dab in the middle of that minefield. One wrong move and her heart, her life would be decimated.

Kissing Maureen on the cheek, Ryan walked directly to her. Without a word he curved one arm around her waist, linked his other hand with hers. A Johnny Mathis song played, but it was a faint sound, because all her senses were attuned to the man holding her, the man she loved.

"I missed holding you," he whispered.

"Me too," she murmured, listening to the erratic beat of his heart.

"Ryan, you're not following the four-inch rule," Ezekiel told him.

"I beg your pardon?" Ryan said.

"At least four inches should separate dance partners on ballads." Ezekiel glanced down at the space between himself and Nettie, then back up.

Traci lifted her head. Her granddaddy was in one of his irascible moods. He liked Ryan, but he loved her.

"You can't be serious?" Ryan questioned.

"Do I look as if I'm joking?" Ezekiel asked, his face serious.

Traci watched Ryan look around the room at the other women. They all looked as if they wanted to laugh. Finally, he looked down at her.

"I have no idea," Traci told him.

Ryan leaned her away from him. "Is this all right, Mr. Hightower?"

"For now." Ezekiel nodded his approval. "I told Maureen she had a good son."

"You tell her how you trounced me at checkers?" Ryan asked as they danced.

"Nope," Ezekiel said. The slow song ended. "I told her what was most important."

"Thank you," Ryan said, clearly pleased. "Is it all right if Traci and I go to the kitchen? I'm starved and the Sisterhood always have plenty of food."

"What do you need Traci for?" her grandfather asked.

With a straight face, Ryan talked over the sudden bursts of laughter. "I need to talk to her about the fund-raiser dinner for the clinic."

Ezekiel rubbed his chin. "I guess."

"Thank you." Grabbing Traci's hand, Ryan went to the kitchen. Once there, he swept her into his arms, kissing her. "I was starved for more than food."

"The same." She hugged him. "I wish we could help Maureen and Simon."

"I talked with Simon and got no place. If Mother cares, as you said, why did she say no? Is it the age difference?" he asked, frowning down at her.

"I know, but I can't say. Sorry," she said.

His fingers threaded through her hair, then cupped her head. "I understand. I'm just glad she has you and the Sisterhood to help her through this."

"Granddaddy is certainly livening things up," Traci commented.

"That he is." Ryan tsked. "Your grandfather is something, but I like him."

Traci traced his lips with her fingers. "He likes you, too, and he also likes to be asleep by ten. I can meet you at the back door at eleven."

"Make it ten thirty."

"Ten thirty." She kissed him again.

Maureen waited until everyone had left to make the phone call.

"Hello?"

Hearing Simon's voice, her legs felt rubbery. She plopped on the side of the bed. She'd debated about the wisdom of this call for the past hour. Now she wasn't so sure. Perhaps she should just hang—

"Maureen."

Too late. Either he had caller ID or was very perceptive. In either case, he knew it was her. "Hello, Simon."

"Have you changed your mind?"

He certainly believed in not wasting time. She moistened her lips. "I thought we should talk."

"We did. I asked you to marry me, and you said no."

The bite in his voice made her wince. "I had reasons."

"That I don't accept," he came back.

"Simon, please be reasonable," she implored, hearing the crack in her voice. "Why do things have to change? Why can't you accept what I can give?"

"Because I don't want to creep to and from your bed at night. I don't want to have to remind myself when we're out not to touch you, kiss you. I want to have the right to wake up with you each morning. The right to go to sleep with you in my arms each night without worrying about getting up before Ryan sees me. I want to share my dreams with you, share yours."

If only that were possible. "We do share things."

"On the surface level," he said. "If you had a problem at the store or with the house or were just feeling blue, who would you think of to call first?"

She closed her eyes as the truth hit her.

"Exactly. I'm the man you sleep with, but not the man you need the way I need you in my life."

"That's not true," she cried. "I love you. I'm miserable without you."

"Then love me enough to say yes, to know that my love for you won't change because we won't have children," he said.

Her grip on the phone tightened. "I can't."

"Please, Maureen."

"I don't want to ruin your life."

"You already have."

She gasped at the pain his words caused.

"This conversation is over."

"Simon," she pleaded, but all she heard was the dial tone.

Hand in hand, Traci and Ryan crept up the stairs to her room.

"You're sure he's asleep?" Ryan whispered. Not even in his wildest days had he ever done anything like this.

"Shhh," Traci admonished, and opened the door to her bedroom.

Ryan breathed a sigh of relief, then forgot to breathe as

Traci stepped away from him and slipped off the black silk robe she'd worn. The material whispered over skin as it slithered to the floor. The room was bathed in candlelight, but it was enough to see her lush body in a low-cut gown, enough to make his mouth water, his body hard.

"All I want you to think about is me."

He walked to her, his gaze roaming hotly over her body, anticipation pumping through his bloodstream. He touched her breast with one finger, felt her tremble. Her body was as responsive to his as his was to her. "Beautiful."

Her smile was slow and beautiful and powerful. "I'm going to do bad things to you tonight, and you're going to enjoy every one of them."

He hardened even more. He didn't know whether to ask for mercy or enough stamina to keep up.

She unbuttoned his shirt, tossed it aside, then reached for his belt. He didn't think it was an accident that, as she shoved his pants and silk briefs down, the back of her hand grazed his erection. Air hissed through his teeth. He toed off his loafers, kicked his pants and briefs away.

"You're asking for trouble," he said, air rushing through his lungs as her hand stroked him.

"No. Pleasure," she practically purred the words.

If he had any control, it left him with those two words. He whipped her gown over her head. His head dipped, his lips closing around the pebbled hardness of her distended nipple. He sucked one rigid point, then the other. His hand found her softness. She was hot and hungry for him.

While he still had the strength, he picked her up and mercifully made it to her bed across the room. Then he remembered the condoms were in his pants pocket. He didn't think he could make it there and back.

"Protection," was all he could get out. He saw her reach under the pillow and produce a foil package. He almost sagged in relief. Then she dropped a kiss on his bulging member, and he groaned. "Hurry."

As soon as she finished, she was on her back on the bed and he was over her. Blood pounded in his ears. He wanted nothing more than to surge into her moist heat, to feel her clamp tightly around him, but he could hold it together long enough to give her the pleasure she wanted, the pleasure he wanted to give her.

He dropped soft kisses on her face, her generous breasts, her quivering stomach. Then he kissed her there. She moaned, thrashing on the bed. He loved her until she whimpered with ecstasy, and only then did he thrust into her waiting sheath. She climaxed, a long moan starting in the back of her throat.

He kissed her, and thrust into her again and again until she was with him again, racing toward satisfaction. She finished seconds before he did, her walls clamping around him, holding him in her body. He'd never felt such completeness, such oneness.

When his breathing evened out, he rolled to one side, holding her to him. He never wanted to let her go. "I—" He barely caught himself before he completed the sentence. *I love you.*

"What?" she murmured, her voice sleepy.

He dropped a kiss on her damp forehead and tried to drag the covers up with his foot without releasing her. "Go to sleep."

Her head lifted. "You aren't leaving me, are you?"

He frowned, puzzled by the near-panic in her voice, then he realized she must have felt the crazy acrobatics with his foot. "No. Just trying to snag the covers. You're stuck with me."

She didn't say anything, just stared at him a moment longer before lying back down.

He finally managed to draw the covers up and pull them over her shoulders. Her breathing was even, so he knew she was asleep. He tried to figure out what had caused the fear in her voice earlier, and finally reached the conclusion that she didn't want them to break up like his mother and Simon.

She wanted their relationship to be status quo. Asking for anything more was asking for trouble. Yet, as he held her while she slept, he recalled what Simon had said about wanting more, wanting all of the woman you loved. Simon had predicted that, soon, what Ryan and Traci had wouldn't be enough.

Ryan stroked Traci's shoulder, feeling that day might have already come.

Growing up in the country, where the weather change could destroy a crop or a wild animal might wander too close to the house, I learned to be a light sleeper," Ezekiel said calmly as he sipped his coffee.

Traci's eyes cut to Ryan, who was sitting at the breakfast table, before she could stop herself. Just as she couldn't stop the flush that crawled up her throat to her forehead. She and Ryan thought they'd been so clever, having him shower, then go downstairs, and ring the doorbell that morning as if he'd just arrived.

"I'm the same way." Ryan forked his pancake. "During my internship and residency, you had to be a light sleeper and prepared for everything."

"A man had to protect his family from vermin that might sneak into the house at night and the chickens from a fox in the henhouse." Setting his cup aside, Ezekiel stared at Ryan. "I learned to be a good shot."

Ryan held his gaze without flinching. "If there were a fox or vermin that only wanted to destroy what's in this house, I'd help you load that gun."

"Anyone for more pancakes or coffee?" Traci interjected into the charged stillness. Neither man paid her any attention.

"Traci is important. Her happiness is important." Ryan shoved his plate aside.

"Men say one thing and mean another to get what they want," Ezekiel countered.

"Granddaddy, I think—"

"He has a right to want what's best for you, Traci," Ryan interrupted.

"I love and respect you, Granddaddy, but I can take care of myself." She turned to Ryan and picked up his empty plate. "I can talk for myself."

"Always was hardheaded," Ezekiel mused, draining his coffee cup.

"So I noticed." Ryan stood and began helping clear off the table. "When all of you finish at the flower show, call and I'll take everyone to an early dinner."

"I'll tell the others." Traci picked up the serving platter. Nettie loved flowers and had suggested the outing so Maureen wouldn't be alone that day. They were all coming back over that morning.

"We haven't finished, Ryan." Ezekiel handed Ryan his cup as he picked up his flatware.

"Never thought we had." Ryan took the things to the sink and began rinsing them.

Traci looked from one stubborn man to the other. "So what I say doesn't count?"

The doorbell rang just as Ryan began stacking dishes in the dishwasher. "The doorbell."

"Doorbell," her granddaddy repeated.

"Behave. No talk of guns while I'm gone." She stalked out of the kitchen wondering how they were going to reconcile her grandfather's old-fashioned values with those of today. Sleeping together did not mean marriage . . . no matter how much she'd thought about just that lately.

Deep in thought, Traci opened the door without looking through the peephole and saw the last person on earth she expected to see.

"Get off my porch!"

Vera Jefferson didn't even flinch at the venom in her daughter's voice. "You were a nasty child who grew into a nasty adult."

Once those words would have brought Traci to her knees. "So you shouldn't want to be around me."

She started to close the door, but her stepfather, Nat Jefferson, planted his palm on the door facing. "We want the old man."

Once, before the booze and late nights of gambling, Nat had been a handsome man. Now his dark brown skin was ravaged. He carried enough bags under his eyes for a weekend getaway. On the porch behind him were Traci's half sister, Carla, and her no-good, unemployed husband, Martin. Traci couldn't see their boisterous seven-year-old twin boys, but she could hear their bickering over whose turn it was on the Game Boy.

"Take your hand off my door before I call the police," Traci told him with precise fury.

"Go ahead and call them. I know he's here," Vera said. "Daddy, get out here unless you want something to happen to Traci!"

"You're wasting your breath." Traci hoped her grandfather wouldn't take the bait, that he'd remember she could take care of herself.

"You leave my baby alone," shouted her grandfather.

She looked over her shoulder. Both he and Ryan were coming at a fast clip. Ryan was the last person she wanted to hear the airing of her dirty laundry.

"I told you he was here," Vera said smugly.

Ezekiel insinuated himself in front of Traci. "Leave her alone."

"It's you we want, old man," Nat said and pulled a thick envelope from his coat pocket. "Just sign over the property and we're out of your life."

"That property's been in the family for generations," Traci reminded them. "And that's where it stays."

"Make her invite us in, Mama," Carla whined. "We got a right to go inside."

Traci shot her half sister a killing look. She and Traci were practically the same size, but where Traci took pride in her appearance, Carla had let herself go. She'd dyed her hair red and the nappy black roots were showing. The dress was a size too tight. "None of you will step one foot inside my house."

"You're no better than us," Martin, Carla's husband, spat from beside her.

"A snake in the grass is better than you, Martin," Traci told him. "If Carla wants to turn a blind eye to the women you chase and let you control the little money she makes at the factory that's her business, but you're still slime in my book."

"You—" Martin began.

Ryan shoved Traci aside. "You want to watch your mouth and your hands."

"Who are you?" Nat snapped.

"Someone you don't want to mess with," Ryan told him, fury in every word. "Now, if Traci doesn't want you in her house, we can discuss this on the porch or you can leave."

"That's telling them, son," Ezekiel said. "Now back up, or I'll get my gun."

They scrambled off the porch. Traci might have been amused at their hasty retreat, but she knew it wasn't over. It wouldn't be until they had what they came for.

Flanked by Ryan and Ezekiel, Traci stepped off the porch. "You wasted a trip. He's not going back with you."

Vera pulled an envelope out of her imitation Louis Vuitton tote and shook it in Traci's face. "These papers give me custodial rights to him. The police told me where you live. They gave me your address. If I call them you'll be put in jail for obstruction of justice."

Traci folded her arms before she gave into temptation and snatched the paper out of her mother's hand and thumped her across the head with it. "You've been watching too much TV. I'm a lawyer, remember, and a darn good one."

Vera sent her angry husband a nervous look. "He's going back with us, don't worry."

Traci's arms dropped to her side. "How much would it take to end this?"

Vera's eyes filled with greed. She licked her too-red lips and looked at the two-story house in front of them. "The property is worth a lot."

"You—" Traci bit the word off as she felt Ryan's hand on her shoulder. She was sickened by her mother's avarice, sickened that he had to know what kind of mother she had come from.

"Don't give her a penny, Traci." Ezekiel put his hands on his hips and glared at his daughter, who shrank back. "I might have set a couple of fires on the stove while I was watching TV, but there is nothing wrong with my thinking. Bring on the tests and, when it's over, you will have lost."

"You think you're so smart," Vera riled. "I already have a buyer for the property."

"Which means squat." Traci had never been happier that she was a lawyer. "While the tests are being run I'll file an injunction against the sale of any properties. You do *not* have power of attorney."

"Traci does." Ezekiel laughed at the shocked expression on his daughter's face. "And if you're thinking to wait until I'm dead, you're still out of luck. The day after Traci came to live with me, I had my will changed, leaving everything to her. I've kept it updated. You and your sorry family get nothing."

"You're lying," Vera screeched.

"Unlike you, I don't lie," Ezekiel said calmly.

"So, Vera, get back in that car you can't afford and leave, because Granddaddy is not going one foot from this property unless he wants to."

"You can't tell me what to do. I have this paper," Vera said.

"She sure does," Nat said. "We'll get that property. It's her right as his only child and daughter."

"Right?" Traci felt the rage that she had held inside for thirty-three years explode. "You dare speak of rights to me? What about the rights of a four-year-old child to be loved by her mother instead of being dumped on her grandfather with two paper sacks of ragged clothes that he threw in the trash?"

"Traci, don't," her grandfather said.

"She'd rather pander to you than care for her own child because you didn't want to see the results of her first marriage, to be reminded that she had been with another man, although that man had been her husband. You spouted biblical verses and she swallowed it and look what it's gotten both of you." Traci shoved her hand toward them.

"Nothing. While I have a grandfather who worked his hands raw to ensure that I had the necessities, but also what was more important, his love." Traci wiped the tears from her eyes. "Get off my property. While you're driving back, you'd better think of what your congregation is going to say when they learn how their holy and beloved pastor and his first lady turned their back on a helpless child."

Fear leaped into Nat's eyes. "You got no right to mess with my church or my life."

"You should have thought of that when you messed with mine. Look for me in church one bright Sunday morning," she told them. "Now scat. If I have to tell you again, I'll have you arrested for trespassing."

The adults scrambled for the car, then had to come back for Carla's twin boys, who were fighting on the lawn. Traci watched the clattering, dented Mercedes back out of the driveway, then speed off. They were gone, but she felt exposed.

"I'm proud of you." Ryan hugged her.

She stiffened. She couldn't face him. Not now.

"So am I," Ezekiel said.

"That's our Traci."

Traci whirled around on hearing Maureen's voice. She wasn't alone. All the members of the Sisterhood were with her. She tucked her head. They all knew her shame. Her mother hadn't wanted her. She pushed out of Ryan's arms, but went only a few steps before her granddaddy caught her by the arms.

"You gave me a reason for living when you came to live with me," he said quietly. "Vera was as mean as her mother. Nothing I did made her happy."

Traci's head came up. He'd never said one word.

"Your mother did you a favor or you might be like Carla, trying to hang on to a man who chases everything in a skirt and children she can't control and who act as if they hate her." Gently he shook her. "You are the blessed one. You blessed me."

"Granddaddy." Crying, she went into his arms. "I couldn't have made it without you." Applause sounded and she lifted her head, brushing away tears. She had real, lasting friends who saw you at your worst and loved you anyway. She'd been truly blessed. "Thank you."

"This calls for a toast," Nettie said.

"Before we do, there is something I have to say." Ryan crossed to her and took her hands in his. "I realized something when I wanted to knock out your stepfather's gold teeth."

"Yes?"

"I want to be around to protect you, to laugh with you, for you to keep me in line."

Her entire body began to shake. Hope blossomed in her before she could stop it.

"I love you. Will you marry me?"

Traci wasn't sure if the gasp came from her or one of the women standing around her. Probably not her, because she couldn't make a sound as she stared up into Ryan's eyes.

"Traci, girl, you'd better say yes, or else I might have to get my shotgun out of the truck."

"He'd do it, too, but he won't have to, will he, honey?" Ryan kissed the knuckles of both her hands. "Say yes."

"Yes. Yes!" She launched herself into his arms. He caught her weight without a stagger or even a grunt. He was definitely the man for her. Lasting love was possible. Ryan would never have to beg.

Laughing, Ryan swung her around, then set her on her feet. "You made me a happy man."

"I'm so happy for you." Maureen, with tears in her eyes, threw her arms around both of them.

Traci promised herself, as she was passed from one Invincible to the other, that somehow she'd help Maureen find her own happiness.

Maureen wasn't in a partying mood, but that didn't seem to matter to anyone.

"This is going to be so much fun," Nettie said from beside Maureen in the front seat of her Beamer.

"I haven't been to the beach in years," Ezekiel commented from beside Nettie. "Thanks for the invitation."

"You're welcome." Maureen took the turn to her house on the Isle of Palm. She was sure Nettie, not the beach, was what drew Ezekiel. In the two weeks since Ryan and Traci's engagement, he'd flown home twice to check on his place for a couple of days, then flown back. If Nettie needed to go anyplace, Ezekiel was there for her.

"Ryan and Traci are already here," Ophelia said.

"They make such a handsome couple," Donna said.

"I can't believe she's asked us to help her find the perfect wedding gown." Betsy sniffed. "I always cry at weddings."

"Me too," Ophelia admitted.

Maureen said nothing. The lump in her throat wouldn't let her. With all the talk about Traci and Ryan's wedding she was reminded, sometimes on an hourly basis, of Simon's proposal and how miserable she was without him. She'd lost count of the number of times Traci or one of the Invincibles, with just a look, said she didn't have to be.

What kept her awake at night was knowing Simon was just as miserable as she. Had she made the right decision or the worst mistake of her life? Love meant trust. Traci had made the giant leap of faith with Ryan. Maureen founded the Invincible Sisterhood for women who overcame, women who were brave enough to face fears and heartaches and come out the other side better. She didn't run from problems. At least, she hadn't in the past.

Deep in thought, she parked in front of the house behind Ryan's car. Lights blazed from the front windows. "We're here." And she wanted to turn the car around and go find Simon, talk to him, have him hold her, hold him.

"Ladies, you go on inside. I'll get the luggage." Ezekiel helped Nettie out of the car, then went to the opened trunk.

"We can help." Maureen slipped her keys into her purse. "We're used to bringing in our own luggage."

"I wasn't here then. Shoo." Ezekiel reached for a midsize suitcase.

"Come on, Maureen." Nettie took one arm, and turned toward the three wooden steps.

Ophelia took Maureen's other arm. "I can make us a pitcher of apple martinis."

"I don't think I want one," Maureen mumbled.

"I think we know what you need," Betsy said.

"We sure do," Donna added, opening the front door.

"Simon," Maureen whispered his name, felt the never-ending ache of missing him.

"Hello, Maureen."

She lifted her head sharply, then blinked. Simon couldn't be here in her beachfront cabin.

"Consider him an early birthday present."

Traci stepped into her line of vision; Ryan was next to her. She tugged Maureen's purse from her and removed the set of keys, then gave the purse back to her. "We'll be back in the morning. We're at the hotel if you need us, but I don't think that's going to happen."

Ryan stopped when he was even with her. "Go for it, Mother."

"Good advice," all the other Invincibles told her. "Make the most of a second chance."

The door closed. Maureen heard the symbolic click of the lock, swallowed hard. Simon looked so strong and handsome, but he had yet to smile at her. "I-I didn't know anything about this."

"I can't say the same." He came to her. "When Traci asked me if I wanted a second chance to get my foot out of my mouth, I jumped at the chance."

"You were so angry," she said.

"And wrong." He drew her gently into his arms. "I shouldn't have given you an ultimatum."

"I refused because I love you."

His hand lifted her head. "That's the second time you've said that, and I haven't been looking at you. Please. Say it again."

Her hands covered his. "I love you."

With incredible tenderness his lips brushed across hers. "I love you. I don't want to live another day without having you be a part of it."

The words went straight to her heart, banishing any lingering doubts. She stared up into Simon's strong, beloved face and wondered how she could ever have been unsure. No matter what, Simon would always be there for her just as she would always be there for him. The strength of their love, not their ages, was what mattered. Fear caused her to forget that one irrefutable fact. Never again. "I feel the same way," she finally said, taking the leap and finding it one of the easiest things she had ever done.

"I'll take you any way I can."

"You mean that?" she asked, already knowing the answer.

"Yes." His steady, adoring gaze never left hers.

"That's good because, if the offer still stands, I accept your proposal," she said, her voice shaky, tears glistening in her eyes. "I was thinking of driving back to Charleston to find you."

His eyes filled with warmth and unending love. "I'm here and I always will be for you."

Her trembling fingers grazed his lower lip. "I finally figured that out."

His head lowered, his hungry mouth finding hers, kissing her until both were breathless and needy. "When?"

She laughed with happiness. Her hands on his wide shoulders, she kissed him back. "Soon."

He swung her up into his arms. "I'll always love you, Maureen."

"I know. We're one of the lucky couples."

"That we are," he said, taking her to bed to prove it in the best possible way.

1. Has anyone ever asked you out and you thought, Not even if you begged? Did you remain firm or did you later go out with the person? What happened?

2. Traci let her deceased husband influence her attitude about men. How do you get over a bad relationship and open your heart to love again?

3. Maureen wanted the deep bond of love again, but thought she was too old for Simon. Can you be "too old" to want love and companionship? Why or why not?

4. Simon was ten years younger than Maureen. Should age matter in a relationship? Does it matter if the man or woman is younger/older?

5. Traci was confident about her full figure until a teasing word caused her to doubt herself. Why is it that a man can make a woman second-guess herself?

6. Maureen and Traci had an argument that almost cost them their friendship when Maureen said things that Traci told her in confidence. Has a friend ever betrayed you? Answer this silently. Did you lose your friend?

7. Ryan didn't react very well to his mother dating. Why is it that males are often overprotective of their mothers? Are they being selfish or are they just concerned?

8. Although Elisa was mentally ill, how difficult is it to get over being in love with someone when they don't love you back? How do you move on?

9. Ryan and Simon didn't give up on trying to get Traci and Maureen to go out with them. How persistent should a man be if a woman says no the first time? Have you ever said no and regretted it later? Have you ever said no so as not to seem too anxious? What was the outcome?

St. Martin's
Griffin

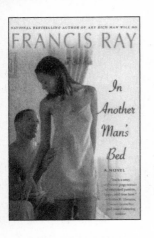

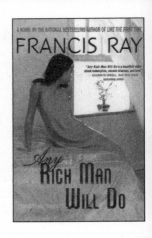